Chattanooga

A Novel by

Chet Raymo

and Dan Raymo

Published by Platypus Multimedia Solutions
8 Old Post Road, North Easton, Massachusetts 02356, U.S.A.
www.platypusmultimedia.com

ISBN: 978-0-9836810-0-7

Book and cover design by Dan Raymo.

Cover photograph licensed by iStockphoto.com.

Authors photograph by Michael Raymo.

If sex were all, then every trembling hand could make us squeak,
like dolls, the wished for words.

— Wallace Stevens,
Le Monocle de Mon Oncle

Time: Summer, 1944

Place: Chattanooga, Tennessee

Characters:

Mamie Buffon, 67, widow of Nelson

Ignatius (Iggy), 72, her bachelor brother

Mamie's daughters:

Wanda, 32

Roger Goody, 35 her husband

Ellen (Tootsie) 11, their daughter

Anne Frances (Button), 30

Vincent (Buddy) Cioffi, 30, her husband

Emily Sue, 28

Lynette, 25

Rebecca (Becca), 24

Alma, 22

Eileen (Bitsy), 19

Eva, 80-something, the cook

Tometta, 17, her great-granddaughter

Prologue - Buddy:

Summers in Chattanooga tend to be taxing once the oppressive heat and humidity make their way over Lookout Mountain and settle into the valley, but nothing could quite prepare us for the monumental life-changing madness the summer of '44 would heap upon us. Until that time, as far as anyone was concerned, we were just an ordinary family, living an ordinary life, in an ordinary house. Now we've become famous, or more accurately *infamous*, and newspapers quote neighbors as saying things like, "They were a nice quiet family, always seemed perfectly normal." I suppose we were normal, or at least seemed normal, until fate, the war, a missing boy, and a dime store canary conspired to expose us for what we really are – a bunch of raving loons.

Iggy:

Imagine livin' in a house full of women. How many? Seven? No, eight. My sister Mamie an'er seven daughters. Lawdy, how them hens prance aroun'. Titterin'. Posin'. Grousin'. Course, they resent me, havin' to bring my meals an' tend my bedpan. 'Casionally helpin' me to the bathroom fer a li'l wash-up. Not that they hafta do these things of'en. God knows there's enough of 'em to share the load. Once or twice a gosh-darn week they might have to pay me a li'l never mind. But Lawdy, how they bitch! *Yap, yap, yap.* Thousands of gals in uniform nursin' bedridden G.I.s day in, day out without complaint – an' you'd reckon I was askin' these Miss Prisses to smoke a horde of nips outta some Pacific hell-hole, never mind carry a tray up the damn stairs. "Here Iggy. Here's your eggs and Spam," their nose in the air. *Ha* – that ain't the real reason they resent me. It's 'cause I'm takin up a room to myself, while the rest of'em are packed in like rats. There's one advantage bein' the only man in a house full of women.

Course, I'm forgettin' Roger an' Vincent, those two pansies that're married to Wanda an' Button. Those boys take up some space too, but not much. Roger, why he's almost never here. Always out huntin' birds. Ha...not shootin' at 'em mind ya, jus' spyin' on 'em. Reckon that fool cares more 'bout his birds than goddamn people. When he ain't buildin' bombs for Uncle Sam, he's traipsin' aroun' the National Cemetery or up on the mountain, huntin' birds with his spyglasses. Only comes home to sleep, far as I can tell. Or to muck about in that la-bor-a-tory he's got in the cellar. Can't say as I blame the boy. That wife of his is all pout an' bother. Wanda, I mean. A train would take a dirt road jus' to avoid that gal. A real fuss-budget. Wanda's the only woman aroun' here that's too good to take her turn bringin' me a meal. Acts like she can't stand the sight of me. But I see her. Oh, yes. I see her out in the side yard takin' the sun, in her skimpy sun suit. Half naked, fer Chrissake. I suppose she thinks no one's watchin'. But I see her out my window here. An' I'll tell ya this, someone else is watchin' too. Vincent. Button's husband. If Wanda's sunnin' in the yard, sho' as shootin' Vincent'll be bird-doggin' aroun' soon nuff. Makin' his way through my room, out to the sleepin' porch, slappin' the Saturday Evening Post 'gainst his thigh – jus' to make sho' I see he's got some readin' planned. Ha – readin' the Post! Spyin' on Wanda is what he's up to. Lawd knows what that horndog sees in her. Skinny as a rail. Why that boy ain't satisfied with his own wife Button, I'll never know. As pretty as a Georgia peach, she is. An' sweet as a peach too.

Button's my favorite. Besides li'l Tootsie, I mean. Tootsie is Roger an' Wanda's girl. She's eleven. Or is she twelve yet? I don't usually include her when I'm totin' up the women aroun' here. I s'pose in another year or so she'll get that same snippity air that goes with bein' a woman in Mamie Buffon's house, but right now Tootsie's my pal. My eyes an' ears, so to speak. Without her, I wouldn't have an inklin' what's goin' on aroun' this nuthouse. What's *really* goin' on I mean, not jus' what they want me to know. Yep, good ole Tootsie, my eyes an' ears.

But it's Button I was goin' on about.

Was me, wouldn't ya know, that gave her the nickname. Back when she was just a li'l mite. *Cute as a button*, I'd say when I came a callin', an' I reckon the name jus' stuck. Mamie's husband Nelson was alive back then. Well, a course he was – there was still five more girls to come before he met his maker. Damn fool fell down the cellar stairs. Stepped on one a Button's roller skates an' went flyin' into space. Damned if he didn't land in a cupboard a peach preserves at the bottom of the stairs. They found him in a messa broken glass an' syrup. I s'pose there's somethin' to be said fer leavin' this earth in such a fashion – quick an' easy. Sho' beats lyin' aroun' in bed, jus' waitin' for the inevitable.

Anyhow, was 'bout that time that Mamie asks me to move in here, justa have a man aroun'. *Why not?* I says. I wasn't hitched. No point in payin' rent an' all when Mamie was offerin' a free room. But if I'd a known 'bout Button, I might a thought diff'rent. But, I came. How old was I? Fifty-two? Fifty-three? Let's jus' say I was no spring chicken. Button, she was thirteen. Pretty as a picture. I reckon I sort of fell in love with 'er. Mind ya, I shouldn't be confessin' this, her bein' my kin an' all. Not to mention so young. But I couldn't get her out of my head. Now don't go gettin' all highfalutin'. I never laid a finger on her. Never said a word. Kept my secret best I could. I know it weren't right. But Lawd know when that feelin' strike a man

– he jus' take leave of his senses. Ever' time I saw the girl my heart near leaped out of my chest. But I never did nothin'.

Never could figure why Button up an' married Vincent. That mystery will go unsolved to my dyin' day. I reckon he's OK to look at. The girls all seem to like him, with that slick black hair an' rabbity eyes. But that boy is slippery as a weasel. All sweet-talk an' bullshit. I wanted to tell her. I wanted to say, *Watch out, Button, that sweet-talkin' charmer will break yoah heart.* But I kept my tongue. Who was I to say anythang? I was invited to the weddin', of course, but I stayed home. It would've broke my heart to see Button walkin' down the aisle with that dago smoothie.

An' now he comes slippin' through here to spy on Wanda. An' don't imagin' it's jus' Wanda. He's sniffin' aroun' the other gals too. Dancin' with 'em down there in the parlor most ever' night. Jitterbug, they call it. Boogie-woogie. *What's the racket*, I ask Tootsie. "Oh, just Buddy dancing with Becca and Lynette," she says. *Buddy*, that's what they call him. Not me. I call him Vincent. Vincent, the no-good lay-about. That boy's so lazy he follows the shade round the house. Ain't seen hide nor hair of a job since he was discharged from the Navy. The Japs put a piece of shrapnel in his knee at Pearl Harbor. The war lasted but all of five minutes fer Private Vincent Cioffi. Got his Purple Heart an' ain't done a lick of work since. That wound in his leg don't keep him from dancin' with Becca an' Lynette. Swing an' sway with Danny Kaye. Meanwhile Button sits in her room readin' the Post. Or she's out in the kitchen helpin' Eva with the dishes. That boy ain't fit to wipe the sweat from Button's brow. Button's too good fer Vincent. Too damn good fer the likes of him.

I could teach Private Vincent Cioffi a thang or two 'bout bein' a war hero. I went into Cuba in '98. Santiago. Wasn't a whole lot of shootin' to speak of, but the skeeters down there was bigger'n bullets – an' more dangerous too. I'll tell ya this, I'd rather be dodgin' Jap bombs than them damn Cuban skeeters. Once those monsters got hold of ya, they'd suck yoah blood till yoah was dry as a bone. Half the troop was sick with malaria, dysentery, typhoid, or yella fever. I damn near died on the ship back to Tampa. Right into the hospital I went. Never did get my strength back. I reckon that's why I never married. Always pantin' an' wheezin' like a old steam engine. Ain't been able to catch my breath since. No self-respectin' gal'd take two looks at me after that. An' there weren't no one tryin' to pin a medal on my chest. Did I complain? Not once. That's what bein' a hero's all about. Goin' to war without complaint an' takin' what comes. Now look at our boy Vincent, burnin' up the carpet with the gals. But he goes out of the house an' he's hobblin' aroun' like a pirate with a wooden leg. Makin' sho' he stays out of the service is all that goldbricker's worried about. The worse they'd give him is a desk job anyhow. Yep, Private Vincent Cioffi with his Purple Heart. Had it fixed up in a fancy frame. Damn fool put it up over his bed, right next to the crucifix, or so Tootsie tells me. Apparently Button ain't all that impressed. Tootsie tells me that sometimes Button sleeps on the floor. An' who'd blame her, married to Vincent? *Pffft*. What was that woman thinkin'?

Now Roger – well, he's a good egg I reckon. At least he's got a job. It's Roger's paycheck that keeps the house goin'. That an' my pension. That job of his keeps him out of the war too. He's a engineer at the TNT plant out by Tyner. Reckon Uncle Sam figures he's more valuable makin' bombs than gettin' his fool head blown off at the front. Can't say I know exactly what he does out there. "Loose lips sink ships," Roger tells me. I suppose he thinks I'll hop outta bed, run down to the telegraph office an' drop a wire to Tojo. But it's Tootsie who tells me he's workin' on bombs – that girl finds out ever'thing. *How's it going at the plant?* I ask Roger. "Would you believe it, Iggy?" he'll say, "I saw the most gorgeous Rose-breasted peckerbeak on my lunch break." Lawd knows how he gets any work done at all. He don't leave the house without his damn spyglasses hangin' round his neck, even goin' to the plant. If we was countin' on Roger to win the war, the Japs'd be marchin' down Ninth Street right now. Anyhow, his job pays the rent – I'll give the boy that.

If I live to be a hundred, I'll never figure why folk marry each other. Wanda an' Roger couldn't be more mismatched if they was a woodpecker an' a block a granite. Well, at least he might take a look at her if'n she was a woodpecker. Wanda's bored as the day is long, an' Roger's interested in nothin' but his birds. What the Christ were those two thinkin'? Course, they'd been in school together since they were knee-high to a grasshopper. I can remember Roger comin' ovah here fer birthday parties an' such. But they never paid each other no never mind, least not in high school. No courtin' at all, far as I can tell. Then damned if Roger doesn't show up one day an' announces they's gettin' married. Straight outta the blue. With Wanda all moony-eyed on his arm. She wasn't knocked up either, mind ya. Tootsie didn't come along till ten months after the weddin'. That was eleven years ago now, an' far as I can figure there ain't been much baby-makin' since. Can't figure it out. You'd think two semi-intelligent adults like Wanda an' Roger would know what the hell they want.

The big mystery is – how's it that nobody's ever happy with what they got. Always hankerin' fer somethin' more. Give a man the purdiest wife in the world, an' a barrel of money, an' he'd still be sniffin' aroun' fer sometin' better. An' women, they ain't no better. Worse I'd say. God himself don't know what makes a woman tick. Watchin' the women round this house has been a real education. These gals are the luckiest human bein's on the face of the earth an' still they grumble. Complainin' about this. Bitchin' about that. Not enough men. Not enough rationin' stamps. Not enough nylons. Not enough boogie-woogie. I s'pose I mighta been the same when I was their age. Lawd knows, I had my moments too, wantin' what I didn't have. Wantin' what I *shouldn't* have. But sooner or later a bit of perspective settles in. At my age, you feel lucky jus' to take a decent crap.

The only one aroun' here that seems to know what she wants is Alma. How old's Alma? Nineteen? Twenty? Alma's religious. An' when I say "religious", I mean "*crazy* religious." Maybe you gotta be religious to know what you want. Alma don't pay no never mind to what happens here on Earth, 'cause she reckons ever'thing will come out right up in heaven. Ohh, does Tootsie go on about Alma – with her little shrine of statues in her bedroomm and how she puts cinders in her bed. *Mor-ti-fi-cation of the flesh*, she calls it, or somethin' of the sort. Alma an' Bitsy share a bed, an' Alma puts cinders in the sheets. Jus' on her side mind you, but the stuff sifts over to where Bitsy's sleepin'. Bitsy complains to Mamie. Mamie cleans the sheets. Alma puts the cinders in ag'in. I'll never understand that kinda religion. I reckon it's on account of Alma bein' spoiled, like the rest of the gals aroun' here. Always had ever'thing they wanted. Treated like princesses. If Alma'd been a coughin', wheezin' wreck all her life, she wouldn't be needin' to put cinders in her bed. Those goddamn Cuban skeeters gave me enough *mor-it-fi-cations of the flesh* to last a lifetime. But, then, I can't rightly say I was ever particularly religious. Sho', I went to church on Sunday like ever'one else, but can't say as I took it seriously. An' don't be expectin' me to get all religious now cause it's almost time to meet my maker. If the good Lawd's willin' to let me through the pearly gates, then Amen. If he's got other plans – so be it. I reckon I'm like that dumb-ass woodpecker outside my window in the chestnut tree. Damn thing been out there fer a week now, knockin' its brains out 'gainst that tree, bangin' its fool red head 'gainst that tree day in, day out. What does it get for its trouble? I'll tell you what it gets. *A goddamn headache*. That's me – dumb an' stubborn as the day is long.

Now don't let me give the wrong impression. My life ain't been all bad. No, there's been some mighty special moments. Moments to make it all worthwhile. Oh, I could tell ya thangs. I could tell ya thangs that could melt a man's heart.

Tootsie:

Uncle Iggy hurt Sugar, my canary. It wasn't my fault Sugar escaped. Grandma made me clean the cage and Sugar flew away when I took off the bottom. Sugar flew into Iggy's room and woke him up from a nap. Iggy whacked Sugar with a badminton racket and knocked her against the wall. She was just lying there on the floor and I was sure she was dead. I picked her up, and it turns out she wasn't dead – only stunned. She's ok now, but I'm still mad at Iggy.

I suppose I shouldn't blame Iggy. He's an old man. Becca says he's crazy. *Crazy as a loon* is what Becca says. She says that people get crazy when they get old. I don't think Iggy is crazy. I think he's just lonely. I think he wants someone to talk to. But he sure doesn't like canaries. Iggy hates Sugar.

Iggy told me a rhyme:

> *One day a little bird flew by*
> *And dropped some whitewash in my eye.*
> *But I was brave, I didn't cry,*
> *I just thanked God that cows don't fly.*

I didn't know what whitewash was and asked Iggy. "Bird shit," he yelled, "whitewash is bird shit." I don't know why he got so mad – it's not like they teach us what whitewash is at school. I suppose he thought it might have ruined his joke. Iggy says birds belong outside where they can fly around. "No goddamn bird belongs in a cage," he yells. He says I should set Sugar free. But I know he's wrong. Sugar's not an outside bird. If Sugar went outside she'd be killed. By a cat. Or by other birds. That red-headed woodpecker in the chestnut tree would probably peck Sugar's eyes out. And what would Sugar eat? Iggy says, "If that bird was outside she could drop her goddamn whitewash wherever she wants, and nobody would have to clean up after her." But I don't mind cleaning her cage. Next time, I'll just be more careful not to let Sugar fly into Iggy's room.

I don't think Iggy's crazy. Uncle Buddy's the crazy one. Everybody else thinks Buddy is wonderful. Becca and Lynette dance with him most every night. But I would never dance with Buddy. *Not ever*. Not even when I get older. He's mean to Button. I hear them at night in their room. My bed is next to their wall and I can hear them talking. They kind of whisper, but I can still make some of it out. He asks her to do things she doesn't want to do. I don't know exactly what he's asking her to do, but Button says no. Then Buddy gets mean. He calls her nasty names – names I wouldn't want to say. Bad names. Sometimes he makes her sleep on the floor. He says, "If you don't want to share my bed you can damn well sleep on the floor." And she does. I know because I've looked into their room in the morning, after Buddy's gone down to breakfast, and I've seen Button sleeping on the floor. She probably prefers it. I wouldn't even want to sleep in the same room with Buddy. I feel sorry for Button. Button's nice.

Iggy says that Uncle Buddy spies on my Mom.

I would tell Dad that Buddy spies on Mom, but Dad is such a fraidy-cat that it's not even worth it. It would only make Dad feel bad. He's afraid of Buddy. Buddy is just mean. He's mean to Dad sometimes too. Everyone thinks Buddy is just fooling around when he calls Dad "Birdy-Man" and things like that. Everyone laughs. Dad even laughs. But I can tell that Buddy is being mean. He's trying to make Dad feel like a sissy. He's trying to make himself look better than Dad in front of the girls.

Becca and Lynette are always fooling around with Buddy. Last night Becca asked Buddy to draw lines on the back of her legs with an eyebrow pencil so it would look like a seam in her liquid stockings, and Buddy did it. Becca and Lynette were laughing their heads off, but Button wasn't laughing. Button was there in the parlor with the rest of them, but she didn't think it was so funny. Buddy drew the line almost up to Becca's underpants, until she made him stop. Everyone was laughing like crazy. Even Emily Sue was laughing. But Button didn't laugh. Button went to the shack out back to talk to Eva.

Eva is grandma's negro cook. She lives in the shack out by the alley. The shack belongs to grandma, but Eva lives there for free. She's older than grandma, older even than Iggy. She hasn't been feeling too good lately, so her great-granddaughter Tometta is staying with her and helpin' with the chores. Eva has two children who are still alive. Her son lives in Nashville. Her daughter is a school teacher, but I don't know where she lives, only somewhere near Chattanooga. Buddy doesn't ever call Eva by her name. Only once did I ever hear Buddy call Eva by her name. They were on the back porch one day, and Eva had a big armful of clothes she had just taken off the line, and Buddy said, "You're a useless old nigger, Eva, you're lucky we still let you live here." Eva didn't say nothing, just shook her head. Grandma says only ignorant people use the word nigger. I'm sure Buddy wouldn't use that word in front of Grandma.

Dad likes Eva. Dad and Eva are good friends as far as I can tell. Sometimes on nice evenings they will sit in the glider under the tree by Eva's shack and talk and talk. I don't know what they talk about, but Mom says that Dad talks to Eva more than he talks to her. That's what Mom says, but it seems like every time Dad tries to talk to Mom she doesn't pay any attention, so I don't think it's his fault. Dad always asks Mom to come with him when he goes birding, but she says it's a waste of time. I don't think it's a waste of time. I like to go on bird walks with Dad. Sometimes in the morning, when it's not a school-day, I get up early and go with Dad to the National Cemetery. We walk between all those gravestones, and we're very quiet, and Dad shows me lots of birds. We don't hardly talk at all, Dad just squeezes my hand and points to where I should look. I suppose we'd scare all the birds off if we talked too much. Dad says, "God gave us two ears and one mouth, because we can learn more by listening than talking." He must know what he's talking about, because he knows more about birds than anyone I've ever seen. Most birds look alike to me, but he knows the differences. He'll say, "See that bird with the little brown cap and the button on its vest," and I'll look and the bird has a brown cap and a button, just like Dad said. Or he'll say, "See the bird in the Lone Ranger mask," and sure enough the bird has a mask. Sometimes I think about all those dead soldiers under the grass – there must be a million of them – and I wonder why birds come to that place at all, but I'm glad they do because they make my Dad happy.

It's really nice to be in the cemetery in the mornings. There's nobody there but us, and the German prisoners that mow the grass and dig graves, and the soldiers that guard the prisoners. Dad says the German prisoners are people just like us, except they happen to be born on the wrong side of the ocean. I sometimes wonder about that – about where we are born. I mean, why was I born in Chattanooga, instead of Germany, or China, or anywhere? It's like I could have been born anywhere and if it happened to be Germany then planes would be dropping Dad's bombs on me – except he wouldn't be my Dad of course. These are the kind of weird things I think about on our bird walks. Sometimes we walk to the top of the hill where the flagpole is, and we lay back in the grass looking up at the sky, and maybe there'll be a bird up so high that we can barely see it at all and Dad will know exactly what it is. He can tell by the shape or its call. "Yep, it's a sparrow hawk," he'll say. *How many kinds of birds are there?* I asked. "Not nearly enough," he said.

Roger:

There are twenty-seven kinds of warblers that visit Chattanooga, and I've seen them all. For a long time I had never seen a Duck Creek warbler. The guidebooks say Duck Creek warblers don't come this far north, only to about the latitude of Atlanta, but someone told me he had seen Duck Creek warblers down in Chattanooga Valley, so I went down there every Sunday morning during March and April, and on the last Sunday of April I saw them. Six of them. Such pretty little birds. Yellow with an olive hood. A softer, sweeter yellow than many of our other warblers. I wish Tootsie could have been with me and seen them. Anyway, I've seen them all now. All twenty-seven.

Of course, I wasn't supposed to be driving to Chattanooga Valley. I have a C sticker for my car because of my war work, so I can get most of the gasoline I want. But I'm not supposed to use the car for unnecessary journeys, and I guess you'd have to say that driving down to the valley to look for Duck Creek warblers doesn't contribute to the war effort. Not that it matters much now. I'd say the war is almost over. The Allies have broken out of the beachheads at Normandy. Pretty soon the Germans will give up, and then the Japs will surrender too. Once the war's over, we'll have all the gasoline we want.

I wish Wanda could have seen the Duck Creek warblers. Or more to the point, I wish she had some desire to see Duck Creek warblers. I don't understand Wanda. Sometimes I wonder why she even married me. Before we got married she seemed to be interested in birds. And in my work, too. But no sooner did we walk down the aisle than she lost interest in everything about me. She just sort of moped around the house. Until Tootsie was born, that is, and then she got interested in life again, took a job at Woolworths and even became a manager. Bought some pretty new dresses. She seemed real happy. She was always bringing Tootsie things from the store, mostly damaged merchandise or things the store was going to throw away. Or pets. Lots of tiny turtles and goldfish in paper cartons. A chameleon once. And Sugar. That bird must be four years old now, because it's been nearly three years since Wanda worked at

Woolworths. She hasn't worked there since the war started – back to just moping around.

Judging by how cranky Wanda gets whenever Becca and Lynette bring home soldiers or airmen from the USO, I think maybe she's sorry she married me. I suppose she'd rather be single like her younger sisters. When I married Wanda she had a nice figure, pleasingly full, you might say, but now she's skinny as a bean pole. Seems to think the skinnier she is, the prettier she is. Stands in front of the mirror for hours on end, in her bra and panties, brushing her hair. She doesn't close the door, either. In fact, she conspicuously leaves it open. I can't imagine who she wants to see her. Buddy isn't interested. Buddy's interested in Becca, certainly, and Lynette, but not Wanda. Anyway, I know it isn't me she's primping for. I tell her to close the door, but she just laughs and says, "No one's looking. Who do you think is looking?" She thinks I'm a prude. I'm no prude, but I do believe in modesty. Is that so bad? Wanda sure isn't the modest type. She suns herself in the yard with her shorts hiked right up to her crotch, and her top rolled up so it barely covers her breasts. It's tacky. I can't imagine what the neighbors must think. I try to tell her she should be more modest, but she pays no attention to me.

I'm not quite sure what Wanda wants from me. I try to be a good husband. I put up with her moods, and God knows that's not always easy. I keep our bedroom tidy. Meanwhile, she leaves her underwear and stuff all over the floor for me to pick up. I try to be a good dad to Tootsie, too. Sometimes I wonder if Wanda has forgotten that Tootsie is her daughter. When Tootsie was a baby, Wanda doted on her, but she certainly doesn't dote any more. Come to think of it, she doesn't pay much attention to anyone, these days – least of all me. I keep telling her she ought to get a job. There are lots of good jobs for a woman as smart as Wanda, especially now that most of the men are in the service. She could get her old job back at Woolworths, or she could get a job at the Volunteer Life Insurance Company, or the TVA. There are lots of jobs around that Wanda would be good at, jobs that would keep her mind occupied. But she just mopes. I just wish I knew what the heck she wants from me.

I even asked Mamie what Wanda wants. Mamie said that Wanda is "going through a stage." I don't know what that means, *going through a stage*. Seems to me like that's all any of us do, day in and day out as long as we live, just go through stages – one stage after another. I suggested to Wanda that maybe when the war is over we might go on a second honeymoon, so to speak, to Daytona, maybe, or New Orleans. She said, "What for?" I said, *Oh, I don't know, maybe just to get to know each other again.* She said, "What for?"

I know Wanda resents my birdwatching. She never has anything good to say about it, but at the same time she seems to be glad that I'm out of the house. Once a week or so I'll ask her to come with me, like she did when we first got married, but she won't come. She calls my birding a waste of time. I suppose it *is* a waste of time, but what is time *for* if not to waste? I spend fifty hours a week designing explosives for the War Department – bombs to kill people – and nobody considers *that* a waste of time. I drive down Bailey Avenue on my way to work and almost every house has a star in the window, and every one of those stars represents a kid in the service, and a lot of those kids won't be coming home. When I'm out at the Ordnance Works working for the government, I'm thinking that the bombs I'm making are going to blow some poor Japs and Germans to kingdom come. And it's not the generals and politicians that get killed, it's the ordinary people – especially young men, like the POWs working in the cemetery. But of course nobody considers *that* a waste of time. That's war work, that's patriotic. Well I'd just as soon waste my time with looking for a Duck Creek warbler. At least I'm not hurting anyone while I'm watching birds. Except maybe Wanda.

Button:

Buddy has his eye on Wanda, I'm sure of it. I *see* the way he looks at her with those leering goo-goo eyes. At supper they play footsie under the table and you'd have to be blind not to notice. Oh yes – he has his eye on her, I'm sure of it. Not that I really care. Let him chase whoever he wants, but I do feel sorry for Roger.

Poor Roger and his birds. When he's not at work, he's out in some old woods or swamp with his binoculars and that silly cap with the ear flaps. He is a dear sweet man, but hopelessly naïve when it comes to Wanda. Everyone around here thinks that I'm the naïve one, but next to Roger I feel positively sophisticated. I'm sure Roger has no idea that Buddy is fooling around with Wanda, I mean, how could he know, he is never here except for a few hours a day, and then he's asleep, and I'm not criticizing him for that, if it wasn't for Roger's job this family would be in the poor house, because none of the rest of us make enough money to put food on the table. My part-time job at the drug store doesn't pay enough to give Mother any help at all, and Buddy – Buddy is worse than useless.

They all feel sorry for me – my sisters, I mean – that I married Buddy. They don't say as much, but I can tell what they're thinking. They're edgy when they are around Buddy and me together, and they give me guilty glances when they flirt with Buddy. I don't blame them for that. I can see why they flirt. He's handsome, funny, and he can be really sweet when he wants to be. He knows how to make a woman feel special – to feel pretty. I was watching Buddy draw lines on the back of Becca's legs – like stocking seams, to go with that awful leg-makeup – and he moved the eyebrow pencil along her legs really sexy like and I could tell Becca liked it. Even Emily Sue was laughing, almost as if she knew what was going on. But I couldn't bear to watch. Seeing him taking those girls in, I just couldn't bear to watch. If Becca and Lynette knew what Buddy was *really* like they wouldn't be so apt to flirt.

I don't know what happened to Buddy. He was different when we met, or at least he seemed different to me. We were both twenty-five and I was working at the candy counter at the Tivoli theater and Buddy was an usher. When the movie was on, he would come out to the lobby and talk to me. He was handsome as could be in his uniform with his little bellhop cap and flashlight. When I finished my shift at the candy counter I would stay for the next showing of the movie, sit in the back row, and Buddy would slip in by me, and we would hold hands, and sometimes we would kiss, and he was so gentle and sweet and handsome that when he asked me to marry him I said yes. I mean, I hardly knew him, but I said yes, and then we started dating, and Buddy came to our house every Sunday, and a year later we got married. We had our own little apartment on Cameron Hill, just two little rooms in a big old house, but it was a nice place and Buddy was a good husband. We tried to have a baby but – I don't know, I guess one of us isn't fertile because we tried very hard up until the time Buddy signed up for the Navy. I never knew why he signed up. We had only been married a year and I thought things were going OK, but Buddy said he had to – I don't remember exactly what he said, something about "getting experience" or something silly like that. Anyway, it was supposed to be for three years, but it turned out it wasn't long at all, because he was at Pearl Harbor when the Japs bombed, and he was wounded and came home. That's when our troubles began. He wasn't so sweet anymore. He wouldn't work – he just wanted to have sex all the time, and do things I didn't want to do. I mean, it seems to me that if two people really love each other then they will want to be close and gentle, and – anyway, I guess we weren't really happy any more. *Aren't* really happy anymore, I should say. It's still the same.

I don't care. I'm sick of sex, sick of all the tension, sick of constantly wondering what I'm doing wrong, and of trying to make him happy when I don't even know what it is that will make him happy. And if having sex twenty-four hours a day is the only thing that will make him happy – he's out of luck. Sometimes I think that Emily Sue has it best of all. At least she isn't always worrying about how some man wants her to behave. I mean, Emily Sue may be, you know, retarded, but at least she's free, sort of. She's not a slave to constantly seeking acceptance. Take Becca and Lynette for instance – all they think about is men. Even if they are just going to the drug store they primp for twenty minutes, brushing their hair, putting on lipstick, shaving their legs. I suppose I was like that before I married Buddy, but it all seems so silly now.

Buddy always used to buy me salt and pepper shakers for my collection. I have three-hundred-and-twenty-seven pairs of shakers and Buddy must have bought me at least fifty of them, especially the love birds. I have sixteen different pairs of love-bird shakers and Buddy gave me most of them before he went into the Navy. Those are the ones I keep on the windowsill in our room. I like to see them there, because they remind me of what it used to be like with Buddy, before he came back from Pearl Harbor. When he came home from the service, it was like he had forgotten all about my collection. He had changed. Maybe it was his leg, he was very self-conscious about his leg. He shouldn't be, of course. You'd hardly notice his limp. It's only a slight favoring of his left leg, but he worries about how it makes him look. Buddy has always been very conscious of how he looks – with women, I mean. It's silly. I never cared about how he looked. I mean, I wasn't sorry that he was so handsome, but I would have loved him even if he wasn't handsome. He was so gentle and sweet.

I remember when Buddy gave me the first love bird shakers, two plump yellow birds with blue eyes, and when you put them together the heads and necks of each bird curled about the other. We were sitting at the lunch counter in Woolworths on Market Street having a cherry Coke, and it was our second date, and I told him about my collection, and he said, "Wait a minute," and he got up and went to the other side of the store, and when he came back he had bought this pair of salt and pepper shakers – the love birds – and they were the same ones that Wanda had given me, but I didn't tell Buddy, I thought that it was a really sweet thing to do – to give me love-bird shakers, I mean.

Maybe if we'd had a baby that first year, maybe then Buddy wouldn't have joined the Navy, and – well, I guess he would have been drafted sooner or later anyway, but I keep thinking that maybe if we'd had a baby, things might have stayed the same as they were. I don't really understand Buddy, and I know I'll never make him happy, but I'm not going to feel sorry for myself, or guilty, because I don't think it's my fault, and if Buddy wants to make a fool of himself with Wanda or the other girls, then let *them* try to figure out what will make him happy. Good luck to them.

Buddy:

The coloreds in this town are getting too damned big for their britches. I was in Loveman's yesterday and this darkie is drinking from the white water fountain. The colored folk's fountain was right next to it for chrissake, but this thick-headed sonofabitch was slurppin' away at ours. I said to him, *Can't you read, boy? That sign there says "Whites."* He didn't say a thing, but I'll tell you this – he stopped drinking.

Something's really got to be done. If we don't put the coloreds in their place soon, they'll take over. Already they own half of Ninth Street, and they're creeping closer to Mamie's house all the time. There's another *For Sale* sign in the 400 block of Ninth Street, another white family getting out. Moving to Brainerd or some place like that. A colored family will buy that house and in two months time the grass will be gone, the paint will be peeling, and the front yard will be full of old automobile tires and junked ice boxes. Somebody has to stand up to them, somebody's got to say *Enough*. Don't expect the politicians to do it. They all live up on Lookout Mountain or out on Missionary Ridge, so what do they care what happens to a neighborhood like ours? The politicians don't care if downtown residential neighborhoods are destroyed. They don't care if people like Mamie Buffon lose everything when the bottom falls out of the real estate market. Who'd want to buy Mamie's house with the negroes only a few blocks away?

I'll tell you what the problem is, it's those colored soldiers coming home from the service. They think they're war heroes, hanging around on street corners in full dress, acting like big shots – like they own the place. The colored girls draped all over them. It was a big mistake letting the niggers fight in this war. Nothing cockier than a black boy in a uniform. Just wait and see, when the war is over they'll be asking for everything – I mean – just look at that spade at Loveman's yesterday. Now the white folk in Beaumont, Texas and up in Detroit, that burned down the colored neighborhoods may have carried things a bit too far, but I can't say as I blame them. If we whites don't stand up for our rights soon, there'll be no stopping the coloreds later, I'll tell you that.

Becca and her friends went to the Dixie to see *White Savage*, and when they came out there were four colored boys standing there in front of the theater, and one of them says, "How was the movie, ladies?" Can you imagine? Like the girls would say, *Super-duper, why don't you boys take us out for a soda and we'll tell you all about it*. Christ, there was a time when smart-mouthed niggers like that would've been run out of town on a rail – or worse. I can't bear to think of them boys eye-balling Becca and her friends, never mind talking to them. And you just gotta know what they were *thinking*.

I told Becca that if she and her friends ever need an escort to the movies to make sure they're treated with respect, I'd be glad to do it. Becca's friends are A-OK. Don't even get me going on that Sandra girl from North Chattanooga. What a dish! The tits on that girl would make your eyes spin in their sockets. I sure as hell wouldn't mind watching *White Savage* with *her*. And that look she gives you with those big brown eyes, like she's got nothing on her mind but you-know-what. Talk about the icing on the cake – *she's a nurse too!* I don't know what it is about nurses, but they always run hot. That's no lie either. Out at Pearl, the nurses were the hottest women on the island. I'll admit I never scored one, but while I was in the hospital I must have heard a hundred stories from guys who did. The way they talked, short of getting your pecker shot off any old wound would be worth getting just for the chance to meet those nurses. I don't know if a gal becomes a nurse because she's hot, or if bein' a nurse makes her hot, but take my word for it – the nurses out at Pearl were fucking hot.

I was a married man mind you, so it's not like I was chasing skirts. But I was no saint either. I probably shouldn't talk about these things, but there was a gal out there that will be etched on my brain when they're putting my lifeless corpse into the ground. It was the night before the Nip attack, a Saturday night, and a couple of my buddies dragged me into Honolulu, to a place where you could have any girl you wanted for a couple of bucks. Oriental dames. I suppose they were Japs – American Japs, I mean. Or Chinese. I'll tell you this, they were sweet little pieces of ass. Anyway, this one gal was giving me *the look*, trying to get me to take her to the rooms out back. I felt funny about it at first, on account of her being a Nip and all, but damn she was something. Anyway, we head out back, and

I'm telling you she was nothing like the gals in Chattanooga. She couldn't get my pecker out of my pants and into her mouth fast enough. I didn't even have to ask her. She loved it. I mean – Button had sort of done it to me a couple times, but with Button it was like getting a kid eating Brussels sprouts – with that little Jap angel it was like it was her last meal. The funny thing is, I can't even remember her name – Kikie or Kakie or some such thing – but I sure as hell won't forget the way she went down on me. I couldn't believe it. It was like – well, sufficed to say I didn't sleep a wink that night. I was still lying awake in my bunk thinking about it when the bombs went off.

Everyone thinks I was lucky to get wounded – out of the war with nothing but a gimpy leg and all that. But let me tell you, I wouldn't have minded hanging out at Pearl for a while longer. With the likes of Kikie around, who wouldn't? And I sure as hell wouldn't have minded kicking some Jap ass either. Imagine what it's like being stuck in a place like Chattanooga with all the other guys off to war – with no one around except pansies like Roger. That guy pisses me off. C'mon, what a *nothing*. Imagine a guy his age being interested in nothing but birds? And messing around in the cellar with all those bottles of chemicals like some crazy mad scientist. Setting off explosions, even. I wouldn't be surprised if he was queer. He sure as hell doesn't show any interest in women. I'll tell you this, he doesn't satisfy that wife of his. Wanda is way more woman than Roger can handle. I wouldn't mind getting a piece of Wanda myself, and I'll tell you this, I'm startin' to think she might not mind if I did. I'm standin' in front of her bedroom door the other day while she calmly brushes her hair in front of the mirror, wearing nothing but her panties and brassier, with me just standin' there watching. And believe you me, that little tease knew I was there. Hell…the whole show was just for me. *Mmm…mmm….*the things I'd do to that woman. Good Lord, Roger, what the hell is wrong with you?

Button would be pissed if she knew the thoughts I was having about her sister. Button's such a stiff-assed goody-goody. If only she'd married Roger instead of me, all would be right in the world. Those two were made for each other. Neither of 'em with an ounce of interest in sex, as far as I can tell. How I ever allowed myself to marry someone like Button, I'll never know. Stupid! It's not like she's not nice to look at, and she's a hell of a nicer person than Wanda, but it ain't right. You don't trick a guy into marrying you just to treat him like a cold fish. A guy has needs. It's *especially* hard for a guy in this house, with Wanda parading around half naked, and Becca and Lynette always gammin' about, and even Emily Sue – well, she may not have all her marbles, but she ain't bad to look at either, and Bitsy, too, in a half-hearted way. Don't even get me going on Tometta, that colored gal was built for screwing. The only one around here not trying to turn you on is Alma. Good lord, poor Alma. Now that girl is weird, and I mean *really* weird. Any man that would mess around with that gal needs to have his head examined.

It's not like I *try* to hurt Button, but when a man ain't getting what he needs, he just ain't himself. I told her she was frigid the other night, and she cried. I apologized and said I didn't mean it, but the damage was done. But I did mean it. She is *frigid*. The thing is, she just won't admit it. How can she just lie there like a sack of potatoes staring at the ceiling when we're having sex? Say something! Do something! Maybe if she'd admit it, then we could do something about it. It's my own fault, I suppose. I should have seen the writing on the wall even before we were married. Like when we used to make out in the back row of the Tivoli. She was an eager kisser, and she'd use her tongue and everything, and she'd let me slide my hand up her sweater, but when I tried to get my hand into the business district, that was the end of the line. Even when we became engaged, she wouldn't let me touch her pussy. There was no convincing her to put her hand in my pants either. "When we're married," she always promised. What kind of woman holds that over a man. I should have seen it then. What in God's name was I thinking? Well, I guess we know the answer to that – I wasn't thinking, at least not with my brain.

The first year we were married, Button lived up to her promises. I have to say, it was pretty damn good. We were in the sack all the time. She wanted a baby. I don't know why she didn't get pregnant. It sure as shootin' wasn't from lack of effort on my part. I think maybe getting pregnant has something to do with the mindset. A woman's got to be thinking about sex to make it happen, and Button just wasn't thinking about it. At least she wasn't thinking about it the way I think about it. She was just going through the motions. The longer it went without her getting pregnant, the less interest she showed. I was always the one that had to try and initiate things. I could feel myself getting mean and resentful. I had to get out of there before I went nuts. That's why I joined the Navy. Well that, and I wasn't about to wait around and be drafted into the Army – *dumb grunts*. In any case, I thought the time away from each other would do us good. Once I was gone, I figured she'd see what she was missing. I couldn't have been more wrong. It was worse than ever when I came back. Seems like she was always avoiding any situation where we might have sex. Anytime I tried, she'd just lie there like a bump on a log. And all I could think about was that Jap girl in Honolulu, and how she couldn't wait to go right down. That's what sex should be all about – two people making each other happy.

It's Becca and Lynette who are having all the fun. Those girls are out almost every night at the USO or the Service Men's Club, with lovely Sandra and their other friends. You'd think they'd be too tired to party, with their jobs and all. They tell Mamie they're volunteering at the USO to help with the war effort, but trust me, they're not making any big sacrifice. Those girls are the biggest vamps in town. Sometimes on a Sunday afternoon they'll invite half the U.S. Army home for dinner, and when *that* happens – well I eat down at the drug store. I can't bear to be around here, watching those girls flirt and tease. I guess it reminds me too much of what I'm missing. I ask Becca when she's getting married and she just laughs. *Ha*, that gal has the right idea. Stay single. Play the field. Keep your options open. Don't get trapped in a marriage like mine.

Tometta:

Lawd give me strength, goin' on two months stuck in this house. If Mista Cioffi ain't the devil himself, then I reckon I don't know who is. I can live with his eyes runnin' all ovah me, but the way he treats Nana leave me ready to slit his fool throat – *Lawd forgive me*. After all she done fer these folk ovah the years, it's a downright sin. Would it kill the man to give Nana a kind word? To show some respect? To treat her like a human bein'? Nana says, "Pay him no never mind, we all git what's comin' to us in the great hereafter." But there jest ain't no call for one human bein' to treat another in such a manner, in this life or the next. "The Lawd jest be testin' us, Tometta," Nana says. I guess she right – I jest ain't sho' why God reckon negroes need so many more tests on this earth than the white folk, an' it be wearin' my soul thin.

Why I jest run into my friend Mary on the bus this very mornin' – didn't she have a story 'bout Mista Cioffi. Her daddy be down at Loveman's an' took a drink from the *white only* water fountain. An' Buddy Cioffi, with a crowd of his *pals*, says to Mista Washington, that be Mary's daddy, "Can't you read boy?" Well, Mista Washington gave Buddy a mighty stare an' jest walk away. Mary's daddy is near on sixty, but he could whup Buddy if'n he set his mind to it. But ya jest don't do that round here, if'n you a negro that is. Mista Washington lost one son fightin' fer this country an' has another still in the Pacific, I don't s'pect he feels like he ought be tol' where he can git a drink of water.

Mary says, "I don't know how ya put up with that man, Tometta, you gotta find you a proper family to work fer. There be a tonna white folk out in Brainard, in beautiful houses, that don't be actin' like that, an' pay a good wage to the right girl. I can ask Missus Stevenson if she knows any families who be lookin' fer a girl, if you want?" *No thanks Mary*, I says, *I jest helpin' my Nana fer a spell, don't reckon I wanna be housekeepin' much longer then need be.* "Don't know what you turnin' ya nose up at, you git a nice family in Brainerd, yoah ain't gonna git much better work round here," she says. I didn't wanna come off like I thinkin' I be better then her, so I says, *Maybe you be right, lemme think on it, Mary.* An' I *don't* be thinkin' I's better than her. She sho' is right, there ain't much better work round here fer a negro woman. It jest seem to be givin' up, sayin' this is the best I can do, this be my lot in life. After bein' in this Buffon house two months, one thing I know sho', it can't git much worse.

It only be Missus Cioffi that make it tol'rable. She one of the finest white folk I ever did come to meet. Dunno how she come to hook up with that husband of hers, but aside that, she be won'erful. Treat me like a true friend. "Call me Button," she always say. I could never do that, poor ole Nana'd have a fit. Nana say, "You be respectin' yoah elders, Tometta, yer Momma didn't raise you like that." Course, Nana don't pay no nevermind when they be callin' her Eva, and when I be fool nuff to point this out, she says, "Tometta, all ya can do in this life is do right by yoahself."

Poor Nana in her eighties now and time startin' to git the best of her, cookin' and cleanin' fer this bunch of do-nothings be more than she can handle fer the moment, so I come to help her till she git back on her feet. Nana don't have much here, 'cept her shack, food to eat, an' a small wage, but she be a proud woman an' it'd break her heart to be put out. So I take the bus ovah ev'ry Monday mornin' an' stay with her till Saturday evenin', 'fore I head home to Momma's. I don't mind the work, I done much worse growin' up, but I could sho' do without that Mista Cioffi lurkin' about. God willin', Nana git her strength back, an' I can get outta this crazy house. Better still, once my William get out of the army, we can git married, git us a small house an' have Nana come live with us. Maybe move up north.

William be my *fee-ance-say*. I've knowed William 'bout far back as I can remember. He be our next-door neighbor where I grew up on Holly Street. He was married to a woman named Martha, 'bout the prettiest woman you'd evah see. I only be 'bout five years old back then. William and Martha always be playin' with us neighborhood chillins, squirtin' us with the garden hose on hot summer days, laughin' at our foolery. Well, William and Martha was gonna have a baby, and never a happier couple you evah see. But God love 'em, both poor Martha and the baby done die durin' chil'birth. We didn't see much of William after that – he barely come out his house, 'cept to go off to work. As the years got on, William start to spend more time tendin' his yard an' garden. But he wasn't the same man. Still frien'ly, but quiet, an' always a sad look about him.

One day – I reckon I was near on 14 at the time – I says *Hullo, Mista Jackson*, as I always done when I seen him in his yard. He say back, "Hullo Tometta. You ole nuff, I reckon you oughta start callin' me Willie." I says, *I dunno Mista Jackson.* He says, "Please, I'd sho' like that." I says, *How 'bout I call you by yoah given name – William, like William Shakespeare – That'd be more proper.* He smile and says, "That'd be fine Tometta, an' who be this William *Shake-spear* anyhows? He must be one fine lookin' fella with a name like William." I giggled and tol' him 'bout the book I be readin', *Romeo and Juliet.* He says, "Tometta, you keep workin' at that. Learnin' to read an' write the most 'portant thing you can do. It be the only way you gonna get a fair shake in life." *Did you learn to read and write, Mista Jackson?* I asked. He says, "No, 'fraid I spent too much time jus' gettin' by when I be growin' up." I says, *I could teach you to read an' write.* He said nothin' fer a spell, but I could see he was thinkin' on it. He says, "Well there be nothin' in this world what would make me happier than to read an' write, but I reckon you best ask yoah momma first."

So I started spendin' 'bout an hour most evenin's teachin' William to read an' write. I reckon I'd always been kinda in love with William, on account of him bein' so handsome an' nice. *Puppy love*, I s'pose you call it. But bein' with William ever' evenin' – well, the love sunk deeper an' deeper into my heart. William be all I could think 'bout. Course, I never tol' him. And he never did show the slightest interest in me – I mean *that kind* of interest. Ovah time, the hour become two, then three. I even read books to him — books he couldn't yet read hisself, *Treasure Island, Tom Sawyer.* We'd laugh when we come to words I didn't know. The two of us lookin' it over like a couple of scientists, soundin' it out, scratchin' our heads.

It was las' June. William an' I be settin' on his front porch, sippin' lemonade, so hot we was grateful fer even the slightest breeze. We jest finished readin' the final chapter of *Black Beauty* an' I was fixin' to go on home. William got a real gentle look on his face an' says, "Tometta, our lessons gonna hafta go on hold fer a spell, I done gone an' enlisted into the Army, I be leavin' next week." My eyes welled with tears, an' my tongue stopped a workin'. Williams says, "Aw, don't you worry, we'll pick it up soon as I get back." Still, I could say nothin'. I'd never let myself imagine our lessons comin' to a end. William leaned towards me, touched the back of my head with his hand, an' kissed me on the lips. Then bein' afraid fer what he'd done, he says, "I'm sorry Tometta, I shouldn't a done that." *Why?* I says, *it felt jest right.* Now he sat there speechless, an' his eyes were wet with tears. I stood up and says, *William, look at me, I's a woman, not the li'l girl next door no more, I's a woman in every way an' I'm in love with you.* Well, Willam might've been struck by lightnin'. He took me in his arms an' whispers, "I love you too" an' kissed me on the lips like I never been kissed before.

Roger:

Have you ever seen a Painted Bunting? Painted Buntings don't usually come as far north as Chattanooga. They're mostly a Gulf Coast bird. But every now and then we get a few, when the summers are especially warm. Today, I saw a pair of Painted Buntings on my way to the Ordnance Works. I was driving along Wilcox Boulevard out by the tunnel when I caught a glimpse of the male bird out of the corner of my eye. You can't mistake a Painted Bunting. What a gaudy little thing he is – red, green, and indigo – like someone took apart a Tanager, a Green Warbler, and an Indigo Bunting and put the pieces back together all mixed up. I pulled to the side of the road and got out my glasses. The Painted Bunting is also called a Nonpareil and, I'll tell you, the name's appropriate. That bird is something to look at. But, boy, is it shy. It's not a bird for the casual birdwatcher. You've got to be patient. You've got to make yourself inconspicuous and stand stock still. When you've made yourself completely indistinguishable from the background, then – just then, maybe the birds will show themselves, maybe you'll be rewarded with a little activity. A warble. Or a chip. I must have watched that pair of birds for half an hour. I was late for work and my supervisor read me the riot act, but it was worth it. Those were the prettiest little birds I have ever seen.

What I missed at work were the first ten minutes of a bombing-run damage-assessment film of a night raid on Hamburg, the Brits dropping our 500-pounders from Lancasters. You could see a thousand cotton puffs springing up across the city as if by magic, until the entire field of view of the camera is tufted with cotton like a North Georgia bedspread. The guys in the screening room are shouting "Yahoo!" with each successive wave of detonations. And I'll admit there was a kind of beauty about the images on the film, as if the city were being blown kisses, smothered in kisses. The bombs fell from the belly of the plane into – well, like into another world, like there's no people down there, and all the time our slide rules were clicking in the dark screening room as we refined, one more time, the precise mix of high explosives and incendiaries that will cause maximum destruction to the German cities. Cotton puffs raced across the industrial districts, the dockyards, the old quarter, the suburbs. "Yahoo, yahoo!" the guys shouted. I was sick. I guess I kept thinking about what was happening under the cotton wool – the firestorm with temperatures of eighteen hundred degrees Fahrenheit, the asphalt of the streets ablaze, trees uprooted and flung through the air, automobiles whirled skyward. In tunnels beneath the city, tens of thousands of men, women, and children suffocated as the air is sucked out of their refuges, then incinerated as superheated air rushes in to replace what has been drawn out. I know all of this, everyone in the room knows it, but we put it out of our minds. Or we try to put it out of our minds. There's a war to be won. The Nazis must be stopped. The world must be "made safe for democracy" and all that rubbish. Strangely, I found myself thinking of the birds – the birds down there in Hamburg's parks and suburbs. When the bombs fell I imagined thousands of birds going puff in the air like Chinese firecrackers – tiny explosions of flesh, little starbursts of singed feathers.

"You were late, Roger," said my supervisor. Mel is from Massachusetts, and he hasn't quite gotten used to living down south. He twitters like a chirping sparrow, a real Nervous Nellie. Always looking over his shoulder, as if someone will find him out. I lied: *I had a flat, not a tread left on my tires*. He wasn't mollified: "You can have your tires recapped at Sears, Roger, no ration certificates are required. You've got to make allowances for these things. You must allow time for emergencies. Our airmen risk their lives to make these films. These films are the only way we have to evaluate our work." *I've seen that film six times before,* I said. He looked at me over his glasses: "That's not the point, Roger. We wouldn't be screening the film unless we believed there was something more we can learn from it. The higher-ups say the mix is wrong, wrong for urban targets. We've got to find the right proportions of blast and burn to scare the hell out of German civilians – sap their will to fight. You've got the wrong attitude, Roger. Remember, you could be over there, getting shot-the-hell up. Deferment is a privilege, and the government expects you to earn it. And so do I." Mel is a pompous Ph.D. chemist from Harvard. He expects everyone to call him Doctor Kelsen. I call him Doctor Mel – to his face. He doesn't quite know what to make of it. He doesn't know if I'm joking, or if I'm making fun of him, or if I'm just a country bumpkin that doesn't know any better. That's what drives him crazy – not knowing. Anyway, he says I have an "attitude problem." You can't fault him for that. He's probably right. My trouble is, I don't know what sort of attitude I'm supposed to have. About my work, I mean. I don't like the idea of making explosives, but I'm good at it. In fact, I'm damn good at it. I seem to have a knack for it. I'm not a chemist, just a plain engineer and not even a chemical engineer. But I know about explosives. I understand the way the stuff behaves. I can feel in my bones exactly how a bomb is going to explode. When we test a new device I can usually tell the other engineers exactly how the bomb will detonate – with what pressure, to what effect, and so forth. That's why they need me, and that's why Mel backs off. A few of the bigwigs want me to go to Oak Ridge, near Knoxville. Something big is going on up there, some kind of superweapon, I think, although no one seems to know exactly what. There's a factory that's more than a half-mile square, I know that for sure. I've got no desire to leave Chattanooga, but sooner or later, I suppose they will make me go. I'm happy enough right here, happy enough with the bombs I'm making now. Or *unhappy enough*, I should say.

As a matter of fact, I think I might be on to a new kind of explosive, something I've worked out all by my lonesome – a way to self-catalyze TNT. I know my new mix will be at least twenty percent more effective than the stuff we are producing now but I haven't figured out yet what to do about my idea. It's my *attitude problem*, I suppose. I know that twenty-percent might not sound like much, but making a bomb that will do twenty-percent more damage is like increasing your weapons production by twenty-percent, and the boys in the Washington would love that. As soon as I realized the potential of my new idea, I stopped working on it at the Ordnance Works and started tinkering in my own lab in Mamie's basement. If the idea works out, then maybe I'll tell the Army and maybe I won't. It seems to me as if the war is almost over anyway. No point adding one more bit of nasty stuff to the world. I don't know what I'll do, but for the moment, I think I'll keep my idea to myself. I've made myself a testing chamber out of an old hot water tank. I've been detonating milligrams of my new compound and let me tell you, this stuff is fierce, especially if I add jellied petroleum. Ten minutes after ignition, it's still burning on the walls of the tank. *Fire-paint* I call it.

Can you imagine what would happen if it got on skin? That's what I keep thinking about. I keep thinking about kids over there in those German cities with this stuff on their skin. Fire-paint. The effect is almost too terrible to think about, although I suppose it can't be a lot worse than what we are using now.

I almost told Button about my idea. When I came home from work she was sitting on the back steps shucking peas. I was feeling kind of low – I suppose because of what Mel had said – so I sat down with Button. I almost told her. I almost asked her to come down to the basement and watch one of my miniature explosions. It just seemed to be the right thing to do at the time, like she was someone I could trust. But I didn't. Instead, I just sat there and watched her shuck peas. Every now and then she would look up and smile. I don't know why, but when she had finished the peas and went inside, I felt much better.

Button:

Roger is a sweet man, but I can't say as I really understand him. He seems to walk around in a kind of fog. I know he works hard, and he certainly is generous with the family, but somehow it seems that he doesn't belong here with the rest of us. He almost never joins us for supper, even when he's home – he just grabs a sandwich or something and goes off to that lab of his in the basement, and an hour or two later there'll be a boom and the house will shake a little and everyone will look at each other and shake their heads as if to say, "Roger is at it again."

Last evening he stopped on his way into the house and sat next to me on the back steps. I was snapping peas to help out in the kitchen on account of Eva being sick. Roger sat there and watched. It seemed like he wanted to say something, but he never did. He just watched. He's a sweet man but I hadn't any idea what to say to him, I mean, really. So I didn't say anything.

I feel kind of bad for Roger because of Wanda. I know that I should take her side because she's my sister and all, and when we were little she was my best friend, but I don't think that their troubles are Roger's fault. It seems to me that if Wanda just paid a little more attention to the things that Roger is interested in, then they might get along OK. But Wanda's all caught up in her own world. She was always like that, even when she was a little girl.

Once, when I was six years old and Wanda was eight years old, we both got dolls for Christmas, really nice dolls with eyes that closed when you laid the dolls down, and brown lashes, and pretty dresses. My doll was blonde and Wanda's was a brunette. She wanted my doll, even though her's was just as nice. She said bad things about my doll – that my doll was a cry-baby, that my doll didn't have a mother, that my doll was dirty, things like that – and she said good things about her doll – that her doll was going to be a movie star, that her doll could dance, and so on. Finally, I asked Wanda if we could swap dolls, and we did. Then – well, you can guess what happened. Suddenly it was the blonde doll that was going to be the movie star, and all the rest. Wanda, of course, ended up with the doll she wanted all along. She was always like that, she always got what she wanted, and usually what she wanted was whatever I had. But I didn't mind, because Wanda was my best friend, and anyway, I never really expected to have what I wanted, even when I was a little girl.

When Daddy died – I was eleven – it kind of seemed to me like it was the expected thing to happen, like he was meant to go away. But Wanda was terribly sad. She hardly talked to anyone for months, she just stayed in our room sulking whenever we weren't at school. She didn't talk to any of her friends. She didn't even talk to me. Daddy died at just about the time when Wanda was beginning to become a woman, when her body was beginning to develop, I mean. Somehow I think the two things got all mixed up in her mind. She became very preoccupied with her body. She wasn't so skinny then, and she really did have a very nice figure, clear skin, and lovely breasts. She went about our room naked – at bedtime, I mean, or when she was getting ready for her bath – I just couldn't believe it. She wanted me to see, wanted me to be jealous of her beauty, I suppose, wanted me to see that she had breasts and I didn't. But I wasn't jealous. I thought Wanda was pretty. I was proud that she was pretty. She was my best friend. She was my sister.

And now Wanda wants Buddy. Poor Roger isn't good enough for her, she wants my husband. Not that getting Buddy will take a lot of doing. Buddy falls down over anyone in a skirt. Any fool can see the way he keeps his eye on Wanda. He doesn't think I know what's going on, but I do, I know, I mean how could I *not* know, he thinks he's being so subtle but anyone with eyes can see. Wanda spends half her time laying about half naked and Buddy can't keep his eyes off her, although there's really not that much to see, I mean, she's a real string bean. Oh, she'll get him, all right if she hasn't already. But right now Buddy has someone else on his mind, too. Eva's great-granddaughter, Tometta. Tometta is taking care of Eva while Eva is sick, and helping out with Eva's chores. She's – I don't know, really – seventeen, maybe eighteen, going on *thirty*. And really beautiful, with skin like Chinese lacquer, and Ipana teeth. What's really sad to see is Buddy panting after this beautiful negro girl when he's the biggest bigot in the world. I mean, you'd think he would be ashamed of himself, he treats Eva like she's the scum of the earth, and whenever Tometta comes into the house he suddenly finds a hundred excuses to be in the kitchen. Of course, Tometta doesn't give him the time of the day, and, really, why should she, she's got way too much sense for that. Tometta is nobody's fool, she knows that Buddy treats her great-grandma like trash, but still, it's pitiful to see Buddy lurking around the kitchen with his big silly Italian eyes crawling all over that young girl's body.

I suppose I should resent the way Buddy behaves, he being my husband and all, but I can't say as I do. I know it's a terrible thing to say, but as long as he's chasing after someone else, he's not bothering me. Of course, he's meaner than ever when he's crazy on someone like Tometta or Wanda. That's when he really takes it out on me. He calls me frigid, and a prude, but I don't care anymore. Maybe I am frigid. So what? I tried to be a good wife to Buddy. I tried to be everything he wanted me to be. One time I even took his – *thing* into my mouth. He'd been torturing me for months, really, saying the ugliest things to me, or looking at me with those Barney Google eyes, and pretending to be hurt, like, trying to make me feel guilty. But I don't feel guilty. I don't think a person should ever have to do something they don't want to do, I mean, if two people love each other then it seems to me the first thing they would think about is what the other person wants, which is why, I suppose, I finally did it, took his *thing* in my mouth, I mean. I mean, what's the big deal?

Tometta is a sweet girl, I can understand why Buddy finds her attractive. She usually lives with her mother over in East Chattanooga. Her grandmother is an English teacher at Howard High School – the colored high school – and Tometta is as smart as a whip. If there was ever anyone who should go to college, it is Tometta, that girl always has a book in her hand, but of course she won't – go to college, I mean. There's really no where she could go, there's not a college for negroes in Chattanooga, and she could never afford to go away from home. Lord knows what she will end up doing. Probably a maid or something, in one of the houses up on Lookout Mountain. You know, that girl is as sweet as pie to Eva, watches over her great-grandma like an angel. Tometta's made herself a little bed in the corner of Eva's shack, and just seems to be as happy as can be, like a bug in a rug. Really, the only thing that bothers her is Buddy.

Sometimes I wish that I had gone to college. I could have gotten into the University of Chattanooga, and Uncle Iggy said he would pay for it, but Mother didn't want me to go because it wasn't a Catholic college, although God knows what she expected could happen to me, I mean, it's not like I was going to Nashville or Atlanta or something. I really should have gone. I was at the top of my class at Notre Dame High School, and I used to read all the time, I mean, I must have read about a thousand books when I was in high school, I mean, everything – murder mysteries, romances, all the classics, everything. Maybe if I had gone to college I could have gotten away from Chattanooga, gone somewhere really different. I would really like to have gone to California. Who knows what would have happened with my life if I had gone to California? I wouldn't be married to Buddy, that's for sure, and I wouldn't be stuck here in this crazy house with all these crazy people.

Iggy:

That Button sho' is sweet. Still cute as a Button, too. She come up an' chewed the fat with me fer a spell this mornin', tellin' me all about her job at the drug store, about the folk that come in an' the crazy things they ask fer. Tellin' me about Mrs. Reynolds comin' in an' askin' fer somethin' fer her hemorrhoids an' pretendin' like it was fer her husband, an' other such malarkey. Damn if that gal didn't have me in stitches. Why I'd say that Button should be on the radio, have her own comedy show or somethin'. She be settin' right here on the edge of the bed, an' when I wasn't laughin' like a darn fool, all I could think on was how much I used to fancy that girl when she was a youngin'. I'll tell you this, there's one good thing 'bout gettin' old an' that's not havin' women cloudin' up your brain all the damn day an' night. Why, when I first come into this house, that girl damn near drove me crazy. Sometimes I reckon *I was crazy*, her bein' my niece an' all, an' her bein' jus' a kid not even half my age – hell, barely a quarter my age. Jus' no explainin' the way them things work, you see, it's like some part of your brain has a life all its own an' the rest of you can't do a damn thang about it.

Button brought Eva's great-granddaughter up to see me. Tometta, they call her. I says, *I don't reckon I ever did hear that name before*, an' she tol' me that her pappy's name was Tom an' her mama's name was Etta, so they done call her Tometta. A nice girl I reckon, but I don't think Button ought be bringin' her upstairs on social calls, her bein' a colored girl an' all. I held my tongue, of course, her bein' jus' a girl, an' I don't reckon I oughta speak of it to Button neither. That Button's jus' too damn nice fer her own good. When Button was a youngin' she'd bring home every stray cat an' dog in Chattanooga. You'da thunk this place was the city pound, what with all the darned strays aroun'. Mamie used to raise sand over it, but that didn't stop Button from bringin' home the critters. It's not that I *personally* mind Tometta comin' upstairs. I ain't got nothin' against colored folk myself, but there been too much trouble brewin' lately, an' nuthin' good'll come of gettin' too – how should I say, *intimate* with 'em. Folk is folk, an' it seems to me that different sort of folk should keep to their own kind. There's lots of trouble goin' on out in Texas, an' up North, an' some folk think that once this war's ovah all hell gonna bust loose an' there'll be a race war an' all. Tootsie tells me Vincent heard the colored people are stockpilin' guns, hidin' 'em away, jus' waitin' on the Japs an' Germans to surrender, an' then there's gonna be an' uprisin'. Tootsie says Vincent done heard that the nigra soldiers comin' home from the service are keepin' their guns an' ammo an' grenades, an' squirrlin' them away. Now, mind you, I don't put much stock in what that fool Vincent says, but Toostie says that Becca heard the same things. In fact, Becca reckons, the coloreds ain't gonna wait fer the end of the war. 'Cordin to Becca, there's gonna be an uprisin' soon, maybe even this summer, while all the white men are away. I ask Button what she reckons, an' she pooh-poohs the whole idea, but Button is too trustful. I don't exactly know if any of this stuff about a nigra uprisin' will come to be, but it sho' wouldn't be takin' me by su'prise. Lawd knows the nigras got enough reason to be mad, but I don't rightly know what oughta be done about it. I reckon it's best if things jus' go on as they are. It's easy for those yankees up north to talk about in'egration an' all, but they don't have the same number of nigras we got.

I've seen the way the colored folk live. Fer some twenty odd years I sold life insurance fer Southern Mutual an' spent most of that time workin' in the nigra community. I reckon I've been in nearly every colored house in Chattanooga, so when I say I've seen the way they live, I sho' as shootin' know what I'm talkin' about. They ain't the kind of folk you'd want next door, that's fer sho'. They ain't got no idea how to keep up a piece of property. Ain't hardly a house I visited that couldn't of used a coat a paint. Course, that ain't the real problem. The *real* problem is the mixin' of the races. Once you have in'egration, it's inevitable that there's gonna be mixin' of the races. Jus' look at that Tometta girl. Any damn fool can see that she's pretty, too damn pretty fer her own good, if you askin' me. Tootsie says Vincent's been followin' Tometta aroun' like a tomcat in heat, an' God knows that Vincent ain't got the time of day fer colored folk. I reckon, if Vincent is chasin' afta a colored gal, then it's inevitable that with in'egration you're gonna have mixin' of the races, an' I don't know *anyone* who thinks *that'd* be a good thang. I remember one house I was in, over off Third Street, with a mixed-race couple – well, they both called themselves nigras on the insurance papers, but the woman, why she sho' *looked* white – an' the two wee girls in that house both with somethin' wrong with 'em, somethin' mental, or least that's the way it looked to me. That's what'd happen if we start mixin' the races, we'd have a nation of bloomin' morons, that's fer damn sho'. If there's gonna be a nigra uprisin', this neighborhood'll be the first to go. God knows the nigras are but a few blocks away. It won't be the folks up on the mountains or out in Brainerd or North Chattanooga that'll pay the price, it'll be us folk downtown. I tol' Mamie five years ago she ought sell this house an' move to one of the suburbs, but she wouldn't hear of it – stubborn as a mule. "This is Nelson's house," she says, "and I'm not fixin' to sell it." Well, if poor ole Nelson was still kickin', he'd sell up faster than green grass goes through a goose. The only white families still livin' down town are too poor to go. Anyhows, if'n an uprisin' comes to pass, we'll be the ones on the front line, so to speak, an' that's worth givin' some thought to. Tootsie says Vincent is fixin' on buying a gun, an' Becca an' Lynette are eggin' him on. I don't put much stock in Vincent an' his hare-brained ideas, but this time the boy jus' might be on to somethin'. It can't hurt to be careful. If I wasn't stuck in this damn bed, I'd go out an' git me a gun myself. Afta all, I'm the only one aroun' here with an inklin' how to shoot the damn thangs. Vincent was a sailor an' couldn't hit the side of a barn if he held the barrel 'gainst the boards. I was a pretty damn good shot when I was in the Army, the best in the troop. Got myself an Expert's badge, an' if I hadn't come down with dysentery I woulda shot me a few Spaniards, that's sho'. Actually, when you think on it, *I jus' might be* of some use. This here window looks right down Ninth Street, an' that's the way they'd come. I could sit right up here in this window an' pick em off one by one as they come over the hill. Yep, now that you think on it, it might not be such a fool idea. I think I'll have me a li'l talk with Tootsie.

Tootsie:

Iggy wants me to get him a gun. He wants me to talk to Billy Joe Alaska. He wants me to tell Billy Joe to bring him a rifle. Iggy says Billy Joe has lots of guns and that I should tell him to bring one to our house, real secret like. Billy Joe is Iggy's friend. He lives on Eighth Street, just a couple of blocks away, and he comes by here every Christmas and Easter to see Iggy. Alaska's not Billy Joe's real name, but everyone calls him that because he used to live up in Alaska. I don't know what his real name is, but everyone calls him Billy Joe Alaska. I don't think I should do it. Get the gun, I mean. Iggy says he wants the gun because the colored people are going to have a revolution or something and he wants to be prepared. I asked Tometta if the colored people were going to have a revolution, and she just laughed. She asked me, "Who tol' you such a thing," but I didn't tell her it was Iggy, I just said it was something I heard on the radio. She said, "Well, they ought not put such things on the radio. It'll get the white folk all riled up an' they'll take it out on us." I said, *Buddy and Becca say that the colored people are hiding guns and that they're going to shoot all the white people.* Tometta said, "Lis'en, chile, if anyone's gonna get shot, it'll be us colored folk, jes like it always be."

I believe Tometta. I think if there was going to be a revolution, Tometta would know about it, and I don't think she's lying. But I'm scared anyway. I wish there was someone I could ask about the gun, but Iggy made me promise I wouldn't say anything to anyone but Billy Joe. If Iggy is crazy like Becca says he is, then he shouldn't have a gun. A couple of weeks ago he said, "If I had a gun I'd shoot that goddam woodpecker outside my window." I thought he was just kidding, but now I'm not so sure. Dad wouldn't want Iggy shooting any woodpeckers.

I don't like Billy Joe Alaska. He gives me the creeps. He lives all by himself in a big old house with a bunch of guns, and he has hair in his nose. When he came to see Iggy at Christmas, he brought him magazines with pictures of naked ladies. Iggy didn't want the magazines, but he took them and pretended to like them until Billy Joe went away, then he asked me to take them out to the trash. I'm glad Iggy didn't look at the magazines. "I'm too goddamn old fer that sorta stuff," he said, "it jus' makes my eyes hurt." I looked at the magazines before I threw them out – by myself out in the garage – and they were really bad. Not like the pin-up girls in the Esquire magazines that Buddy reads. Billy Joe's magazines had real photographs of real ladies with their clothes off. You could see between their legs and everything. I think the ladies were ugly. Anyway, that's why I don't like Billy Joe.

I have another secret too – besides Iggy wanting a gun. It's a secret about Bitsy. Bitsy has a boyfriend. The secret is that he's a German. I mean a *real* German, a *real army German*, one of the German prisoners at the National Cemetery. Bitsy was walking by the Cemetery and stopped to talk to one of the prisoners through the fence. The prisoners stay in a guardhouse that's right on Bailey Avenue, and Bitsy stopped to talk. There's a big fence, with barbed wire on the top, and an American soldier that watches all the time, but the guards don't mind if anyone talks to the Germans. Bitsy talked to a boy named Horst. He's just the same age as she is, nineteen. He doesn't speak much English, and she doesn't know any German except *donkey-shane*, so I don't know how they talk, but they do. Every afternoon when the prisoners stop working Bitsy goes down to the cemetery and talks to Horst. The first few times she asked me to come with her because she was scared, but now she goes by herself. I think Horst is her boyfriend. She said, "He's not a Nazi, you know." Bitsy says that Horst didn't want to fight the war, only Hitler made him fight. Bitsy says that Horst just wants the war to be over so he can go home and see if his father and mother are still alive. They live in a place called Essen, and I know that we have dropped lots of bombs there because Dad said so. I asked Dad if the Allies bombed Essen, and he said they had nearly blasted it off the face of the earth. I didn't tell Bitsy what Dad said, because she might tell Horst and he would be even more worried about his parents.

I feel sorry for Bitsy having a German boyfriend. They can't go to the pictures or for a walk or anything. All they can do is talk. Bitsy brings Horst chewing gum. If she stretches all the way across the wall she can almost reach the wire fence, and if Horst sticks his fingers through the wire he can reach the gum. But they can't touch fingers. Bitsy said that she and Horst tried to touch fingers, but she can't quite reach far enough. Horst told Bitsy that he loves her. He said *eek-leeba-dick*, or something like that, and she didn't know what it meant so when she came home she looked it up in Grandpa's German dictionary and it means "I love you." Bitsy cried. I asked Bitsy if she loves Horst. She said, "I don't know, but I think so." I think it's OK that Bitsy has a German boyfriend, but she made me swear not to tell anyone. She's afraid people will think she's a traitor of something. She's especially afraid of what Buddy would say. Buddy hates Germans.

Bitsy goes to work early in the morning at the Central Avenue Dry Cleaners, so she can't see Horst when he is at the guard house in the mornings. So she asked me if I would take things to Horst, notes and things. She writes little notes in English, mostly about what's happening in the war and about herself, and I take them down to the cemetery and throw them to Horst. And he sends her presents too, little animals and dolls that he carves out of wood. Horst has a penknife that one of the American guards gave him so that he can carve – it's his hobby – and every day he gives Bitsy a little figure. She keeps all the little figures behind food jars in the pantry on the back porch. They are lined up there like little soldiers. She won't keep the figures in her room because she is afraid that Alma will find them. She says that Alma is always looking for things and she can't keep anything secret from Alma. I don't think anyone will find them in the back porch pantry because nobody hardly ever goes there. Back when the war started we had a Victory Garden on the badminton court, and Mamie and Eva put up lots of vegetables in Mason jars. Lots and lots of vegetables. We ate some of them, but now Eva thinks they may have gone rotten, 'cause she won't use what's left. So the jars just sit there, in the pantry on the back porch, and that's where Bitsy hides her presents. Bitsy has pretty blonde hair, and she says that Horst especially likes her hair. I think Bitsy is the prettiest of all my aunts. Some people think that Becca's prettiest, but I think Bitsy is. She's the only one with blonde hair, and pretty green eyes, and she always looks so nice with her hair pulled back with barrettes. When she goes to see Horst, she always puts on red lipstick and nail polish, and she paints her toenails too, but Horst can't see her toenails because of her socks.

This morning I went to the cemetery with Dad and the Germans were digging graves. Horst saw me and waved, but I pretended not to see him. Dad didn't notice because he was looking at some bird or another. I don't think Dad would mind about Bitsy and Horst. Dad doesn't think all Germans are bad. I would have liked to tell Dad about Bitsy and Horst, because I don't like having so many secrets, but I didn't, because I promised Bitsy I wouldn't. I won't tell Iggy, either. Iggy wants me to tell him everything, but I won't tell him about Horst.

Bitsy asked me if I think Horst is handsome. I said, *Yeah, I guess so*. He has blonde hair like Bitsy, and a blonde mustache, and blonde fuzz all over his arms. He's the youngest of the German prisoners. There are three German prisoners, and Horst is the youngest. The other two look like old men, and I think that maybe Horst misses young people and that is why he likes Bitsy. The prisoners have to wear gray suits all the time, and on the back it says POW. Bitsy asked me if I knew what POW means, and I did know because Dad had told me. Dad said the prisoners are lucky, because they get a nice bed and good food, and if they were still in Italy or France they might get killed. But I don't think Horst is happy. He hardly ever smiles and he has sad eyes. But he has a sweet face, and I don't think he's a Nazi.

I have one more secret – a secret from *Bitsy*. I kept one of Horst's wooden figures, a little boy holding a lamb. I don't know why I kept it. It wasn't meant for me, but it was so cute, I just kept it. I keep it under my pillow and I hold it in my hand when I sleep.

Buddy:

Who does that nigger think she is, that's what I'd like to know? Everyone knows colored girls are as horny as all get out, so where does she get off acting all high and mighty? I just gave her tit a little squeeze. And let me tell you, that gal has got herself some sweet titties. She was washing dishes at the kitchen sink, with those bee-u-ti-ful breasts hanging over them dishes, her wet dress clinging on for dear life. Good Lord, even thinking about it now gets my blood flowing. So I say *How's it going*, and she says "Jest fine," so I reach around from behind and give one of her titties a little *how do you do*. Damned if she didn't jab me in the ribs with her elbow, and, I mean hard. She says, "Don't you ever be layin' yer dirty paws on me ag'in." I say, *Listen girl, you come in here showing yourself off and you can expect a little attention*. She says, "You ever touch me ag'in an' I'll be stickin' you with sometin' more'n my elbow." And I believe it, too. That girl has a violent streak in her. I said, *You're lucky to have a job here, and don't you forget it*. She said, "I ain't got no job here, I's jest helpin' my Nana." I said, *Wouldn't your Nana like to know what a whore you are*. She said, "Ohh...you won't be tellin' my Nana nothin'." I said, *Don't push me, girl*. She said, "If Missus Cioffi know what you done, she'd cry with shame."

Where does she get off acting like that? You'd think she'd appreciate the fact that a white man finds her attractive. My ribs are still smarting where she jabbed me, but hell, I'd say it was worth it. That Tometta has fantastic tits, and she didn't have a bra on either, just that thin cotton dress. I'd like to slather that gal in butter, and eat her like a stack of wheat cakes. But I'll tell you this, I'm going to be careful next time, because when Tometta says she'd stick me with a knife, I thinks she means it. Niggers are nuts – *violent* nuts. I think it's in their genes – what you might call the *law of the jungle*. That's why I'm nervous about what's brewing. It's all over town that something big is about to happen, some kind of race riot. They say the police found a cache of dynamite in a shack over by Howard High School, and Becca heard that a whole rack of M-1 rifles was stol'n from the Armory. It makes sense that the coloreds will make their move now, while all our boys are tied up overseas. The police won't be able to do anything to stop it – they're just a bunch of tottering old fools who're scared of their own shadows. That's why I got myself a gun. A fine little thirty-eight revolver, as pretty as can be. It cost me twenty-four-fucking-bucks but worth every penny. And two boxes of ammo. You should see the way that little sweetheart lays in my hand, like a baby in a cradle. I showed it to Becca and Lynette. Lynette was fascinated, but wouldn't go near it. Becca couldn't wait to get her hands on it. That girl wasn't scared a bit. I said, *Be careful, it's loaded.* And she just points the gun at Mamie's clock on the mantle and says, "Kablooie!" I just love the way Becca holds that thing, she's not afraid of it at all. I said, *If you want, I'll teach you how to use it.* She said, "And where did you learn how to use a gun?" I laughed, *I was in the service, you know.* She said, "They certainly didn't teach you how to use a thirty-eight in the Navy." I said, *Listen, a gun's is a gun. It's a skill, like riding a bike. Once you know how to do it, it's as easy as falling off a log.* She said, "OK Wyatt Earp, teach me how to shoot it." So I'm going to teach Becca to shoot. Come Saturday morning we are going to the cave in the National Cemetery, and I'll show her how to use it. I just love the way Becca holds that thing – with both hands, those pretty little fingers curled around the handle, like this – *Kablooie!*

Becca's the sister I should have married. I'll tell you this, Button would never touch the thirty-eight. If Button knew I bought a gun, she'd be out of her mind. I made Becca and Lynette swear not to tell her. You know, I had this thought, just daydreaming, where I'm showing Button the gun, and explaining it to her, sort of, and the gun just happens to go off. I'm not serious, it was just a passing thought, but if something was to happen to Button, an accident like, then, well, I could start over, have another chance, maybe find myself a girl like Becca who wasn't such a cold fish. It's just a thought. I'd never actually wish anything like that to happen. I shouldn't even be thinking it. It was just a thought. I don't like thinking things like that, but I'll tell you, sometimes I think I'm going crazy. I'll be sitting at the table, say, looking at Emily Sue, and she'll be sitting there looking so pretty with those big dumb eyes of hers, and her hair cut short like a boy's and sticking out every which direction, and food all over her face, and I start having thoughts, like, well, hell, I get a boner just sitting there, and the next thing you know I'm thinking about Button, and I wanna smack her. If she were taking care of me like a wife should, I wouldn't be havin' such thoughts about Emily Sue. Maybe I'm hard on Button, but damn, any guy knows what I mean. I'm sure some poor soul stranded in the desert doesn't think about much of anything but water. Sometimes I think about that girl Kaki – or Kiki – out at Pearl, and I think that when the war is over I could just disappear, get up and go, out to Hawaii, and start over. I'll tell you this, those islands are going to boom after the war and whoever gets in on the bottom floor is going to make a fortune. So here's what I'd do. I'd cash in my life insurance policy – that'd be about four-hundred dollars – off to Hawaii, and buy some land on the beach – it'd be dirt cheap, if you got there as soon as the war ended – and I'd build myself a little house, and find myself a girl like Kiki, not marry her, just live with her in this sweet little house on the beach, and when the boom came, I'd sell off the rest of the land for a big profit, and then I'd be set for life. Nothing but sunshine and pineapples and hula girls – and hot little Kiki. Hell, now that I think of it, Becca would look pretty damn fine in a coconut bra and a grass skirt.

When I was a kid I used to dream about going to some place like Florida or Texas, where the sun shines all the time and the living is easy. My dad had a delicatessen in New York City back in the twenties, and when the depression came he lost it – the bank took the whole building and dumped dad's business on the street – and he said, well, OK, we'll just go down south, because he had heard the depression wasn't so bad down south, so we packed up and took the train to Chattanooga, and we weren't here for more than a month when my mother died of the flu, or pneumonia, or some damn thing, and then the life just went out of my dad. I watched him get old right before my eyes. He wasn't much older than I am now, maybe thirty-five or thirty-six – a big, strong, virile guy – and after Mama died, it's like he turned sixty overnight. I couldn't bear to watch it. He was doing just any old work he could get, and getting paid peanuts for doing it. Like a fucking old man. And I used to think, there's no way I'm going to end up like him. I would go to Florida, or Texas, and find a way to make a good living, and keep it simple – just sunshine and the good life. But somehow I never did. I ended up hanging around Chattanooga, and then I met Button at the Tivoli, and well, the next thing you know we were married, and living in that little apartment on Cameron Hill, and it was like everything I had hoped for had gone up in smoke. It's not like anything had happened that I hadn't foreseen, it's just that something started eating away at me, and whenever I'd see my dad all alone and seeming twice his age I'd end up depressed and thinking, *That's no way to live a life*. I don't know what it was I wanted, but Button wasn't giving it to me. I tried to talk to her about it. I figured we could work it out if we could just talk about it, but she wouldn't talk. She'd say, "Buddy, there's no point in talking, you're going to be unhappy no matter what I do." And that's when I realized that she was probably right, and that's when I decided to sign up for the Navy. I knew that if I didn't get the fuck out of here, I'd end up like my dad. I still feel like that. I'm thirty fuckin' years old and I haven't had a life. Can you believe it, Button is the only woman I've ever done. Oh, I fooled around a lot with other girls before I met Button, and, well, there was that Jap girl out at Pearl, but Button's the only woman I've ever actually fucked, and I think, that's goddamn pathetic. I just wasn't meant to get married. Some guys may thrive on it, but I wasn't meant to get married. Damned if I know what can be done about it now. That's why all those awful thoughts come into my brain. I'd never want any harm to come to Button, but you can see why I'd think about it. There's got to be some way out of this godawful mess.

Damn, I can't get Tometta out of my mind. She is one fantastical piece of ass – like a big piece of Belgian chocolate. Just thinking about touching that titty of hers sends shivers up my spine. You could tell she didn't have a brassiere on, and I reckon a girl like that probably doesn't wear panties, either. You just know that some black boy is getting into that sweetie-pie's pussy, and I'll tell you, that's one lucky nigger I wouldn't mind trading places with.

Tometta:

Good Lawd, someone's gone put in Tootsie's head that the negroes are gonna revolt, scarin' the poor girl half to death. Anyone with half-a-brain know us negroes ain't fool nuff to think takin' up arms would do us a lick a good. Least of all in *Chattanooga*. We so much's spit on the sidewalk, an' they's ready to string us up from the nearest tree.

William says there is a revolution of sorts goin' on. A revolution in how folk think. He reckons things is gonna improve fer us after the war. He writes me real regular from Fort Hood in Texas. At first, when he be at Camp Claiborne, I couldn't make much of his letters, so much be scratched out by the Army censors, but now they post the letters when they's off base. His letters are writ real nice too. William done made a friend who helps him with his spellin'.

...You better look out Tometta, I gots me a new teacher down here who just might take your job. Ha ha, just teazing, he be awful smart, but you got charms he don't have. His name be Jim Tanner and he from up north and even went to a college - the University of Massachusetts. Jim says up north is the place to be for the negro. He say it ain't perfect, but he can't believe how bad it be down here in Texas. Jim says after the war you and me ought move up north. Says he'll help us find a place to live and even a job. Course you'll be having to convinse Nana to come with us. You know how stubborn that old lady be. Hu ha just funning, you best not read this to Nana or we both be in big trouble. Lot of talk of us finally shipping out. All the guys say we sure to get some leave before we do. My heart akes to see you again and hold you in my arms. I will let you know soon as I knows for sure...

"University of Massachusetts" wasn't in William's hand. I reckon Jim figure the war'd be ovah fore he could call out all the letters to William. I can jest picture William drivin' poor Jim crazy, "Jim, how you spell this – Jim, how you spell that."

I wonder if it be possible fer us to move up north after the war, an' even fer me to go to a college like the University of

Massachusetts. Missus Cioffi always be sayin' I should be in college. I reckon she thinks I could throw on one of Bitsy's sweaters and skirts and march down to the University of Chattanooga and start takin' classes. But I don't say nothin'. I reckon it all be outta kindness, her way of payin' me a compliment. Her way of sayin', things jest ain't right. An' it ain't right. I reckon that be why William so keen on movin up north. Am I crazy to think I could go to college there?

With William coming home soon, I shouldn't be wastin' thoughts on such foolish dreams. This prob'ly be the last I see him 'fore he ships overseas. He be training in Louisiana an' Texas for near a year now. William didn't figure 'em to ever actually ship out. William says they don't trust the negro troops to go into combat, but I reckon things must be gettin' desp'rate. William be in a tank battalion, the 761st – *The Black Panthers* they call themselves. Most of the negro troops are sent to places like San Diego to load ships, or off to some place like China to drive trucks. I wish William was goin' off to load ships. The thought of him in combat scares the livin' daylights outta me. Still, I can't be more proud. This be the first armored division of colored troops. William says, "If we expect to get the same rights as the white folk in this country, we's gonna hafta fight an' die for her jes' like the white boys." I reckon I jest gotta be positive an' trust the Lawd to watch ovah him.

I mus' say, the whole idea of William going off to fight in Europe has put some thoughts into my head. Thoughts which prob'ly shouldn't be there. The thought of him dyin' on a battlefield in some God-fersaken place, an' us never havin' made love together, well I don't want his last thoughts to be regret, is all. An' if I said I wasn't wanting to do it myself, I'd be lyin'. When William be kissing me, feelings take me, an' I sho' want him in the worse way. Course we ain't had much time together – together as a couple. He was off to the army soon as we realized we was meant to be together. He been back three times on leave, and I mus' say, it got a might passionate at times. Mostly kissin', and sometimes touchin', but he always stop there. I know he wants to do more. Last time he be home, he had me in such a state, I says, *I wouldn't mind whatever you want to do with me, William.* He says, "Sugah, when I get outta the army, I's gonna make an honest woman outta you, and God help ya then." An' that was it. He stopped kissin' me, closed his eyes, put the sweetest smile on his face, like he was in some magical place, an' jest held me in his strong arms, rockin' me ever so gentle. I reckon that be the reason I love him so in the first place. Lawd I miss him. He can't be here soon nuff.

I jest hope that fool Buddy has the sense not to be lurkin' round when William get here. I could never tell William what that man done to me. I can't imagine what William'd do to Buddy if'n he found he put his hands on me. What kinda man jest go an grab a woman like that? Of course, once it all be said an' done, William would end up bein' the one in trouble. That Buddy Cioffi even call me a *whore*. An' he no better to his own wife. I dunno how that poor woman take it. If that man gits through life without someone killin' him, it'll be a miracle. I jest gotta make sho' it ain't William who be the one who do it.

Roger:

Tootsie says that Buddy has bought a gun. You'd think there was enough shooting going on in the world these days without Buddy going out and buying a gun. He expects the colored people are going to come marching down Ninth Street, looting and raping and all that malarkey. Becca and Lynette believe every dumb rumor they hear at work, and pass them all along to Buddy, and of course that's like throwing fuel on a fire because he hates the negroes anyway. Any fool knows that colored people aren't going to do anything. Those poor folks are beset on every side by nitwits like Buddy and every other hooligan red-neck in a bedsheet. All those rumors about caches of guns and stol'n weapons are put out by the Klan to stir up hatred – like out in Beaumont, Texas. Everyone resents that the negroes are getting jobs that used to go to white people, that's the real crux of the matter, but there isn't any alternative if we are going to win the war. That's what people don't understand.

All Buddy's got to do is go flying off the handle and somebody's going to get hurt. Tootsie said that Buddy showed the gun to Becca and Lynette. Now that's really crazy. Those girls have no business playing with dangerous weapons. I don't understand why Buddy doesn't just let those girls be. I said to him, *Buddy, I know you've bought a gun, and I just hope you'll be careful with it.* He said, "How'd you know I have a gun?" I said, *Never mind how I know, I just know. I can't imagine what you are going to do with it.* He said, "I'm going to shoot every goddam bird in Chattanooga, that's what I'm going to do." That's what I mean about Buddy being crazy.

But I wouldn't put it past him. Buddy would just as soon take a pot shot at a bird as look at one. It's beyond Buddy to understand how someone can love natural things. He calls me Birdy Man. He thinks that's funny. But, you gotta agree, birds aren't doing nearly as much harm in the world as people. That's why I like birdwatching. It's a peaceful activity. I could sit for hours waiting for a glimpse of a rare bird. Somewhere I read that John James Audubon used to shoot birds so he could paint them. I can't figure that out, how anyone who loves birds would shoot them, even to paint them. Sometimes I wonder if Audubon really *did* love birds, or whether it was just something he did for a career, to make himself rich selling portfolios of his prints. I don't know, I'm probably wrong or there wouldn't be Audubon Societies and all that, but it just doesn't make a lot of sense to me.

I was talking to Button yesterday evening. She was sitting with Tometta in the glider when I came home, and I sat with them for a spell. I didn't tell her about Buddy's gun because I knew she would be upset, but I kind of fished around a bit and I could tell that she doesn't know about it. She and Tometta were talking about books. Button was saying that she used to read all the time, but that she never reads any more, and Tometta told her she should start reading again. Tometta went into Eva's shack and fetched a book for Button – I think it was something by Daphne du Murier – and she was telling Button all about it. That Tometta is one smart girl, smart as a whip for someone so young. I enjoyed sitting there listening to the women talk. It was such a beautiful evening, and the lightning bugs were flickering all over the badminton court – or where the badminton court used to be before we dug it up to make a garden. There was something about their voices, so peaceful, talking about stories they had read, and Button saying she was going to start reading again.

It's funny that I'm living here in this house. I guess I've been coming here since I was knee high to a grasshopper, maybe since I was seven or eight years old. We lived just across the street, my sister and I, and the two of us were always invited to birthday parties at the Buffons – and in a family with seven girls there were plenty of those. I guess I've known Button and Wanda for as long as I've known anybody. The funny thing is, I always thought that Wanda was the smartest sister. She always had something clever to say, and she made me feel like I was smart too. Button was very quiet all the time. But it turns out that Button is the smart one. As I was listening to Button talking to Tometta, I realized that she is quite a sensible woman. It seemed like almost everything she said made some sort of sense. And Tometta too. I could have sat there all evening listening to those two girls talk, watching the lightning bugs, and swinging back and forth in the glider.

After a while Tometta had to go inside to see about Eva, so I sat there with Button. We didn't have much to talk about. I guess I was fishing, trying to find out if she knew how I could fix things up with

Wanda. But I didn't know exactly how to ask what I wanted to know. I asked her if she thought Wanda was happy or unhappy. She shrugged. And I shrugged. That's kind of how the conversation ended. I thought again that I might ask her to come down to the basement and watch one of my experiments, but I couldn't figure out how to ask it without being embarrassed. Then I thought, *it would be nice if Button could go birding with me, maybe some Sunday morning down to Chattanooga Valley.* There's a great flyway there because birds going north or south must fly right along the side of the mountain. You're likely to see something interesting there at almost any time of the year, and I was sure that Button would enjoy it. But I wasn't sure what Button would think if I asked her, like maybe she would think I was being unfaithful to Wanda, so I didn't say anything. Mostly we just sat there watching the lightning bugs.

It's occurred to me that maybe Wanda and I should get a divorce. The trouble is, the Buffon's are Catholic and Catholics are not allowed divorce. I suppose you'd say that I'm Catholic too. I wasn't raised a Catholic, but I became one when I married Wanda. Mamie didn't want her daughter to marry a Lutheran, so I agreed to take instructions and be baptized a Catholic. It didn't make a lot of difference to me. I wasn't much of a Lutheran to start with, and I haven't been much of a Catholic since, so I did it to make Mamie happy. Wanda didn't care. Even back then, Wanda only went to church because she had to. Wanda's only got one religion – a religion called Wanda. But I don't see that there's any possibility of us getting a divorce, at least not until Mamie dies, and there's not much likelihood that'll happen soon. Besides, I don't exactly know what I'd do if I divorced Wanda. I like living here with the Buffons, being needed by all these people, helping to take care of the family. After all, they're my family now. I'm the only one with a real job, a man's job. Becca's a spinner at the Peerless Woolen Mills, and Lynette is a typist at the Red Cross, but neither of them makes much money. Button and Bitsy both work part time. Of course, Emily Sue can't contribute, and Alma – well, it's hard to imagine what kind of job Alma could hold. So it really comes down to me, and I don't mind at all. My own parents were divorced when my sister and me were just kids. We were dumped in with our grandmother right here on Ninth Street, so we never had much of a family at all. I guess that's why I like having the Buffons for a family.

And, of course, there's Tootsie.

I worry a lot about Tootsie. I wouldn't want Tootsie to have divorced parents, although you'd hardly say she has much of a mother now. Wanda hardly ever pays attention to the child. I try to be a good father, but my job keeps me busy, and that's why I'm glad to be living here with the Buffons – it gives Tootsie some stability in her life. It was Wanda's idea to move in here. At first it was supposed to be only until we could find the right apartment, and that stretched on and on, and every time I suggested that we move, Wanda found some excuse to stay. Which suits me fine. And Tootsie too.

The thing I worry about with Tootsie is that she's growing up too fast. She is only eleven years old, but sometimes you'd think she was another one of the sisters. She's never had any friends her own age. It's always Tootsie and her aunts, and mostly it seems to be Becca and Lynette that she likes most. Those girls are boy crazy pure and simple, and I'm afraid it's going to rub off on Tootsie. Becca and Lynette talk about everything in front of Toostie, and I mean *everything*. I can't imagine a thing that the girl doesn't know about. Tootsie hasn't menstruated yet, at least not as far as I know, but she has started to develop breasts, and I wish she had a mother that she could talk to about these things, but I can't imagine her talking to Wanda. I take Tootsie with me birding every chance I get, and she talks to me about the others in the family – she told me about Buddy's gun, for instance – but she never talks about herself. It just doesn't seem right to me that Tootsie is going to learn the facts of life from the likes of Becca and Lynette.

That's something else I thought I might ask Button. I thought I'd ask her about Tootsie. Maybe Button could give Tootsie some good advice, answer any questions she might have, that sort of thing. I mentioned it casually to Tootsie, I said, *You know, if you ever want to talk about girl things, and you don't feel comfortable coming to me or to your mother, then you might talk to Button.* Tootsie shrugged and said, "Thanks, Dad." It's a lot for a father to be concerned about.

I guess I should be grateful that Wanda and I didn't have more children. Tootsie's was an extremely difficult delivery, and Wanda swore she would never go through it again. And that was the end of marital relations for Wanda and me. When I suggested using a rubber, she acted like I was a Protestant heretic or something, but I don't think the issue of rubbers had much to do with it. Wanda just decided that we were finished and that was that. Oh, she pretends and all, so that no one will know. She'll say things to the others that imply we are still having sex, but it's a lie. Not that I care. I keep myself busy and I don't think about it.

The astonishing thing is, I don't really miss it all that much.

Iggy:

The house is in an uproar ovah Alma. That girl's always been a little strange an' now she's gone off the deep end. It's her hands. She's got open sores in the palms of her hands an' she won't go see a doctor. Tootsie says that ever'one wants Alma to see a doctor, but Alma just sits in her room with her hands squeezed up in fists. Tootsie says that Bitsy was the first one to notice somethin' was wrong, when she found blood on the sheets of her an' Alma's bed. Bitsy told Mamie, an' Mamie an' Button had a hell of a time gettin' Alma to show 'em what was wrong. Button finally had to pry open Alma's fists, an' that's when they found the sores.

Course, there was this big discussion on account of Alma bein' so religious an' all, an' Becca an' Lynette sayin' it was the *stigmata*. Button says that Alma picked the holes in her palms with her fingernails. Mamie – she doesn't know what to believe. An' Alma ain't sayin'.

I'll tell you what the problem is, it's sex pure an' simple. That girl's hysterical, that's what. Too many female hormones is what it is. I don't put much stock in all this religious stuff, mind you. It's not natural fer a girl of Alma's age to be thinkin' on religion all the time. She should be out havin' a good time with the fellas, like Becca an' Lynette, 'stead of goin' to church all the damn time, lightin' candles an' stayin' in her room sayin' prayers. Somethin's gone haywire in that girl's head, an' I reckon it's to do with sex, pure an' simple. As far as I can see Alma was always a little strange. That girl hasn't said five words to anyone in this house fer as long as I remember. Even the nuns at the high school used to say that Alma was odd. Course, they wouldn't come right out an' admit there was somethin' crazy about Alma's religious devotions – they wouldn't say *that* – but they thought her solitariness was extreme. Morbid, that's the word they used, "We're worried that Alma might be a bit too morbid." I'll say. If there was a prize for morbid, Alma would win han's down.

Becca an' Lynette used to try to get Alma to go out on dates, but she never would. Finally they got Alma to come with them to a dance at the USO. That was 'bout two years ago, when I was still up an' about, so I saw the girls as they were settin' off, an' let me tell you, Alma looked as pretty as any one of 'em. She had a nice blue dress with a cardigan across her shoulders – jus' one little button at the neck, that's all, right here – an' ribbons in her hair. She looked right fine. But they weren't gone long, that's sho'. Accordin' to Becca an' Lynette, some soldier made a pass at Alma, put his hand on her fanny, somethin' like that, an' Alma went kind of nuts an' started cryin', an' that's when Becca an' Lynette had to bring her on home. Becca an' Lynette were too embarrassed to go back to the dance. So that's what I mean when I say it's sex pure an' simple. I mean, anybody in their right mind doesn't go makin a scene jus' 'cause some fella put his hand on yer fanny. All this stuff with the sores on Alma's hands is jus' normal hormones workin' themselves out in an abnormal way.

Button says that Alma should see a doctor, but Mamie won't hear of it. Mamie says that Alma jus' going through a stage. So the whole house is in an uproar, an' no one knows what to do with Alma's hands bleedin' an' all. Too bad they don't ask me. What I'd do is bring that soldier boy in here an' have him keep pattin' Alma on the fanny 'til she snaps out of it.

Button:

Sometimes I wonder who's the craziest around here. I mean, if I left this house tomorrow I wouldn't miss the place one bit. But where would I go? And who'd help Mother when things get really crazy, like Alma getting sores on her palms? The only other person around here with any sense is Roger, and he's hardly ever home. And it's not really his family anyway. That poor man can't be expected to sort out all our problems. Becca and Lynette are the worst. They are convinced that Alma's sores are some kind of religious thing, a stigmata sort of thing, and they think Mother should tell a priest – Father Sayers or Father O'Neil. But can you imagine what would happen if one of those men got in here. Next thing you know the whole parish would think that Alma's crazy. Well, she probably is crazy, but that's no reason for the whole parish to know it. Alma should see a doctor. She's all confused and withdrawn into her shell, and she keeps digging at her palms with her nails until they are sore and raw. It's tension, pure nervous energy, that's all, and a doctor could probably straighten things out in no time at all, but Mother won't hear of it. Mother says that all those psychological doctors are quacks, but, you know, the real problem is she's embarrassed. She won't admit that her daughter needs help.

Alma's problem is that she's too sensitive. I mean, it's like she takes all the problems of the world onto her own shoulders. She feels responsible for the war, and for all the soldiers dying, and for any little thing that gets hurt, even a fly. She's always been like that, ever since she was a little girl, and maybe it has something to do with our Daddy dying when she was only three or four years old. But I think what started this current bout of craziness was those war films that Roger brought home from Fort Oglethorpe. They were training films, you know, the kind of films they show the troops to get them ready for combat, and anybody that wants to can borrow them, so that's why Roger brought them home, just because he thought we might want to see what the war is really like. Roger had a projector and a screen from work, and he showed the films right here in the living room. I wouldn't watch. I saw just a few seconds of the first film and it was too bloody for me, I mean, these were *real movies of real soldiers* getting killed and all, stuff they wouldn't show in the news reels. I can't understand why anyone would want to watch such things, but Roger said we might as well know what is really going on. Becca liked the films, and Buddy did too, but I wouldn't watch, and Lynette wouldn't either. Alma watched, and I think that might be what caused her to start picking at her hands. I mean, somehow she thinks it's her fault that all of those terrible things are happening.

What I don't understand is why Becca liked the films. Becca says she is sorry she is not a man so that she could go and fight in the war, and I asked her why she didn't join the WACs, and she said it's not the same thing. That girl is very independent. She and Lynette didn't get home last night until after one o'clock, and God knows where they were all that time. They say they went to the Service Men's Club at the Memorial Auditorium, but that place closes at 11 o'clock and Becca and Lynette didn't get home for hours after that. I mean, it's none of my business, those girls are old enough to take care of their own lives, and if anybody is going to speak to them it will have to be Mother. But I doubt if Mother even knows that the girls were out so late. It used to be that she would never go to sleep until everyone was home, but now she falls asleep in her chair and nothing really wakes her up. I don't know where Becca and Lynette were until one o'clock, but I know they weren't alone. They were out on the front porch for a long time before they came into the house, and I could hear them whispering with someone. I'd hate to see those girls taken advantage of. Most of the service men they meet downtown are just passing through Chattanooga for a day, on their way to Fort Forrest, or some such place, or waiting for a train, and to them Becca and Lynette are just pick-ups, someone to take advantage of. Lynette is the one I worry about most. She is a year older than Becca, but it's Becca who is the instigator of all their crazy ideas. Becca is absolutely boy crazy. You should see the walls of her room – Becca and Lynette's room, I mean – the walls are covered, and I mean covered, with pictures of guys cut out of movie magazines. And when they bring servicemen here to the house on Sundays, you should see the way Becca flirts, like – well, it's not the way I'd behave. And the worst of it is that Buddy sees all of Becca's flirtatiousness and it just makes him miserable.

Right now he's in one of his terrible moods. He said awful things to me, and he's being just downright vindictive, you know, doing mean things without any rhyme or reason. I went into our room after breakfast this morning and I noticed that one of my love-bird shaker sets was gone from the windowsill, the very first one that Buddy gave me, the one he bought at Woolworths, the yellow birds with blue eyes. I searched all over the room, but I couldn't find them anywhere, and I couldn't ask Buddy because he had gone out, but I suspected it was him who had taken them. When he came home at lunchtime, I said, *Buddy, do you know what happened to my yellow love birds?* He was making a mayonnaise sandwich in the kitchen, and Tometta was there, and he just shrugged, but after a few seconds he said that he had thrown them out in the garbage can. I said, *Why did you do that?* And he said, "I couldn't stand to look at them anymore," and I said, *Then why didn't you just tell me and I would have put them away?* and he said, "I didn't want them in the house." You know, I couldn't believe it and I went out to the garbage cans behind the garage and found the love birds where he had thrown them, but he had smashed them before he threw them away so I just left them. I came back into the kitchen and said, *Buddy, why in the world would you do that?* He didn't say anything, he just threw his mayonnaise sandwich against the wall over the kitchen sink and left the house.

I was embarrassed that all of this happened in front of Tometta. I said, *I'm sorry, Tometta.* She picked up the pieces of sandwich and wiped the mayonnaise off the wall. She said, "Oh, don't you worry, Missus Cioffi." I said, *Do you have any idea why Buddy is in such a bad mood?* "No, Ma'am," she said. But I know why Buddy is in a bad mood. Buddy gets in these moods regularly. Buddy wants to be with every woman he sees – with Wanda, and Becca, and heavens knows who else – and he gets all frustrated and blames me. Still, I can't believe he would break my love-birds and throw them away. I went upstairs and took the rest of the shakers off the windowsill and hid them away in the closet in Mother's room where Buddy wouldn't find them. And I added the other set of yellow love birds, the ones that Wanda had given me that were just the same, the ones I never told Buddy about.

When I came back to the kitchen Tometta was wrapping up the pieces of Buddy's sandwich. I said, *Tometta, what do you think I should do?* I don't know why I asked Tometta that, it just seemed like I had to talk to someone and Tometta was the only person I could talk to, and besides she is such a smart person. She said, "That's not fer me to say," and I said, *But I'm asking you, Tometta, I just need to talk to someone,* and she said, "That Mister Cioffi jest has a mean streak," and I said, *He used to be such a sweet man, and he still can be sweet when he wants to be, but lately he just seems to blame me for everything,* and she said, "I s'pect he be too full of spirit." And, you know, right then I knew that something had happened between Buddy and Tometta, I mean I don't blame Tometta, I'm sure that whatever happened had nothing to do with her, but there was something about the way she said, "I'spect he be too full of spirit," kind of low-key like, and with her eyes looking down, that – well, you know, I could just tell that something had happened. I can see why Buddy would be attracted to Tometta, she's pretty and she's the sweetest girl, but the funny thing is Buddy hates negroes. Still, I could tell that something had happened. I said, *I'm sorry, Tometta.*

I wish I knew how I could make Buddy happy. Sometimes I wish he would just go ahead and have an affair with whoever he wants, I mean, it would make my life a lot easier. If he's not happy with me, then I wish he would just have an affair with whoever he wants. What Buddy needs, I think, is a job. Buddy needs something to keep his mind off that thing in his pants.

Buddy:

Becca may not have the biggest tits in the world, but, like they say, more than a handful's wasted. I'll tell you this, she looked damned fine when I took her to the National Cemetery to teach her how to use the gun. She didn't want to be seen leaving the house together, so I met her down on the corner of Central Avenue. She was wearing those short shorts of hers with the little bows by the sides of her long legs, and a pretty pink blouse, and she had undone the bottom buttons of the blouse and tied the ends in a knot so her lil' tummy was peeking out as sexy as can be. Becca always cuts her hair short in the summer, and with her little tits she looks almost like a boy – but let me tell you, she's no boy. That girl really knows what it means to be a woman. Just walking with her across the viaduct was an experience.

I said, *Becca, You look terrific*, and she smiled. I said, *Mmm…mmm, I'd even venture to say you look good enough to eat.* And she said, "You'd better behave, Buddy or I'll tell Button." But I could tell she was just kidding. I showed her where I had the gun in my pocket and asked her to touch it. She said, "Is it loaded?" I said, *Oh yeah.* She said, "Aren't you afraid it might go off in your pants?" I said, *Now don't you go worrying your pretty little head about anything going off in my pants. Besides, It's got a safety. It can't go off if the safety's on.*

When we got to the cemetery, the German POW's were sitting there eating their lunch – sandwiches or something – and I said, *It'd be fun to take a pot shot at them, not hit them or nothing, just scare the pants off 'em.* Becca said, "That young German with the blond hair is cute." And I said, *You gotta be kidding, those guys are Nazis.* She said, "Oh, I don't know, I like his mustache." I said, *If those guys got out of there, you'd be glad that I have this gun.* She said, "You're big talk, Buddy." I'll be damned if those Nazi POW's weren't giving Becca the once-over, so I gave them the finger.

The cave in the National Cemetery is a perfect place to take Becca shooting. It's not a real cave exactly, it's sort of an artificial cave that has been cut out of the rock to make a kind of underground room, I don't know what for, maybe for something back during the Civil War. There's an iron gate at the entrance, but it isn't locked, and we were able to pull it open. It's a perfect place to shoot, because plenty of light comes in through the entrance, and you're far away from anyone that might hear the shots. I asked Becca if she'd ever been there before, and she said lots of times when she was a kid. "It's creepy," she said. I flashed her the gun. *It's a Smith and Wesson thirty-eight,* I said. She took it in her hands, and turned it over and over, and then pointed it at the back of the cave and said, "Kablooie!"

I knew there would be lots of Coke bottles and other junk in the cave, so I set up a bunch of bottles at the back of the cave and then took the gun from Becca. I showed her how to take off the safety, and I showed her the shells in the chambers. She said, "OK, hot shot, let's see you hit the bottles." So I aimed and shot, and God almighty there was a terrific racket, like a huge echo, and Becca was scared that the ceiling of the cave might collapse. I missed the bottle. "Some shot" she said. I said, *It's been a while, I just need a little practice.* I shot again and this time I busted a bottle. It wasn't the one I was aiming at, but Becca didn't need to know that, and she was duely impressed.

OK, now you try, I said. She took the gun, and pulled the hammer back with both thumbs, and – *whamo!* – that thing went off and almost knocked Becca on her keister. I don't know where-the-hell the bullet went, I never saw it hit. I said, *Let me help you, Sugar.* So I got behind her, and put my arms around her, and helped her steady her hands. She said, "Don't get fresh, Buddy" but I could tell she was only kidding. Let me tell you, holding her like that and the smell of her hair, it almost drove me crazy. I had my cheek right up against her hair, and I could feel her tight little ass against me, and I thought, *Something just might go off in my pants.* My dick was as hard as a rock. She pulled the trigger, and there was a godawful noise, and her shoulders slammed back against me, and God knows where-the-hell the bullet went, and Becca laughed, and I snuggled up against her neck and gave her neck a kiss. She said, "Buddy, I told you not to get fresh." And I said, *Give it another go.* So she took aim, and I helped her steady the gun, and – *whamo!* – damned if she didn't hit a bottle and the glass went flying all over creation. She said, "Yow-ee!" And I said, *You see, it's not so hard*, and she turned around and looked me in the face and – well, I couldn't help it, so I gave her a kiss on the lips, and it's not exactly like she stopped me. She actually let me kiss her for just a second, and then she pushed me away and said, "Buddy, cut that out or I'll tell Button."

She said, "Let me try it by myself." I said, *You sure you don't want me to help*, and she said, "Yeah, Buddy, I know how you want to help." So she took the gun all by herself, and pulled the trigger, and the bullet must have ricocheted off a rock, because it came flying straight back our way and pinged off the iron gate. Becca screamed. "I felt it," she hollered, "I felt it go right past my ear." She started crying and threw the gun on the ground. I said, *Hey, take it easy Sunshine, that thing cost me an arm and a leg*. And she ran to the gate and opened it and started marching home.

Well, I let her go. Let me tell you, I was shaking like a leaf. When I realized how close that bullet had come to killing Becca, I started shaking like a leaf. Can you believe it, that bullet came close enough to her ear that she could *feel* it. I hate to admit it, but it really scared the shit out of me. I sat right down there in the cave and shook and shook. But the funny thing is, when I got home Becca acted like nothing had happened. She was as cool as a cucumber, like nothing had happened at all. And she didn't say anything about the kiss, either.

But I'll tell you this, I didn't forget it. That was the sweetest little kiss I ever had. I couldn't get it out of my head. I mean, Wanda was out in the yard taking the sun and I couldn't give a crap – all I could think about was Becca. But well, there's absolutely nothing I can do about it. Button's a ball and chain. As long as I'm married to Button, I don't see that I'll get past first base with Becca. Wanda, now that's different, I think if I put the right proposition to Wanda she would jump in the sack, but Becca's not going to get serious as long as I'm married to Button. It ain't fucking fair. Sometimes I wish Button would simply disappear. It's not that I don't *like* her, it's just that I can't stop being mean to her, and, to tell the truth, I don't think it's my fault. Take that salt-and-pepper set, for instance. I didn't set out to break it. I was just going to hide it for a while, just to be mean, because every time I looked at it it reminded me of how I used to feel about Button before we got married. I took it out to the garage because I knew that Button would never look there, and I accidently dropped one of the birds. It didn't break just chipped off the tip of a wing. She'd hardly have noticed it. But I don't know, something just went snap in my head, and I picked it up and smashed it against the floor. And the other one too. I can't explain it. I know it seems like a childish thing to do, but I couldn't help it. And I don't think it's my fault. I never could figure out why she kept those particular salt-and-pepper shakers on the sill in our room. She's got hundreds of the damn things, and it's the love birds that she leaves on display, just to piss me off. If she wasn't so frickin' frigid, it'd be different. But she keeps me tensed up like a bomb ready to go off, and then leaves those damned love birds right out there for me to see, like she's rubbing my nose in it. That's why I smashed the damn things, and who would blame me?

The thing is, though, what am I going to do about Becca? She's convinced the niggers are about to do something – cause a riot or something – so I wouldn't be surprised if – after she gets over being scared – she might go back with me again to the cave in the cemetery. I have a feeling she'd like to know how to use a gun, just in case something happens. And let me tell you this; if I get Becca in the cave again you can bet your bottom dollar there'll be more than shooting going on. OK, so she pushed me away, but she did let me kiss her for just a second, and – well, that means she's *thinking* about it. I know for sure that she said something to Lynette, because tonight Lynette said to me, "Buddy, I hear you're a real sharpshooter." I said, *What do you mean?* She said, "Becca told me all about your little escapade in the cave." I said, *Oh yeah, what did she tell you?* And she said, "Oh, she told me everything." I said, *Everything?* And she said, "You'd better be careful, Buddy, because if Mother ever finds out what you're up to, you'll be out on your ear."

Well, let me tell you, there's no way Mamie's going to find out unless Becca or Lynette tell her, and Becca's the one who'd catch hell, you can be sure of that, so she won't tell her. I'm surprised that Becca told Lynette about what happened in the cave – about the kiss, I mean. Those girls don't have any secrets at all.

Tootsie:

Buddy kissed Becca – yuk! I heard Becca telling Lynette all about it. Becca said, "That Buddy is crazy." Lynette said, "Was he a good kisser?" Becca said, "Yeah, I guess so." Lynette said, "You gonna tell Button?" Becca said, "Are you kidding." Lynette said, "You gonna to let him do it again?" Becca said, "I dunno. Buddy's nuts."

I told Iggy about Buddy and Becca. He said, "That Buddy is a horny toad." I don't know what that means, but I think it means that Buddy likes Becca. Iggy said, "I knew somethin' was up – Buddy hasn't been sneakin through here lately spyin' on yoah mama."

Iggy asked me again about the gun. He asked me if I'd talked to Billy Joe Alaska. I said no and Iggy got real mad. It's the first time I've seen Iggy really mad. He said that it was important for Billy Joe to bring him a rifle, that the colored people are coming, and if he doesn't get the rifle then they'll burn down the house and everything. I don't know if Iggy is telling the truth, but I'm scared because of Teddy Carr. Teddy Carr is a boy that lives over on Eleventh Street. He's ten years old, and he goes to Park View School. I know Teddy from the playground. Anyways, he disappeared. Just disappeared. Nobody knows what happened to him. The police have been all over the neighborhood. They came by our house and talked to Button and Grandma to ask if they'd seen anything strange. The police say maybe it was a kidnapping, or maybe Teddy got lost. Nobody knows what happened to Teddy, but Becca heard that the negroes kidnapped him and are going to use him as a hostage when the riot starts. A lot of people are really mad at the negroes and blame them for taking Teddy. Buddy says that the Army ought to round up all the colored people and put them into a concentration camp until they say what happened to Teddy. Buddy said to Becca, "See, I told you we needed that thirty-eight and you're crazy if you don't learn how to use it." That's why I thought – maybe Iggy is right about the rifle. So I went over to Billy Joe Alaska's house and knocked on the door. I took Emily Sue with me 'cause I didn't want to go alone. Billy Joe said to come in, but I wouldn't go in, 'cause – I don't know, it just didn't seem the right thing to do. I don't like Billy Joe, he's creepy. He kept looking at Emily Sue. I told him that Iggy wanted him to bring a rifle, but to keep it a secret so nobody would know. Billy Joe said, "What does Iggy want a rifle for?" I told him what Buddy and Becca said about the negroes. Billy Joe said, "The niggas ain't gonna do nothin – they're scared shitless of white folk." I told him about Teddy Carr, and how Becca heard that the negroes are going to use Teddy Carr as a hostage. He said, "That boy probably just wandered away down the railroad tracks. He'll show up in a couple of days." So I asked him if he was going to bring Iggy a rifle, and he said, "Why don't you come in and pick one out," and I said that I didn't know anything about rifles, and that he should just bring one to Iggy or Iggy would be mad.

This afternoon Billy Joe came to our house, but he didn't bring a rifle, at least I didn't see that he was carrying one. He went up to Iggy's room, and he was up there for a long time. I tried to hear what they were talking about, but Billy Joe closed the door. When Billy Joe came downstairs, he talked to Buddy. He asked Buddy what he had heard about Teddy Carr, and Buddy said he thought the coloreds had kidnapped him and were probably torturing him, and that they would use him for a hostage. Billy Joe said, "The niggers won't do a thing, and if they do, they'll be sorry." Buddy went upstairs and got his gun and showed it to Billy Joe. Billy Joe said, "That little pop gun won't do a thing." Buddy said, "Oh yeah, it'll do just fine."

Ever since Teddy Carr was kidnapped, my Dad won't let me go away from the house alone. That's why I took Emily Sue with me when I went to Billy Joe Alaska's. But now I can't go to the cemetery to deliver notes for Bitsy. I suppose I could take Emily Sue – she wouldn't know what's going on, but maybe somebody would get suspicious. Bitsy is crazy about Horst. She goes down there every afternoon and talks to him. When she gets home from the dry cleaners she puts on her prettiest clothes and goes to the cemetery. One of the American guards is her friend, and Horst's friend too, but the other American soldier told her that she should stay away because the Germans are dangerous and that Horst is just using her to get gum and cigarettes. Bitsy says that Horst loves her, and when the war is over he wants to marry her and take her back to Germany. Bitsy doesn't want to go to Germany, but she wants to marry Horst. She showed me one of the notes Horst wrote, about how pretty she is, and how he can't wait to make love to her, and how he's going crazy because he can't be with her. Bitsy made me swear I won't tell anyone about Horst, and I haven't told anyone, not even Iggy.

Bitsy gave her picture to Horst, a really pretty picture that was made when she graduated from high school, with a white blouse and a black tie. Horst said he wants a pin-up. He said the other prisoners have pin-ups, and he doesn't have one, and he wants a pin-up of Bitsy. So Bitsy asked me if I would take a pin-up picture that she can give to Horst. I said yes. She snitched Lynette's Kodak away from Lynette's dresser and bought a roll of film, but neither one of us knew how to load the film into the camera. Bitsy asked Dad to load the film, because Dad wouldn't care whose camera it was or why Bitsy wanted to use it. The only pin-up picture Bitsy knows about is the picture of Betty Grable that all the soldiers have, so that's the kind of pin-up she decided to give Horst. She put on her swim suit, and we went out to the sleeping porch where there was lots of light, and I took a whole roll of pictures.

Bitsy couldn't leave the pictures at the drug store on Central Avenue, because that is where Button works, so she took them to the drug store downtown. When she gets the pictures back she will give one to Horst.

I think it's romantic about Bitsy's boyfriend. And I don't think he's a Nazi.

Iggy:

Good Lawd, Tootsie showed me a photograph she took of Bitsy. A "pin-up," she calls it. She says it's fer Bitsy's boyfriend. I asked, *Who in tarnation is this so-called boyfriend who wants to see Bitsy posin' like a floosie in her bathin' suit*, but Tootsie says it's a secret. I says, *I thought you an' I don't have secrets, Tootsie*. She says, "I'm sorry, Iggy, but I promised Bitsy I wouldn't tell." Offered her a quarter, but she kept her mouth shut. Mind you, I'll find out. I'll find out sooner or later. Mr. Ignatius T. Ferguson has his methods.

Back in my day, no self-respectin' woman woulda displayed herself so saucily fer her man-friend. These days you see pictures in Life Magazine of soldiers with pin-ups plastered all over the walls of their Quonset huts like wallpaper, hundreds of half-naked women – hell's bells, naked women even. Weren't nothin' like that when I was in the service back in '98. When I was in the hospital in Tampa, if one of us convalescents was to put up a picture of his lady friend, the matron would have taken it down quicker than a bat outta hell. I was in that hospital fer four months after we was shipped back from Cuba. Hotter than the gates of hell, that's sho', an' insects was all ovah the place. I'd say there's no place on earth with more bugs than Florida. Anyways, for months we laid there sweatin' like pigs on a slaughter-house truck, an' the bugs as big as crabs, an' a bunch of old biddy nurses watchin' over us, an' if we was even so much as to think about puttin' a pin-up on the wall the matron came down on us like a ton of bricks. I had me a girlfriend before I went off to fight. Kathleen her name was. Kathleen Fitzgibbons. As pretty an Irish lass as you'd ever lay yoah eyes on. I had a photo, too. It wasn't no pin-up, that's sho', but it was as pretty as can be. I kept it in the Bible they gave us at the hospital, right by my bed, an' God knows I looked at it plenty. If eyes can wear out a photograph, then it's a wonder that photo lasted at all. I must've looked at it a thousand times a day. Nurses thought I was readin' the Bible, but I was a lookin' at Kathleen, her bein' so purdy an' all. Then, when they finally sent me home to Chattanooga, the girl had done gone away. Up an' moved away with her family, that's what, up north somewhere, an' didn't even leave a message about where she was goin'. I still have her picture though. I have it right here by my bed.

an' when I think of that trashy "pin-up" photograph of Bitsy, makes me downright proud that Kathleen was never like that.

There was a time when I'd a been ashamed to say this, but Kathleen was the only lady friend I ever had. We kept company for a year or so before I went off to Cuba. Then, when I came home, she was gone, an' – well, my health bein' so bad an' all, the ladies wouldn't pay me no mind at all. It sho' wasn't easy. I wasn't any different from any other young man, had the same urges as the next guy. I would've settled down in a minute if'n I could've found a woman who'd marry me. But with all my coughin' an' wheezin', the ladies wouldn't look at me twice. God knows, there ain't no use cryin' ovah spilt milk. I got on with it, that's what. Tried to put it outta my mind. An' next thing you know, I was too damn old to care.

Too old to care about "pin-ups," too. Ever'thing is pictures these days. Movie pictures. Magazines. Seem like ever'where you look you see pictures of gals in skimpy clothes. I don't go to the movies myself, but I see the ads in the paper. Like fer instance, take that ad fer a movie called "Somethin' of the Islands," with an actress named Arquanetta posin' in almost nothin' she was. Now, I'm no prude, but I reckon an ad like that has no business bein' in a newspaper that youngins read. An' speakin of youngins – why, hell, the comic strips are the sauciest things of all. This Daisy Mae character in "Li'l Abner" runs round in a itty bit of a dress hardly bigger than a hankerchief. An' that Miss Burma lady in "Terry and the Pirates" took her dress clean off to use as a flag. Stark naked, she was. Mind you, they don't actually show her buck naked, but you know she is. I've always said, imaginin' a gal with her clothes off is sexier than seein' the real thing. An' don't think I haven't seen the real thing. I was in New Orleans once, when I was enlisted, before they shipped us out to Cuba, an' the things I saw – Lawdy loo, those New Orleans striptease gals didn't leave nothin' fer the imagination.

Maybe it's the war, but it seems young folk are a lot more *pro-mis-cu-ous* than they used to be. Take the women around this house. Like bitches in heat, they are. Now, I know it's a hard thing to say about my own kin, but goin' on what Tootsie tells me, an' Tootsie tells me ever'thing. Fer instance, Tootsie's been spyin' on Becca an' Lynette when they come home at night from the dances. 'Cordin to

Tootsie, the girls stand out there by the front-porch rail, smoochin'
with whatever soldiers bring 'em home. Can you imagine that?
Smoochin' with some fella you but only jus' met a few hours before.
Someone ought take those girls in hand an' straighten 'em out, but it
ain't no business of mine. I reckon, if Mamie knew half of what
Tootsie tells me, it would put her in the grave.

But what I'd really like to know – who's the fella that Bitsy's
givin' the pin-up picture to. Somethin' fishy's goin' on, or else
Tootsie would tell me. I'll find my way to the bottom of this
somehow. I'll jus' have to get me a secret that I can trade with
Tootsie. That's what I'll do. I'll get me a secret I can trade with
Tootsie.

Tometta:

Tometta my Love,

I miss you more than you can know. Hope all is well at home. How Nana be? I be fine myself. I think it will be real soon we ship out. It can't be too soon, the men have had it up to thier necks with this place. We are working our tails off to get ready, and you sure would be proud to see what fine soldiers they all are. We beat the pants off the white troops in all the exercises they run us thru. Our outfit is the best in the camp. Still we get treated worse than dirt. The GERMAN POWS they got here at the camp get treated better than us! They can use the PX and go about anywheres in the camp, and we can't use any of the white-only buildings. Imagine those Germans been killing Americans all over Europe and they treat them better than AMERICAN soldiers. Anyone can see. Even the Germans laugh to see that they can go ahead of us in line. I do feel sorry for those Nazis in Europe, the boys are fired up and are ready to kick some butt. God help them once we get there. Sorry to bore you with all my complainin. I will write you again tomorrow, I have to get me to sleep now, they have us up afore the sun.

Miss you!
xoxo
William

Good Lawd, I think Miss Bitsy be in love with a German POW! I never took no never mind of the POW's down the cemetery, but William's last letter put me ta thinkin', so curiosity took me down fer a walk. Jest wanted to see what they look'd like an' all. An' there's Bitsy talkin' to one through the fence. You'd have to be blind as a bat not to see she was mad in love. I had a mind to jest walk ovah and say, *Miss Bitsy, what you wanna be talkin' to them fer, them's the ones been killin' all our boys over in Europe.* Then I realized it wasn't the Germans or Bitsy I was angered at, but Chattanooga, Fort Hood, *America.* Where we's the enemy jest by the color of our skin. Where we keep turnin' the other cheek, jest to have it slapped. I don't wanna be hurtful to Bitsy, she'd never harm a fly. Luck have it, she didn't see me none, account of her bein' all moony-eyed, so I didn't act right quick an' say somethin' foolish. Like Nana says, "Best let dinner simmer in the pot, 'fore you go servin' it up." I jest be so angry, hearin' how William an' them other colored troops be treated at that camp. It seem no matter how hard we try, we never get anywhere in this country.

There be a big story in the *Atlanta Daily World*, a negro newspaper, about William's division, the *Black Panthers*. How they be the first negro tank division. There be pictures too, but William weren't in none – I be starin' at those pictures till my eyes hurt, but he ain't to be found. All the colored folk be real proud, they be passin' copies around after church service. Those could read, read aloud to those who couldn't. Momma be tellin' everyone how my William be in the *Black Panthers*. I musta looked a right fool the way I was beamin'. An' still those troops sit at Fort Hood trainin', while the white troops pass in an' out ev'ry two months. I reckon the good thing is that it keeps William outta harm's way, but you see the pride ever'one has in those men, an ya know it do us all good fer 'em to see action.

I was still in a good mood from church the next mornin', jest cleanin' the breakfast dishes at the sink, thinkin' on William, when I felt eyes on me. I dreaded to look, thinkin' it was Buddy lurkin' ag'in, but when I turn, there was Miss Alma jest standin' there starin', dressed like she was going to a funeral like she always is. *Mornin' Miss Alma*, I says. She don't say good mornin' or nuthin', jest, "You're a good person, Tometta, all you do for your great-grandmother." *Nothin' anyone wouldn't do fer their own kin*, I says. Miss Alma doesn't say nothin' fer a spell, like she be thinkin' or somethin', then she say, "We'll all burn in hell for the things we done to you people." I says, *You ain't done nothin' to us Miss Alma, you been right proper to us.* She says, "I mean negroes in general, slavery and all." I'd known what she meant, but I hadn't known what to say, an' I could see in her eyes she be serious, an' it weighin' heavy on her. I jest put my arms round her, gave her a big hug, an' tol' her, *The good Lawd's only gonna judge you fer who you be Miss Alma, don't worry yoahself on things long since done.* She smile, an' says, "Thank you, Tometta," an' slid out of the room as quiet as she come in. I don't know what come over me to hug her like that – I mean on account of her bein' white an' all – I'd of done it without a thought should it've been one of my colored frien's. I don't know what they be teachin' that poor girl in that church of hers, but seems to bring her nothin' but pain. Ya know, I do believe that be the first time I evah did see that girl smile.

Roger:

I finally got up the courage to ask Button if she would go birding with me. The idea was to have Tootsie come along too, so Button wouldn't mistake my intentions. I don't know why I wanted so bad to go birding with Button. I guess, she is such a nice person, and she seems to be someone who would appreciate the finer points of birdwatching. And, well, except for Tometta, Button hardly has anyone to talk to around here. I just thought maybe she'd like the companionship. Of course, I don't know what Buddy will say. Or Wanda, either, for that matter. That's why I wanted Tootsie to come along.

Button was on the back porch sorting clothes when I came home from work. I said, *Button, I like your hair cut short that way.* She said, "I can't stand it long in the hot weather. I can't remember when the weather was so hot." I said, *Well, anyway, I like it that way. And it does look much cooler.* She's right of course. This has been the hottest summer I can remember, and it's only June. I stood there for a few minutes watching Button fold the wash. I liked the way her hands smoothed the towels and wash rags, with her palms moving slow and flat against the terrycloth. I said, *You know, Button, you ought to come birding with me and Tootsie sometime. If you want to cool down, there's no better way than to get out into the country.* Button didn't say anything. She just kept smoothing the towels. I said, *Matter of fact, we're going up to Lulu Lake on Saturday – if you'd like to come along.* It just popped into my head. I almost never go to Lulu Lake. It's not a good birding place at all, being up on the mountain. But I thought, it's sure to be cool. And I know that Button likes Lulu Lake, and that she hasn't had a chance to go there since the war started. So that's why it suddenly popped into my head. Button didn't say anything when I asked her, but I could tell she was thinking about it. I said, *Well, anyway, we'll be leaving about five-thirty. That way, we'll get there while the birds are active. If you'd like to come, you'd be very welcome.* She said, "We'll see."

Button was waiting bright and early on Saturday morning, but the trouble was, I couldn't get Tootsie to come along. Tootsie had promised Bitsy that she would go somewhere with her, and nothing I could say would change her mind. I offered her a dollar if she'd come birding, but she said, "Sorry Dad, a promise is a promise." I was afraid of what Button might think if I showed up alone. But she didn't say anything. She just got into the car. I made up some cock-and-bull story about why Tootsie didn't come, but Button didn't seem to care. She sat there all quiet sort of, as we drove up to the mountain. I said, *I brought along an extra pair of glasses.* She said, "That's good." I said, *I borrowed them from a friend at work. Actually, they're pretty good binoculars.* She said, "Thanks."

Button is not exactly the talkative sort, at least not with me. When she's with Tometta, she chatters away, but with me she's as quiet as a mouse. She sure looked nice, though. She was wearing pink slacks and a polka-dot shirt, and she had a kerchief on her head. I said, *You're as pretty as a picture.* I couldn't believe I said it, it just kind of slipped out. She squinched up her nose, but I think she was pleased. Anyway, when we got to Lulu Lake we walked down to the place above the lake where the water tumbles down over the rocks. Button sat on the rocks, took off her shoes, and put her feet in the water. I sat down too. It was only half-past six and still nice and cool, although you could tell the day was going to be a scorcher. I thought I should take off my shoes too, but I didn't. I don't know why not. I guess it isn't my style to do things like that. Oh, I'd take off my shoes if I had to wade across a stream or something. But to dangle my feet in the water for the sheer heck of it, well, I guess it just isn't my style. But I liked the way Button's first thought was of putting her feet in the water. Wanda would never do that. That's not Wanda's style, either. Maybe that's why Wanda and I got married. I guess that's what we have in common – neither one of us is the sort of person who would think of putting their feet in the water, first thing.

I heard a phoebe somewhere in the trees across the stream. I whispered to Button, *It's a phoebe.* She listened. I mean, she really listened, all quiet like, like she was at a concert or something. She didn't look for the bird, she just sat there and listened to the bird sing its monotonous note, over and over. Then, the damndest thing – a vireo chimed in. What an amazing song! Button looked up, but we couldn't see the bird. It was somewhere in the trees behind us. *It's a red-eyed vireo*, I whispered. And then, as we listened, I whispered into her ear the words the vireo was singing. *Are you weary? Why is it? We can cheer you; we know the secret; this is it; holy spirit; do you believe it? You know it; you see it; can you hear me?*

Button smiled.

When she smiled, something reminded me of my sister. Something about Button's mouth – a genuine smile, but very tentative. I was reminded of my sister, Flowerree. She was the only family I ever had, except for my grandmother. She was one year older than me, and I guess she was my best friend. Flowerree died when she was twenty years old, in 1929, of leukemia. I used to call her "the reluctant flapper." She was always on the verge of getting some fun out of life, but backed off at the last minute. She was full of good spirits, but afraid to let go. Flowerree must have had a hundred boyfriends. They were lined up on the front porch. But she never had a serious fling with any one of them, never went out on a date. It's not like she was scared, or stand-offish. She was full of life, really. It's like she was waiting for something – waiting for someone to tell her it was OK to have fun. It's like she had all of this wonderful goodness welling up inside her, just waiting to burst out, waiting for the right person, or the right moment. Then she died. Out of the blue. In the middle of summer she complained that she was tired. In October, she was dead. And sometimes – I wonder if it wasn't just as well. I know that's a terrible thing to say, but the only world Flowerree knew was a peaceful world. She was too young to remember the Great War. The twenties were mostly a happy time – birthday parties and pretty dresses. Then, since the day she died, things have gone to hell in a handbasket. First came the depression, then this terrible war, and here I am contributing to all the madness, and the killing, maybe more so than the soldiers who actually pull the triggers and drop the bombs. I'm glad Flowerree didn't experience the war. But I miss her. Sometimes I think I might have been a better person if she had lived. Maybe if Flowerree had lived, she would have kept me from getting involved in all of this explosives business. Maybe if Flowerree had been around, I'd have been a better husband for Wanda. Anyway, there was something about the way Button smiled that reminded me of Flowerree.

I don't know exactly what we did that passed the time, but it was nearly noon by the time we started back down the mountain. We saw the vireo, and the phoebe, and at least a dozen other birds, mostly warblers. After the birds quieted down, we just walked – down the old railroad embankment to the point where we could sit and look out over the valley. All that time, Button hardly said a word. I guess I didn't say much either. Mostly, we walked along in silence, and if I saw something that I thought Button might be interested in – a bird, a wildflower, or an insect – I'd point, and she'd look. It's like – I didn't have to say anything. When I'm with Tootsie, I explain everything we see, tell her what everything is, teach her the names. When I'm with Tootsie, it seems like I'm talking all the time. But with Button, I didn't feel the need to do that. It was like – well, it was like she somehow already knew what she wanted to know, and was content just to look. And she looked, too, really looked. Button's eyes took in everything. Even when I wasn't pointing something out, her eyes were still taking it all in. So we walked along in silence, and then we sat on the rocks and looked out over Chattanooga Valley. We didn't say a word, we just sat, and I don't know how much time passed, but it didn't seem like much, and when I looked at my watch it was nearly eleven o'clock.

I don't exactly know how to say this, but I was glad that Tootsie hadn't come along.

Buddy:

Christ, Button found out about the gun. I had thought Button was at work, so I was cleaning the Smith & Wesson in our bedroom when in she walks. She takes one look and says, "Buddy, what's that?" I said, *Aren't you supposed to be at work?* She said, "Never mind, what's that you're trying to hide?" At that point there was no use hiding the damn thing. So I showed it to her. I tossed the gun onto the bed. Her eyes opened as big as saucers. She looked around as if to make sure no one else was watching. "Is that thing real?" she asked. I said, *What does it look like? A water pistol?* She said, "Buddy, why on God's green earth do you have a gun?"

Well, let me tell you, I can't stand that woman when she's on her high horse. No call for treating me like a child just because I have a gun. Lecturing me on why I shouldn't have it. Telling me it is dangerous, maybe illegal, and all that. So I said, *Where do you get off being so high and mighty? You're the one who runs off with Roger to God-knows-where at five o'clock in the morning.* She said, "Buddy, you know very well that Roger asked me to go birdwatching. I told you I was going. I can't help it if you didn't hear me. You never listen to anything I say." I said, *Maybe I never listen because you never say anything worth hearing. If you want to fool around with Roger, it's no skin off my teeth.* She said, "I wasn't fooling around with Roger, as you know very well." I said, *You're damn right, I know it. The two of you together couldn't generate enough heat to melt a snowball in July.*

Truth be told, I wouldn't mind if Button had something going with Roger. I can't think of anything better than the two of them running off together. That'd solve all my problems. But I wouldn't give her the satisfaction of telling her that. So anyway, she stomps out of the room, sniffing, "That's right, Buddy. You always manage to turn the argument around to me. You have the gun – God knows why – and instead of telling me why you have the gun, you rehash the same old personal insults." I said, *Yes, we know why you're afraid of guns. You're afraid of anything that shoots.*

I don't know why I say things like that. I know I'm being a mean prick, but I can't help myself. I suppose Button has a right to know why I'm keeping a gun in our bedroom. But she would never understand. She's too damn trustful. You'd think that sooner or later she'd wake up and smell the frickin' roses, what with the kidnapping of Teddy Carr and all. There's not the slightest doubt in my mind that the coloreds took that boy, and that it has something to do with the uprising. They'll use him for a hostage, I'm sure of it. The cops have been searching the neighborhood, but they're not going to find him around here. I'd bet my bottom dollar the boy is tied up in a cellar in niggertown. Becca told me last night that the people she works with expect the blowup will come any day. She said that lots of people at the Mills are buying guns, or borrowing guns from friends or relations that live in the country. But try telling that to Button. She'll say, *Oh, Buddy, you're so gullible.* She's reassured by Tometta – as if you could believe a word that girl would say. Let me tell you, it's not me that's the gullible one around here. Anyone who'd believe Tometta when she says the negroes aren't up to something – well, *that's* gullible.

I told Becca that Button knows about the gun, so as she'd be forewarned, but Button had already talked to Becca – asked her if she knew why I had the gun. Of course, Becca told her the gun is to protect the family in case of a race riot. According to Becca, Button's response was, "The only thing this family needs protection from is Buddy." Becca said, "Button, I think Buddy's doin' the right thing." And Button said, "Swell, then let Buddy keep the gun in your room."

Well now, finally Button has come up with a good idea. Becca said I could keep the gun in the top drawer of her bureau. So that's where I put it. Right there under her lingerie, wrapped up in a big white hankie. A revolver never had a sweeter place to hide. You should see the stuff she has in there. I wanted to crawl in myself. Mmm…mmm…mmm, just thinking about the thirty-eight in that drawer, beneath Becca's lovely undies, with Becca sleeping in the bed right next to the bureau, and her sweet little body between the sheets, well – fuck-all, it just makes me all the more pissed at Button.

I asked Becca to come with me to the cave on Saturday, for another shooting lesson, but she had a ballgame at Warner Park. She plays with a softball team – girls from the Peerless Wollen Mills. The Woolenettes, they call themselves, and let me tell you, they sure look fine in their caps and flannels. Real uniforms, just like the pros. But it would take more than nine babes in flannels to get me to watch a girls' softball game. All that bobbling and bouncing of the ball. All that swinging and missing. You'd as soon watch a man with no arms shoot pool. But the day wasn't lost, no sir-ee. I knew what the girls would be doing after the game – the same thing they do every time they play at Warner Park. So I staked myself out at the swimming pool, all casual like – like I just happened to be there. I was sitting there, with my feet in the drink, when the girls came out of the dressing room, tucking their curls into their bathing caps, their locker keys jangling on elastics about their pretty ankles.

The great thing about my sunglasses, the ones I got in the Navy, is you can check out the girls and they haven't a clue what you're up to. And, let me tell you, there's nothing better than checking out Woolenettes in bathing suits. As looks go the Woolenettes are strictly major league, with Becca at the top of the order. The gals lined up in a row at the deep end of the pool – all thirteen of 'em – holding hands, giggling and squealing, and then jumped into the pool together. What a tidal wave they put up! They splashed half the people who were sitting at the side of the pool. The life guard blew his whistle and shouted, "No jumping." The girls just screeched. Rita – that's one of Becca's friends – popped up out of the water just at my feet. "Hey, Becca," she shouted, "look who's here. It's your horny brother-in-law." I said, *If I'm horny, Rita, it's only because your boobies are going to pop out of your suit any second.* She tugged up her suit to cover her tits and swam away with a scowl. Becca swam over and said, "Buddy, who are you trying to fool with those dark glasses. We all know what you're doing here." *Just here for a swim, sweet cheeks*, I said.

You know, sometimes you gotta wonder what life's all about. I'm sitting there at the side of the pool, watching the girls splashing around in the water, and I'm thinking – it doesn't get any better than this. And then you think about all the things that can go wrong – like the niggers kidnapping Teddy Carr, and the rioting in those cities out in Texas and up North, and the war, and all – and you wonder what's the fucking point. I don't mean to sound philosophical – I'm no damned Soc-ra-tees – but I mean, sometimes it seems like life is either all up or all down with nothing in between. And right then, with those girls bobbing around, and Rita popping up out of the water every couple of minutes with her boobs practically hanging out of her suit, well, it was like – it doesn't get any better than this. I thought, *I gotta get away from Button.*

I was sitting there thinking about all of this, when Becca and a few of her pals started pulling at my legs, trying to drag me into the pool. *Hey watch it*, I shouted, and I tried to grab hold of something – anything – but the girls had their legs braced against the side of the pool, and they were pulling with all of their strength, and the life guard was blowing his whistle like crazy, and I started slipping toward the water – and the next thing I knew, I was lying on the tiles with Rita pumping away at my lungs with her big strong arms. I guess I must have knocked myself unconscious when I went into the water – hit my head against the splash guard – and the girls had to pull me from the pool. When I woke up Becca was patting my cheeks and Rita was heaving away at my ribs with a fearsome sort of artificial respiration. It was all rather embarrassing. The first thing I saw when I opened my eyes were Rita's big tits, coming at me like a house afire, and I couldn't think of a thing to say. Anyway, the worst was yet to come. There happened to be a newspaper photographer there, taking pictures of folks cooling off at Warner Park and when I finally came around he asked me to pose with the girls. So there it is in the Sunday Times, a picture of me surrounded by my thirteen bee-yu-tee-ful rescuers and the caption says, WOOLENETTES SAVE VET.

Button:

I'd as soon give a gun to a baby as give it to Buddy. I mean, it's not like I think he would deliberately hurt anyone. It's just that he's so clumsy and careless, and when he gets into his mean streak he can – you know, start acting crazy. That man has so much meanness built up inside him, especially against the negroes, that he could shoot someone for no reason at all and think he was doing the right thing. But at least he took the gun out of our room. Becca seems to think that Buddy is this family's lord and protector, so let her deal with it.

Buddy believes the negroes kidnapped Teddy Carr, but apparently the police aren't so sure. Two officers were around here today, searching the neighborhood. They came to the door and asked if they could look in the basement and the garage, places where a kid might hide, or where someone might hide a kid's body. I said, *Sure*, but then I asked Mother if it was OK. She said yes.

I was scared. Scared they might find Buddy's gun. But of course, I knew the police wouldn't go upstairs into Becca's room, but – heaven knows, it occurred to me that Buddy might have moved the gun to a hiding place in the basement or the garage or somewhere the police might look, and if they discovered the gun, well, Buddy might be arrested, or even be suspected of doing harm to Teddy Carr, so the whole time they were searching I was shaking like a leaf.

Of course, the thing I forgot was Roger's laboratory. The police were very interested in that – the boxes and bottles of chemicals with "Danger" or "Inflammable" written all over them, and that old water tank that Roger uses for his experiments, and, well, you know, the two officers were full of questions, and I explained that Roger was employed at the TNT plant, that his work was highly classified, and that all of the chemicals and stuff were part of his job. The policemen were extremely suspicious, and came back later in the evening to talk to Roger. I guess he was able to satisfy their curiosity. He showed them his security clearance, and convinced them that nothing in the basement was all that dangerous, that the labels on the bottles were intended to keep the family away from his work, and so on. The policemen seemed satisfied – up to a point, but they asked Roger for the name of his supervisor at the plant.

Anyway, they didn't find hide nor hair of Teddy Carr. What really embarrassed me was that they searched Eva's shack. I mean, they looked everywhere – in the cupboards, even under the bed with Eva in it. Poor Eva. I was so embarrassed, but I was too scared to ask the police to leave, which is exactly what I should have done. Tometta stood there with her arms folded, and I couldn't bring myself to look her in the eye. The policemen asked her what her name was, where she lived, and why she was in Eva's shack, and there was no rhyme or reason for it except that she's colored. I mean, they never asked me my name, but they wanted to know everything about Tometta, and you can be sure it's because she is colored – and pretty. I was thinking about the thirty white girls whose pictures were in the newspaper yesterday morning, the Cotton Belle debutantes who were presented Saturday evening at the Cotton Ball in Memorial Auditorium, rich girls from the mountains and the ridge who went to Girl's Preparatory School, and who will now go off to college at Vanderbilt, or Randolph Macon, or Sweetbriar, and how Tometta was prettier and smarter than any of them. She just stood there with her arms folded and answered their questions, but you could tell that she was angry – and who can blame her? Tometta has more class in her little finger than all the Cotton Belles put together.

There was another photograph in the paper yesterday morning – Buddy with Becca and her friends at the Warner Park pool. The caption read, "WOOLENETTES SAVE VET. *Purple Heart navy man knocked unconscious at pool. Pulled from water by members of Peerless Mills softball team. Smiling Vincent Cioffi thanks his pretty rescuers.*" It's the silliest thing I have ever seen. I mean, really, you'd think he would have more pride than to let himself be photographed in that kind of situation. Of course, Becca and Lynette spent the entire day laughing about the photograph, and teasing Buddy, and him with a big bump on his head and begging sympathy from me. In the evening, Roger asked me if I wanted to go birdwatching at the National Cemetery, and I said no – well, because of Buddy whining about the bump on his head and feeling put upon by the photograph in the newspaper. All he needs is ammunition and he'd be at me again, taking his embarrassment out on me, as if there was something going on between me and Roger.

He tortured me all last week because I went with Roger to Lulu Lake. I mean, what's the big deal. I don't understand why a man and a woman can't enjoy a walk together without it being considered some kind of heavy-duty romance. After all, Roger is my brother in law. He's much too sweet to do anything improper. I'm sure that any kind of physical attraction for me is the furthest thing from his mind. He was glad to have someone along who enjoys the same things he does, that's all. To tell the truth, I'm not particularly interested in birds, I mean, they all look the same to me, but I must admit I did enjoy our morning at Lulu Lake. Being away from the house was pure pleasure, as was spending a few hours with a man who wasn't picking at me all the time. It was wonderful and peaceful, and the mountain and the lake were lovely, and Roger made me feel very comfortable. He listened as much as he talked, which is something Buddy never does, and mostly, we just walked along in silence, and – well, the amazing thing is I kind of knew what he wanted to say without him having to say it. I don't understand why a man and a woman can't be friends without everyone considering it a big deal. I mean, I would have been happy to go with Roger to the cemetery yesterday evening – but I knew that if I did, I would pay for it all week long with Buddy.

Last Thursday evening, Buddy and I went with Becca, Lynette, and Bitsy to the War Bond Spectacular at Memorial Auditorium. We had been waiting *weeks* for the show. *A fantastic cast.* Rosemary Lane, William Holden, John Payne, Benny Goodman, Martha O'Driscoll, and Mischa Auer. Al Jolson was the host. I mean, just about everybody was there, the auditorium was jammed to the rafters, and we had terrific seats, right near the stage. Halfway through the show, John Payne was wowing us with "You'll Never Know," when out of the blue, Buddy leans over and asks, "So what *did* you and Roger do at Lulu Lake?" I couldn't believe it. The remark was so inappropriate, and so completely gratuitous. I was furious. I got up and walked right out of the show. Then, as I was walking home, I got madder and madder thinking how he had ruined my evening, and there was absolutely no reason for him to do it except pure meanness. Of course, when the girls asked me later why

I left the show, I lied and said that I was feeling sick, because I was too embarrassed to tell the truth. That night, I couldn't bear to sleep in the same room with Buddy. I was still so mad I didn't know what I would say to him, so I slept on the sleeping porch with Bitsy.

Bitsy is sleeping on the porch because she can't bear to share a bed with Alma. She insists that Alma still puts cinders in the bed, although Alma swears to Mother that she has stopped. Bitsy also says that Alma grinds her teeth all night, and that Alma's hands bleed all over the sheets. Bitsy simply refuses to sleep with Alma anymore, and I can't say that I blame her. No one quite knows what to do with Alma. She keeps picking at the sores in her palms, and we are terrified that the sores will get infected. One of those new antibiotics might help – *penicillins*, I think they call them – but that would mean taking Alma to a doctor, and Mother would be embarrassed for a doctor to know what's going on. Of course, Mother is not too embarrassed to have a priest look at Alma's hands. Against my advice, she asked Father Sayers to come to the house. When Alma saw the priest, she started crying, and I swear she hasn't stopped since. Father Sayers talked to Alma for a bit, and then told Mother that he was almost certain that the sores in her hands weren't the "true stigmata," that Alma was probably hysterical, that it is very common for young women to do these things to themselves, and that the Church takes a very cautious view towards any claim that someone has been afflicted with the wounds of Christ. Father Sayers said a few prayers with Mother – prayers for Alma – then went away. He got no further than the front steps when he came back and asked if Alma had sores on her feet or on her side. Mother didn't know. The priest said that sores in those places might be taken much more seriously. Mother asked me to go upstairs and see if Alma had wounds on her feet or side. I refused, I mean, the whole idea was silly and it was none of the priest's business, and Mother wouldn't go, and Father Sayers said he would not ask Alma to show him her side unless there was a "third party" in the room, and I said it was all too silly for words, that what Alma needed was a doctor, not a priest, and Father Sayers stormed out pretending to be very insulted. So then Mother was concerned that Alma might have other sores that we weren't aware of, so she insisted that I come with her to Alma's room. She asked Alma to take off her dress, and the poor girl was still bawling her eyes out and it turned out that she didn't have a sore on her side, or on her feet either, but she did have a knotted cord about her waist that had rubbed a raw, red stripe right around her body. Mother fetched the scissors and cut away the cord, which in some places was stuck to her body with dried blood, which set Alma to crying even more, and I tried to talk to Alma about the knotted cord, and explain to her why these silly practices weren't necessary, that they had absolutely nothing to do with religion, but she was crying so hard I don't believe she heard a word.

Anyway, that's why Bitsy is sleeping on the porch, and I slept there too, because I didn't want to have another go-around with Buddy. To tell the truth, at this time of the year it is much more comfortable to sleep on the porch than in our bedroom. The only problem with sleeping on the porch is having to listen to Iggy snore.

Tometta:

Jest when I be thinkin' this house couldn't get any crazier – I think Roger be in love with Missus Cioffi. He always be starin' at her all puppy-eyed, findin' an' excuse to be round her. An' Missus Cioffi is all he talk about when he be passin' the time with Nana – "Well Button thinks Eleanor Roosevelt is about the best thing to ever happen to this country... Button heard a red-eyed vireo up at Lulu Lake." Don't git me wrong, I think them two gittin' together would be 'bout the best thing could happen. I'd say, they the only two normal ones in the house. Course in this house, it'd only lead to more craziness.

More craziness is the last thing we need.

The *po*lice be by today lookin' fer the poor white boy that done gone missin'. Course it be Nana an' I who be the prime suspects fer our fine officers of *justice*. They guessin' Nana's shack to be the most likely place for li'l Teddy Carr to turn up. After all, who be more likely to kidnap a white boy than an 80-year-old negro woman and her great gran'daughter. They searched 'bout ever'where but up my dress, an' the way them *po*lice were eye-ballin' me, I thought they jest might. Any time somethin' goes wrong round here, they be lookin' fer some *dumb nigger* to blame it on. They didn't so much as investigate when negro boys went missin' in past years. The colored folk round here ain't foolish enough to expect justice, they jest happy if'n they don't fall victim to it. Once the *po*lice left, Nana said, "I jest hope they find that poor boy afore some colored man get strung up by his neck."

Nana go on an' tol' me the story of a man named Ed Johnson, near 'bout forty years ago, right here in Chattanooga. It seems a young white woman was attacked in a most vile manner on 'er way home from work. The *po*lice done arrived, but there be no evidence to be found 'cept a leather strap used to choke the poor woman. The woman wasn't able to get a look at her attacker, 'cept to say he was a colored man. Well, accordin' to Nana, the *po*lice offer a $300 reward, an' sho' nuff, somebody say he seen Ed Johnson with a leather strap on the day of the crime. The poor man was tried and sentenced to hang. Nana says a local negro lawyer be so upset by the injustice, he went all the way to Washington and tol' it to a Supreme

Court judge. Well this judge – *Harlan*, Nana says his name was – says the trial weren't fair at all an' Ed Johnson ought not hang. You might imagine this didn't go over too well with the white folk back in Chattanooga – they don't much care fer the fed'ral gov'ment buttin' into their business. Soon nuff a mob pulled Ed Johnson right outta the jail, while the sheriff turned a blind eye. Took him down to the Walnut Street bridge an' hung him ovah the Tennessee River. Well, the hangin' seemed too slow fer their likin', so they shot him to death as he hung there. The *po*lice found him the next day with a note pinned to him sayin': "To Judge Harlan. Come and get your nigger now." Nana, she says Chattanooga negroes have been walkin' on eggshells evah since.

Don't help poor Mr. Johnson none, but I reckon some good did come of the whole mess. Nana says ole Judge Harlan was madder than a wet hen once he found out what gone on down here. Soon nuff the gov'ment *po*lice come in and start raisin' sand. The sheriff got put on trial for his part in the lynchin', and was found guilty. Course he only fetched ninety days in the fed'ral prison, an' a hero's welcome when he come on home – near 'bout half the white folk in Chattanooga waitin' for his train, says Nana, singin' *Dixie* as he pull in.

Separate but equal, that be the law. I reckon most color'd folk could live with that, if'n there was a speck a truth to it. But seein' Nana and Mista Goody settin' on the swing on a hot summer night, sippin' lemonade, talkin' so easily, the li'l hugs he give her when she give 'em a good laugh, an' I wonder why anyone'd want to separate themselves from someone jest 'cause of the color of their skin. To cheat yoahself outta Nana's stories, recalled like it be yes'erday, the way she find the deep-down good in ever'one, the way she always knows jest what you be thinkin', always seein' the bright side of it all – to miss out on someone like Nana, jest 'cause she got black skin, don't make no sense. I don't s'pose it make no sense to Mista Goody either.

I tell ya who else don't make no sense – Miss Alma. She come shufflin' inta the kitchen to put a dirty plate in the sink, 'er eyes all red an' puffy – seem all the girl do is cry. The poor thing jest look mis'rable, so I says, *Can I make you a nice glass of lemonade, Miss Alma*. "No thank you, Tometta," she says. Well, I got myself between her an' the door, an' says, *Aww, sit right down, won't take me but a minute. It be too hot to turn down a nice glass of lemonade.* She sat down, an' before I could cut the first lemon, I seen the tears comin' down her face. *What be wrong, Miss Alma*, I says. "I'm a freak, that's what's wrong. I'm just a freak," she cries. *You ain't no freak, Miss Alma, you jest fret too much ovah li'l thangs*, I says. "Little things?" she cries. I suppose she's thinkin' on the war an' all, so I says, *It jest be part of life. All ya can do is be the best person you can be. The Lawd don't expect any more'n that.* "Do you believe there's a hell?," she ask. *Well, I s'pect if'n there is*, I says, *it be reserved fer the likes of the devil himself, nothin' you or I's gots to worry on.* I sat down with two lemonades, an' we jest sat there quietly sippin' them fer a spell. I could see her thinkin' on what we say, an' it struck me it might be her Daddy's soul she be worryin' on. I wish I knew the right words to speak right then, but they wouldn't come, so we jest drank our lemonade.

Iggy:

Button must be havin' another squabble with that dago husband of hers. She's back an' forth through here to the sleepin' porch. "Hi Iggy," she says. "Sorry to bother you, Iggy." "Can. I get you anything, Iggy?" That gal is the sweetest person in this damn house. Always was.

Anyways, havin' Button an Bitsy sleepin on the porch is inconvenient right now, since the only way to git to the sleepin' porch is through my room. Billy Joe Alaska was by here today, bringin' me my – well, I guess I might as well say it – bringin' me my rifle, an' I was scared shitless that one of the girls would come traipsin' through. Billy Joe showed up with a golf bag, jus' two old golf clubs stickin' out the top – those clubs must a been fifty years ole an' I don't know who he was expectin' to fool. Also in the bag was a twenty-two caliber rifle. I says to him, *Billy Joe, that gun won't kill a fly. You should have brought me sumthin' with more balls.* I mean, a twenty-two wouldn't do much to scare off a crowd of nigras that was marchin' up the street. I says, *If'n I'm goin to help this family, I'll need sumthin' better than this.* Billy Joe said, "Iggy, you crazy old coot, I'd be a fool to give you anything 'cept a twenty-two. You should count yoahself lucky." Mind you, Billy Joe is near ole as I am, an' if anyone is crazier than me, it's that man. Imagine, walkin' in here with a golf bag with two clubs in it, like he was goin' to play the front nine at the Chattanooga Country Club. Billy Joe Alaska ain't swung a golf stick in some fifty odd years. Damndest thing I evah seen.

Anyways, the twenty-two is better'n nothin'. I stuck it under my mattress. *What about shells?* I ask. Well, Billy Joe reaches into a pocket on the side of the golf bag an' pulls out a handful of shells an' tees, all mixed together. He tosses 'em onto the bed an' reaches fer another fistful. I says, *Goddamn, Billy Joe, do you expect me to shoot nigras with golf tees?* He jus' laughs. I pick the shells out, one by one – tiny as hen's teeth, they are – an' put em into my denture cup an' brush the tees onto the floor.

"I got somethin' else for you, Iggy," says Billy Joe, "A little somethin' to keep you entertained up here." I says, *Billy Joe, you're a goddamn pervert. Take your damn pictures right back outta here, I gots women folk in this house.* I jam 'em right back into his hands. Lawd knows, I'd be embarrassed out of my mind if anyone was to find such things in my room. An' I sho' don't wanna ask Tootsie to get rid of 'em ag'in. Billy Joe was tryin' to stuff 'em under my mattress, "Come on ya ol' coot, will do ya good stuck in this bed all day, it'll take yer mind off guns," he says. I'm pushin' him away, when in walks Tootsie. Well, Billy Joe straightens up right quick, an' stuffs his magazines back into the golf bag, an' starts actin' all highfalutin, an' backin' outta the room like Byron Nelson was waitin' fer him on the first tee at the country club, an' I'd say I wasn't sorry one bit to see him go, him with his damn pictures an' all.

I said to Tootsie, *if brains was leather, that man wouldn't have enough to saddle a junebug.* "He's got hair in his nose too," says Tootsie. *Well, I'd say he has more hairs in his nose than brains in his head.* Anyways, now I had a secret from Tootsie. I says, *I've got a secret you'd like to know. Tell me who Bitsy's boyfriend is an' I'll tell you my secret.* Tootsie was in a quandary. She wanted to know my secret, but she didn't want to tell me hers. So I says, *You give me a clue an' I'll give you a clue.* She thought on that a bit, an' then she says, "Bitsy's boyfriend is a soldier." Now, goddamn, that was no help at all, 'cause nearly every man in town is a soldier. I says, *My secret is under the mattress.* That really got her curious, an' she starts tryin' to pry up the mattress to look, but the rifle was on the other side of the bed. She says, "Bitsy's boyfriend said to her, "Eek-leeba-dick." I didn't know what the hell kind of clue that was. I said, *What the hell does that mean?* She says, "It's German for I love you." I say, *Is this guy some kind of German spy?* She says, "It's your turn to give a clue."

Well, I couldn't think of a damn thing to say. So I took the rifle out from under the mattress an' showed it to her. "That's cheating," she cries. "You were supposed to give me a clue." I says, *Now you gotta tell me.* I got her. She couldn't back out now. Ha, she'd fallen into Ignatius Theodore Ferguson's trap. So she tells me. Yes she did. She tells me that Bitsy's boyfriend is one of the German POWs at the National Cemetery, by the name of Horst. "You've got to swear you'll tell no one," said Tootsie, "Bitsy will kill me if she finds out I told." Well, that's not half the problem, I'd say. I reckon that Buddy

will kill Bitsy if he finds out she's got a Nazi boyfriend. Knowin'
how Buddy hates the Germans, he'd go nuts, that's fer sho. There's
no *eek-leeba-dick* between Buddy an' the Huns.

Tootsie:

Horst likes his pin-ups. Bitsy put the photographs into an envelope and asked the American guard to give them to Horst. We were standing by the wall when Horst looked at the pictures. He grinned. He looked at Bitsy and grinned. He has pretty blue eyes, and nice white teeth, and when he smiles, he looks so handsome that I can see why Bitsy likes him. Then Horst showed the photographs to the other Germans. They looked at the photographs, and then they looked at Bitsy, and then they looked at the photographs again. Bitsy was embarrassed and wanted to go home, but Horst called her back. Horst loves Bitsy. He says he can't wait for the war to end so he can marry her. Dad says the war will be over soon. The Americans are beating the pants off the Germans in France. Dad says the Allies are dropping so many bombs on the German cities that they will have to surrender. Every night a thousand bombers fly over German cities dropping bombs. I feel sorry for Horst because his family is in Germany. Dad says that unless the Germans surrender, soon there won't be a house left standing in Germany. I wonder if Horst knows what is happening to his family. He tells Bitsy he will marry her and take her to Germany. But Bitsy doesn't want to go to Germany. She wants to stay in Chattanooga. She is hoping that when the war is over, Horst will stay here.

Bitsy has changed since she met Horst. She never used to care much about how she looked. Now she makes herself pretty all the time, especially when she goes to see Horst. She spends all her money on clothes and cosmetics. Last night I helped her with a Charm-Kurl permanent wave kit. We put her hair up in curlers, with some kind of icky solution, and made it all curly. She said, "I'll be so glamorous, I'll make the men clamorous." Today, when we went to see Horst, she wore a new yellow sundress with a bolero. She looked terrific. Poor Horst.

Bitsy should enter the Miss Chattanooga Beauty Pageant. Almost every day there are pictures in the paper of girls who have entered, and I think Bitsy is prettier than any of them. Most of the girls are eighteen or nineteen years old, just like Bitsy. I told Bitsy that she should enter. She says that Grandma would never let her enter a beauty contest. She says that Grandma would never let her go onto a stage in a bathing suit. She says no Catholic girl has ever been in the contest. But I think Grandma should let her do it. The prize is a four-hundred dollar scholarship. If Bitsy won, she could go to college.

I told Mom that Bitsy wanted to enter the Miss Chattanooga contest, but that Grandma wouldn't let her do it. I thought Mom might help change Grandma's mind, but instead Mom got real mad. She said Bitsy wasn't pretty enough to win, and that she didn't have anything to do in the talent contest. I told her how pretty Bitsy looked with her permanent wave and the yellow sundress with the bolero. Mom said Bitsy should be ashamed spending money on clothes when there is a war on. I think Mom is mean. Bitsy works hard. The dry cleaners is a hot and steamy place, especially in summer, and Bitsy is always exhausted when she comes home. I'm glad she spends her money on pretty clothes. I think Mom is jealous. I don't know why, but I think Mom is jealous of Bitsy.

Mom is jealous of Becca and Lynette, too. The girls skipped work today and stood in line at Loveman's to buy nylons. They stood in line for two hours. The limit was three pairs. Becca bought three pairs, and Lynette bought three pairs. Lynette gave one of her pairs of nylons to Bitsy, and Lynette gave one of her's to Button. Mom wasn't home when the girls arrived, so she didn't get any. Later, she asked Lynette if she could have a pair, and Lynette said no, she only had two left. Mom wouldn't ask Becca for nylons. I don't know why, but Mom hardly ever talks to Becca.

Buddy was there when the girls came home, and he asked them to model the stockings. He said, "Let's have a style show, girls." Lynette laughed, but Becca took off her shoes and slipped on the stockings. She rolled them right up her legs, real slow and sexy like. Then she stood up and turned round and round, holding her dress up to the tops of her stockings. Buddy clapped. Aunt Button went upstairs.

This evening, Sugar got out of her cage. I couldn't find her anywhere. I looked in Iggy's room, because I thought Iggy might have whacked her again with the badminton racket. Then I peeked in Grandma's room. Buddy was there. He was standing on the back of a chair looking out the window. He was using the chair like a ladder. I couldn't figure out what he was doing. Then I saw that he was trying to see into the bathroom window. I didn't make a sound. I watched at the door. Buddy was standing on the top rung of the chairback and I knew what he was looking at. He was looking at Becca. Becca was taking her bath.

Suddenly, there was a boom. The whole house shook, and Buddy fell off the chair.

Everyone started screaming at once. Becca screamed in the bathroom. Alma screamed in her room. Buddy hollered that he had broken his leg. Downstairs, everybody was screaming. I knew Dad must have had some kind of accident, so I ran downstairs. Button and Lynette were standing at the top of the basement stairs and smoke was pouring out the door. Mom and Bitsy and Grandma and Emily Sue and Tometta were standing by the stove. Tometta had her arms around Emily Sue, and Emily Sue was shaking like she always does when she gets scared. Button was shouting, "Roger! Roger!" Then Dad came up the stairs. His face, hair, and clothes were all covered with black smoke, but he was OK. He was smiling. He said, "Sorry, I guess I had a little accident."

I never saw Mom so mad. She said, "You almost blew the house up and you call it a little accident." Dad said, "My little accident might just win the war." Grandma said, "War or no war, I don't want any more experiments in this house." Dad grinned. He said, "I was messing around with pentolite." Mom stomped out of the kitchen. Tometta took Emily Sue into the backyard. Lynette was laughing. Dad said, "The trouble was, it blew the cap right off the end of the tank."

Then I remembered Buddy. I said, *I think Uncle Buddy's hurt.* So we all raced upstairs, and Buddy was laying on the floor in Grandma's room screaming about his ankle, and the chair was tipped over. Becca was standing there in her bathrobe. Button said, "Buddy, what were you doing up on the chair." He said, "For Christ sake, I was fixing the curtain rod." Becca said, "Yeah, curtain rod." Button said, "We've got to get you to the hospital."

Dad called from downstairs, "Who let Sugar out of her cage?"

The funny thing is, it was Buddy's good leg that got broke.

Buddy:

Roger is goddamn nuts the way he messes around with explosives. Every building at the TNT plant is surrounded by half-a-mile of empty space, and for good reason too, but Roger explodes the stuff right here in the basement of our house, in the middle of town. Can you believe it? I'll tell you this, we are lucky we weren't all killed.

As it was, I busted my ankle. My leg's in a cast and I can only get around on crutches. Which means I have to put all my weight on my gimpy leg, and let me tell you, that's no picnic. The pain goes shooting right up to the hip. I blame Roger for what happened to my leg, him and his crazy experiments. The government pays him to kill Nips and Nazis, and instead he damn near blows up his own family.

My busted ankle has one advantage – I can't get upstairs without help. Last night, Becca gave me a hand up the stairs. Put her arm right around my waist. That girl is one cocky sweetheart, and I'll tell you this, she smells like a rose. She said, "Buddy, I know what you were doing up on that chair. I hope you got an eyeful, for all the trouble it's caused you." I said, *I don't know what you're talking about.* She laughed. I don't care if she knows. That curtain rod was broken. I had every right in the world to be up there. No one else around this house fixes anything. Besides, I didn't see anything worth speaking of. Just Becca's shoulders. Now, if I had had a few more minutes, until Becca stood up in the tub, well, that would have been different. All I needed was just a few more minutes. That Roger has one hellava bad sense of timing.

I'm not especially proud to be spying on Becca. Or on Wanda either, for that matter. I know it's – well, let's say, it's not the gentlemanly thing to do. I don't know why I do shit like that. Something drives me, like – it's something I have to do. It's not as if I'm hurting anybody and, to tell the truth, I don't think Becca or Wanda mind. They know what I'm up to. After all, didn't Becca help me up the stairs last night, let me lean against her? Didn't she put her arm around my waist? That doesn't sound like someone who's holding a grudge. And Wanda – well, she shows it off to the whole world. If I thought they minded, then I wouldn't do it. A guy's got to have some sexual stimulation in his life, and I sure as hell don't get any from Button. If I wanted someone to blame for bustin' my leg, then maybe I should blame Button.

And I'll tell you this, it's not like women don't want it. The other day, Becca and a whole bunch of her friends went to a street dance in Tullahoma with the soldiers from Camp Forrest. At least a dozen buses took girls from Chattanooga, and another dozen buses brought girls from Nashville. According to Becca, there must have been ten thousand people partying in the streets. The girls left here about three o'clock in the afternoon, and didn't get back 'til three in the morning. Not all of them came back in the buses, either. Becca and Sandra got a ride home with two paratroopers who were shipping out for Europe the next day. I know what happened because I heard Becca telling Lynette. They didn't know I was listening, but I heard everything she said. Becca said that Sandra and her guy "did it," right in the back seat of the car as they were highballing down Highway 41, with Becca and her guy in the front seat. Jesus, I don't believe it. That Sandra girl is getting some soldier off in the back seat of a car, I mean actually doing it with a guy she just met, and you can bet that Becca and her guy were watching from up front – and I'm supposed to feel guilty about taking a peek through the goddamn bathroom window.

But that's not the worst of it. When Becca and Sandra got back to Chattanooga the guys stopped at a bar on Broad Street out by Terminal Station. They were drunk by then, and got into a fight with a couple of uppity black boys. One of the niggers made the mistake of pulling a knife, and the two paratroopers damn near beat him to death. Anyway, that's what Becca told Lynette. She said they all piled into the car and got out of there just as the cops came screaming up with sirens blazing. The fight must have been the start of something, because this morning there was a story in the paper about a big hassle out on Broad Street in the middle of the night, with two cops hurt, some windows broken and a nigger shot. And Becca is telling all of this to Lynette as calm as can be, like she just came back from a Girl Scout jamboree. That girl is as cool as a cucumber.

I'm not knocking it. I say, *more power* to her. Life is meant to be fun, live it up, grab a little ass wherever you can get it. I'll tell you what I'd like to do. I'd like to take Roger's car, invite Becca to come along, and hightail it out of here. Drive to Texas – hell, drive all the way to California. Doing any damn thing that comes into our heads. Drive when we feel like it, stop when we feel like it. Sleep under the stars – or in a feather bed. Eat Mexican food. Take pot shots at stop signs with my thirty-eight. Fuck like crazy.

Trouble is, we wouldn't be able to get enough gasoline. No coupons. So until the war's over, it's just a pipe-dream. But, damn it, I've got to think of something. I've got to start living a life. I'm going nuts, here. It's like I'm living in a loony bin. Hobbling around on crutches, with one gimpy leg and the other in a cast. Married to a woman that doesn't give a blue fuck in hell.

Button:

Everybody's been a little jumpy around here since Roger's bomb went off. This morning there was another bang, and I almost jumped out of my skin. I knew it wasn't Roger again, because he was at work. The first thing I thought of was Buddy and his gun. The thing is, Buddy was nowhere to be seen. I knew he kept the gun in the top drawer of Becca's bureau, so I looked there. The gun was there all right, under Becca's lingerie.

The noise was probably a car backfiring in the street, but we are all so nervous, the first things that came to mind were Roger's bombs and Buddy's gun. It's a shame we have to worry about such things. The saddest thing of all is – Emily Sue was terrified by the noise. When I came downstairs, she was banging her head against the basement door and Tometta was trying to calm her down. She thought something bad was happening in the basement, because of the way Roger looked when he came up after the explosion. Poor Emily Sue. Of course, she can't understand what's going on, but to tell the truth, I can't either. Sometimes I wonder if anyone around here is in possession of their right senses.

I can't imagine what Tometta thinks. I suppose she can hardly wait till Eva gets better, so she can go back to her own home, but in the meantime I'm glad she's here. She contributes a rare bit of sanity to this crazy household. Together, we took Emily Sue out into the backyard and sat her down in the glider. Emily Sue likes the glider, just swinging back and forth, it calms her down, and really, it calms me down too, I mean, there's something soothing about just swinging back and forth, and watching the clouds sail across the sky. Tometta brought out a colander of okra, and we sat there, cutting the okra. Tometta is a fine cook. To tell the truth, she's a better cook than Eva, and I'll not be happy when she leaves, but, I mean, the main reason I'll be unhappy is because she's the only person I have to talk to – I mean, *really* talk to.

I wish she would call me Button. I've asked her a dozen times to call me Button, and occasionally she will do it, all tentative like, but she always goes back to calling me Missus Cioffi. I don't want to make her uncomfortable, but still, it seems like such a sensible start if we could address each other in the same familiar way. Of course, if Buddy heard Tometta call me "Button" he would have a conniption fit, her being a colored girl and all. And the difference in our ages doesn't help, either. Tometta is only half my age, really. When you think about it, she is younger than Bitsy, but I can't imagine talking to Bitsy the way I talk to Tometta.

While we fixed the okra, we talked about the books Tometta is reading. She likes to talk about books, and she doesn't have anyone else to talk to. I never knew a girl to read so many books. She gets books from the colored branch of the Chattanooga Public Library over on Fourteenth Street, and the funny thing is, she can't find any books written by negroes. She says she's been through almost every book in the collection, and hasn't found a single story by a colored person. I said, *Tometta, you ought to write a book yourself.* She said, "An' jest what should I write about?" I said, *Write about yourself. Write about your great-grandmother. I don't know your mother, or your grandmother, but perhaps you could write about them, too.* She said, "Why anyone want to read 'bout us?" I said, *Tometta, everyone's life is interesting. If you tell your story honestly and simply, then people will want to read it.* She said, "No, ma'am, ain't nobody gonna read what I write."

I could tell she thought about what I said, though, because she was quiet for a long time. The thing is, I'm probably not doing Tometta a service by encouraging her in that way. There really isn't much of a chance she'll get more education, and although she has taught herself a lot by reading, the chances of getting a story published are – well, I just don't know who would do it. But really, when you sit there and listen to Tometta talk – you know, it's more interesting than some of the things you read in books. I said, *Tometta, why don't you just write a story about a colored girl growing up in Chattanooga, and you could base it on your own life. A story just for you and me.*

Tometta took the okra into the kitchen, and brought out a basket of apples from the Farmer's Market. Mamie had managed to get hold of a bag of canning sugar, and Tometta was going to put up some applesauce. We have Mason jars left over from when we had the Victory Garden and Tometta can't bear seeing them go to waste. We sat in the glider, with Emily Sue between us, and pared half-a-bushel of green apples. We didn't say much, we just swung and pared, and

Emily Sue babbled on like she does when she's happy, and I knew she had forgotten being scared.

Roger:

When I got to work today, Mel Kelsen called me into his office and asked about my basement laboratory. The police had paid him a visit, and told him what they found when they searched our house. I told Mel that my lab was for private experiments – nothing whatsoever to do with my job. He was skeptical. He reminded me that it was against regulations to remove materials of any kind from the plant. He spoke of the security aspects of my work. He was resentful, and perhaps even embarrassed, that the police had showed up on his doorstep. There's something fishy about Mel. He tries to establish camaraderie when he talks to you, informal like – a pat on the back, a wink and a nudge, and all that – but his attitude is one of pure condescension. Perhaps it's because he is a Yankee who resents having been sent down south, or maybe his snooty attitude goes with the Harvard degree. Anyway, he never lets me forget that he has a Ph.D. and I don't. Whatever it is, he condescends to me, and treats me like a child, though he is no older than I am.

I managed to convince him that my basement experiments are innocent, just a hobby, and nothing to do with dangerous explosives. Nevertheless, he managed to feel put upon, and blamed me for the intrusion into his time. He spieled his standard sermon: "There's a war on, Roger. Need I remind you that every minute of our work helps shorten the war." He asked me again about the possibility of transfer to Oak Ridge, as a kind of threat I suppose. Apparently, Oak Ridge is desperate for engineers with my skills, and Mel certainly wouldn't mind seeing the back of me. I get on his nerves because I don't treat him with the proper deference. On the other hand, he knows that if I left, his department would be sorely beset. No one else around here has quite the knack with TNT that I do.

I asked him again what they are doing at Oak Ridge, and once again he wouldn't tell me. I don't think Mel has the foggiest idea what's going on up there, but he likes to pretend he's in the know. I hear rumors of a giant jet-propelled cylinder – and I mean something really *colossal* – that rolls across the land, crushing everything in its path – buildings, trees, weapons, personnel. I'll admit, it sounds farfetched, but the size of the plant they have constructed up there is, by all accounts, far bigger than what would be required for an ordinary weapon. I know for a fact that the Krauts have jet-propelled fighter planes, and I've heard reliable reports that the Brits are working on jet-propelled land transport, so I would be surprised if we weren't working on the same technology. Still, that sort of thing is no business of mine. I know nothing about jet propulsion. What I do best is explosives.

This afternoon, Mel called a meeting of the engineers. We have bomb-damage assessment films from the first Super-Fort raids on Japan. Our B-29's can now strike Japanese cities at will, and each of those big birds carry as much firepower as five B-17's. We watched a film of the first raid on Tokyo – *over and over and over* – the explosions on the ground like a wall of ash and lava rolling across the city from Mount Fuji. It's all toothpicks and rice paper down there, as far as I can see. Dropping a bomb on a Japanese city is like putting a blowtorch to kindling. Certainly it's a different kettle of fish than bombing European cities, at least as far as civilian populations are concerned. The Air Force wants bombs that will do maximum damage to Japanese cities, and come to think of it, I may have just what they need. My special mix of pentolite and liquid petroleum would do the trick. A dozen five-hundred pounders dropped onto certain neighborhoods of Tokyo would cause a firestorm that wouldn't leave a stick standing. Trouble is, I haven't decided what to do about my private experiments, and my fibs to Kelsen this morning won't make matters easier. I'm not happy about our nation's present policy of bombing civilian targets. It's one thing to level military or industrial targets, but obliterating residential neighborhoods is something else. The Air Force bigwigs that come here for briefings gloss over all of that. They never quite come right out and ask for bombs that will incinerate babies, but that's what they want. Everyone here knows the difference between a weapon designed to destroy a concrete or steel structure, and one intended to ignite firestorms in domestic environments. I keep putting questions to the Air Force officers – holding their feet to the fire as it were – and they hem and haw, and talk about ending the war quickly by sapping the enemy's will to fight, saving Allied lives, and all that malarkey. They never admit even to themselves what's happening on the ground. That's the beauty of high-level bombing – it takes a leap of imagination to recognize what's going on down there under those pretty powderpuffs of smoke. Of course, as Buddy says, "they're only Japs."

I'm not trying to sound self-righteous about any of this. It's just that I'm not especially happy about what I do for a living. And what's worse, I enjoy doing it. I love making bombs. I love the challenge of it. I love the sound and the fury when a bomb explodes. Always did. Even when I was a kid, I made bombs. I cut the heads off matches and packed 'em into Dixie cups, then set the damned things off. I mixed baking soda and vinegar to make erupting volcanoes. I put cherry-bombs under tin cans and blew them sky high. Then, I started getting sophisticated. I'd go down to the railroad yard and collect sulfur, nitrates, coal dust – anything that fell from railroad cars, and experimented. I made fantastic bombs. In one memorable explosion I blasted a garbage can lid over the roof of the house. Once I made a pipe cannon that hurled an aggie all the way across the playground. I'm lucky I wasn't killed. I'm lucky I didn't kill someone else.

I guess I'm still a kid at heart. That's why I'm messing about in the basement. Everyone in the family thinks I nearly blew up the house, but there was never any danger of that. I was off on my estimate of the power of the explosion by about five percent, that's all. I added ammonia and formaldehyde to TNT, along with a special ingredient of my own. I felt certain that I knew just what the result would be – and that my tank would contain it. But that particular mix had a special *poof.* In the bomb-making business, five percent extra is a breakthrough. Kelsen would dearly love to know my recipe. It would make his department look very good indeed. I'll tease him along a bit before I tell him. By then, the war may be over and I won't have to tell him at all.

My experiments are certainly less dangerous than Buddy's gun. When I got home this evening, Button was waiting for me on the back steps. She took me into the side yard and showed me the bird. The woodpecker. The redheaded woodpecker. The one that's been banging away in the dead chestnut tree outside Iggy's window. The bird was on the ground. It wasn't dead, but it couldn't fly; it was flopping about with one good wing. Button wouldn't touch it, but she was concerned and sad. I examined the bird. Its wing had been badly damaged by a shot. Too much damage for a BB gun, so the culprit wasn't one of the neighborhood kids. I said, *Button, I hate to tell you this, but Buddy is up to no good with that gun of his.* She said, "I heard a bang this morning, but I didn't see Buddy, and when I went to look for the gun, it was where he left it." I said, *Well, it's hard to imagine who else might have done it.*

I didn't let Button see how angry I was. Buddy is crazy. Imagine – shooting an innocent bird. I mean *really crazy*, clinically nuts. He probably did it just to spite me. And of all birds, he had to shoot the woodpecker. What a beautiful animal. "Shirttail bird" is what the negroes call it, because of its formal dress. I'll admit that this particular woodpecker has been a bit of a bother. It's a mischievous bird, noisy, and terribly territorial. It can yap louder than a dog if you get close to its nest. But that's no reason for Buddy to shoot it. I swear to God, if Buddy wasn't Button's husband I'd call the police on him. I kept my temper. I said to Button, *I can't imagine why Buddy would do such a thing.* Button said, "Roger, I don't think it was Buddy that did it. Not unless he has another gun."

The problem was, what to do with the bird? It couldn't fly. The wing was too badly damaged to ever mend. We talked about what we might do. Button suggested making a nest of sorts in the garage, and keeping the woodpecker there, but I couldn't see doing that. It would be a crime to keep that beautiful bird cooped up in the garage, and unlikely that we'd be able to keep it alive. The only honest thing was to put it out of its misery. We were sitting there talking about what to do when Tometta came along. As soon as she apprised the situation, she took that bird in her hands and wrung its neck like a Sunday chicken. I said, *Tometta, I don't know how you did that, but I'm glad you came along.* I couldn't have felt worse if I had killed the bird myself. I was so queasy in my stomach, I couldn't eat. All evening long, I stayed away from Buddy. I was afraid of what I might do or say. He didn't mention the woodpecker. If he did, I might have thrown a punch at him. The thing is, I wouldn't want to do anything that would hurt Button.

Iggy:

I may be an ole coot, but I can still shoot straight. I had my
sharpshooter badge when I was in the service. That's more'n forty
years ago now, but I haven't lost the touch yet. I waited till I figured
no one was in the house but Mamie. Mamie, she don't hear much
any more. Hard of hearin', she is. So I waited till the rest of 'em was
away an' then had myself a try with Billy Joe's rifle. Took aim at
that goddam woodpecker that's been driving me near crazy. One
shot. *Pow!* Right 'tween the eyes. Killed that sucker dead as a
doornail.

Sittin' here on my bed is like bein' in a sniper's nest. I got me a
clear field of view right up Ninth Street. I took a bead on a couple of
nigras who were walkin' up the other side of the street. Squeezed the
trigger, easy like. *Pow.* Then the other one. *Pow.* Course, there was
no shells in the chamber. Jus' practice. Aim high, that's the secret
with a twenty-two. Aim high an' let the bullet fall to its target. Given
my druthers, I'd have myself an M-1, or even my old carbine from
Cuba. But if worse comes to worse, the twenty-two will do jus' fine.
If the coloreds come marchin' ovah the hill fixin' to cause harm, I'll
pick 'em off, one by one.

I see in the paper that we had an – an *al-ter-CA-shun* the other
night. Cops an' coloreds down on Broad Street. Two *policemen* were
taken to the the hospital. One nigra killed, an' God knows how many
injured. It's like Buddy says. These are the first skirmishes. The
nigras are testin' the waters, measurin' the resolve of white folk.

Mamie sent Tometta up with my tray this mornin'. Spam an'
powdered eggs. Worse food'n we ever had in Cuba, that's sho'. If
spiced ham is called Spam, then dried eggs should be called Dregs. It
was funny havin' Tometta standin' here, an' me with the rifle under
the mattress – her bein' a nigra an' all. I says, *Tometta, what do you
colored folks have gainst us whites?* She says, "I don't know what
you mean, Mister Iggy." I says, *Goddam, Tometta, ever'one knows
the nigras are out to get the whites. Jus' look what happen up in
Boston the other day. The newspaper called it a "savage battle."
The whole nigra district of the city was in a uproar. Dozens of
colored soldiers an' sailors was arrested, most of 'em fer carryin'
knives. Here we are tryin' to fight a war against the Nazis an' the*

Japs, an' we got to fight another war at home 'gainst you folk. Seems to me as you got nothin' to complain about. She says, "I couldn't say, Mister Iggy." I says, *Oh, I figure you know more than you're wantin' to say. I'd say, most of you folk know what's goin' on.* She says, "Mister Iggy, eat your breakfast now. Missus Buffon is waitin' to get the kitchen cleaned up." I says, *What about Teddy Carr, Tometta? What would you say has happened to Teddy Carr?* She says, "I don't know nothin' 'bout no Teddy Carr." Well, what Tometta says an' what she knows is two different thangs. She's got her secrets an' I got mine. I got my secret right here under the mattress. An' Tometta don't need to know it.

Seems like ever'one round here is carryin' secrets. That young Alma – she doesn't tell anyone what's goin' on in her head. She has secrets from ever'one but God. An' Bitsy, she's got her secret, too. Only thing is, I know Bitsy's secret, 'cause Tootsie done tol' me. Bitsy comes prancin' through here this mornin' an' I says, *Bitsy, how long would you reckon it'll be before we whup them Germans.* I's jus' teasin' her. She shrugged. I says, Bitsy, *I'd say as we should keep all the German POW's in concentration camps, even after the war is won, jus' so they won't start no trouble ag'in. What do you say to that?* She says, "Not all Germans are bad, Uncle Iggy. There's lots of German soldiers who are fighting just because Hitler makes them do it. Lots of German soldiers are as nice as you or me." Now, I don't know why I was teasin' Bitsy. It's jus' her havin' a secret an' all. An' tell the truth, if what Tootsie says is true, about Bitsy I mean, then that girl is in serious trouble an' someone oughta help her out. So I says, *Bitsy, if what I read in the newspapers is true, them German soldiers are a bad lot. Mean as snakes. If'n it was up to me, I'd keep 'em all locked up till they had plenty of time to see the error of their ways. I'd keep 'em locked up till hell freezes ovah.*

I couldn't tell, but it looked as if Bitsy was about to cry. She sho' skedaddled out of the room right quick. When Tootsie came by, I tol' her what I said to Bitsy. Tootsie said, "Iggy, you promised you'd keep a secret." I says, *I didn't tell her nothin'. I jus' asked her a few question, that's all. Jus' tryin' to see if you was tellin' the truth.* So Tootsie said that she could prove the story about Horst. She went away an' came back with a little wooden carvin of a boy holdin' a lamb, which she says Horst made for Bitsy. I asked her how she come to git it, an' she said she stole it, an' that Bitsy doesn't know. Well, as far as I can see, that li'l carvin' was too good to be carved by some German soldier. Tootsie may have stole it all right, but she more than likely stole it from Woolworths than from Bitsy.

Then Tootsie tol' me the darndest thang. She says that Bitsy has signed up for the Miss Chattanooga contest. The contest is Saturday night, an' Bitsy signed up. Paid the $25 dollar entrance fee an' ever'thing. The trouble is the evenin' gown the girls are s'posed to wear. They has to wear an evenin' gown an' a bathing suit. Bitsy's got a bathing costume, all right, but she ain't got no evenin' gown, an' no money to buy one. The only person round here with a evenin' dress is Wanda, an' Bitsy is 'fraid to ask Wanda if'n she can borrow it. So Bitsy wants Tootsie to ask her mother fer the dress. Tootsie says she's 'fraid to even mention the dress cause Wanda is dead set against Bitsy bein' in the contest. So Tootsie is gonna snitch the dress fer the night. She says Wanda will never notice it gone. That's why Tootsie come by my room. She was watchin' to make sho' her mother was out in the yard takin' sun. Then she hustled off to get the dress from Wanda's closet.

I kept an eye on Wanda while Tootsie took the dress. Same as ever' sunny day. Wanda sets out the lawn chair. Then she spreads a sheet across the chair. Then she makes that sunsuit of hers even skimpier. Rolls the skirt right up to her crotch. Rolls the blouse right up to her boobs. Rubs herself all over with some kind of oil till she's shinin' like a sweatin' mare. Then lays herself out on the lawn chair – jus' so, on display. The funny thing is, I haven't seen hide nor hair of Vincent, so God knows who she thinks is lookin' at her.

Buddy:

I'll tell you this, the shit has hit the fan. In the News-Free Press tonight there is a picture of Bitsy. Bitsy with two other girls. New contestants in the Miss Chattanooga Beauty Pageant.

The house is in a bloody uproar. Even Alma drifted downstairs to see what was happening. Mamie is furious. She says that only over her dead body will Bitsy get up on that stage in a bathing suit. Button was trying to calm Mamie down, telling her that beauty contests are good clean fun. Becca and Lynette think the idea is wonderful. They say Bitsy's sure to win. They rushed right out to Memorial Auditorium and bought tickets for everyone. Everyone except Mamie, that is. Mamie refuses to consider going. Mamie says that if Bitsy goes through with it, she'll be too embarrassed to ever go out of the house again.

I doubt that. Mamie will get over it. Meanwhile, Bitsy is the embarrassed one. When Becca and Lynette started making a fuss, she blushed like crazy. They asked her what she will wear, and what she'll do in the talent contest. They are full of suggestions. Lynette promises to teach Bitsy how to dance. Becca thinks Bitsy should sing, but damned if I've ever heard that girl sing a note. Bitsy says she has her own idea, and won't tell anyone what it is. Wanda sneers at the whole thing. Wanda says the competition is rigged, that the people who run the pageant already know who'll win. That doesn't cut any ice with Becca and Lynette. They're already planning Bitsy's trip to Atlantic City.

Bitsy blushes, but still loves all the attention. That girl has been coming out of her shell lately. Wearing makeup. Buying new clothes. Reading Becca and Lynette's copies of Mademoiselle. All of a sudden Bitsy has decided to become a grown-up woman. She looks fine, too. *A-OK*. But I'll tell you this, she doesn't have much sex appeal. Doesn't turn me on at all. I can't explain it, but she doesn't have that certain something that – well, say, that Becca and Lynette have. Bitsy's more like Button. Bitsy's a goody-goody. But who knows, maybe that's what she'll need to win the pageant. That may be just what the judges are looking for – someone nice and wholesome.

The other girls in the picture with Bitsy are from Central High School and Red Bank High School. I'd say Bitsy is the only Notre Dame graduate that's ever been in the contest. Catholic girls just don't do these things. That's what Mamie says, and I'd say she's half right. Catholic girls are either stiff-assed prudes or hot to trot. There's nothing in between. It's like they have a switch that's turned on or turned off – and there's no way to tell which way it's going to be. That's my experience, anyway. Look at Button and Wanda. You'd never guess they were sisters. First of all, they don't even look alike. Button's getting heavier and Wanda's getting thinner. Something's wrong there. Wanda's the hot one. She's the one that should be filling out. Button's got the nicer body, but – so what? What's the point of having a nice body if you don't know how to use it. I'd rather look at Wanda's sweet little tits than Button's boobs. Like I always say, sex is mostly in the mind anyway. Give me a woman who thinks about sex, and I'll show you an attractive woman, no matter what physical attributes she was born with. I suppose if you looked at nothing but photographs, you'd say that Bitsy is the most attractive woman around here, but I'll tell you this, Becca or Lynette, or even Emily Sue, would turn a guy's head quicker than Bitsy.

Tonight after Mamie went to bed, Becca and Lynette put on the radio – Tommy Tucker's Orchestra on WDOD – and started teaching Bitsy how to dance. They figure there's no way Bitsy can go to Atlantic City if she can't jitterbug. They pushed back the furniture and rolled up the rug and went to town. Bitsy didn't want to dance, but Lynette pulled her onto the floor and showed her the moves. Pretty soon Bitsy was bopping like she'd done it all her life. Becca's got a new word – "sensational." She said, "Bitsy's sensational." I sat in the corner and watched. With my broken leg, I couldn't dance, but it helps the girls to have an audience.

Roger stopped by the living room when he came up from the basement. I said, *Roger, what kind of bomb are you cooking up now? Are you going to liven up our party with another explosion?* He turned and walked out of the room. A real brushoff. For the last couple of days, Roger hasn't given me the time of day. I don't know what's eating him. I'm sure it's got something to do with Button. I doubt if those two are messing around, but Roger has his sights set on Button, I'll tell you that. He probably figures that I'm in his way. Well, that's no problem with me. If Roger can get Button to put out, more power to him. No need for him to act so snitty. If one of us has a legitimate beef, it's me. After all, it was his damned bomb that caused me to break my ankle.

Tootsie:

Poor Uncle Buddy. He had to sit on the sofa and watch the girls dance. His leg is in a cast and he's on crutches. Becca and Lynette were teaching Bitsy to jitterbug. There'll be a big party for all the beauty contestants at the Read House on Friday night, and Becca and Lynette think Bitsy should know how to dance. Bitsy doesn't want to go to the party. She won't tell Becca and Lynette why she doesn't want to go, but it's because of Horst. There will be escorts at the party for each of the contestants. Bitsy says her escort's name is Randy. She isn't interested in Randy. The only boy Bitsy likes is Horst.

Becca and Lynette are sensational jitterbuggers. They learn all the latest steps at the USO and the Officer's Club. When the soldiers come to our house on Sundays, they jitterbug with the girls in the living-room, or on the side porch with the Victrola right next to the living-room window so the music goes outside. By the time I'm old enough to jitterbug, the war will be over and there won't be any soldiers.

I borrowed the evening gown for Bitsy. When Mom was outside I went into her closet and took the gown. It was at the back of the closet, behind her newer clothes, so she'll never notice that it's gone. It's a sensational dress. Pink. With bare shoulders. And a big bow at the waist. Bitsy tried it on in her room. Becca and Lynette were there, and they thought it was fun that we had borrowed the dress from Mom. Becca said, "Won't Wanda be surprised when she finds out that Bitsy won the beauty contest in her dress." Becca is sure that Bitsy is going to win.

The gown was too big. Mom must have been bigger when she was younger, 'cause the dress would never fit her now. Lynette pinned up the hem, and Bitsy will baste it so to make the skirt shorter. Becca showed Bitsy how to put hankies in the top of the gown so it will fit better. Becca said to Bitsy, "You should use Nanette Creme so you'd have bigger tits. It's got homones and makes you grow." She sat Bitsy down in front of the dressing-table mirror and made up her face. Becca used Overglow, which she says comes straight from Hollywood. And lipstick. And eye liner. When they were all finished, Bitsy looked like a movie star. "Pretty cute, huh?" said Becca. "Ain't she sumpin'?" said Lynette. *Sensational*, I said.

Everyone wants to know what Bitsy will do for the talent contest, but she won't tell anyone, not even me. Maybe she told Horst. She showed Horst the photograph that was in the News-Free Press, so he knows about the pageant. Bitsy says Horst is jealous, but that he's glad she's in the contest. Jealous and proud, that's what Bitsy says. Horst gave her a little carving of a girl in a bathing suit with a crown on her head. It's supposed to be Bitsy.

The trouble is, Tometta found Bitsy's collection of carvings. She was putting applesauce into the pantry on the back porch, and found the carvings. She said, "Tootsie, I moved your little dolls so I could put the applesauce on the shelf." I pretended the figures were mine. Tometta left them out where anyone could see them. She said, "Them's the cutest things I ever did see." I took Bitsy's figures and hid them in the playhouse that Dad built for me in the garage loft. I lined them up on a rafter above the play bed I made out of old sofa cushions. Except for the beauty queen with a crown. Bitsy keeps that one in her room.

Bitsy's not the only one with a boyfriend. Tometta has a boyfriend, too. No one knew that Tometta had a boyfriend, 'cause he's in the army. Now he's home on leave for a few days and he comes to see Tometta. I went out to the backyard and there was Tometta and her boyfriend sitting in the glider holding hands. He was wearing a nifty new uniform and shiny black boots. Tometta said, "Tootsie, this is William." I shook William's hand. He's older than Tometta, but he has a sweet face. I said, *Hi, William.* That's when Tometta told me she'd moved the figures.

I told Iggy about William. He said, "Nothin' wrong with that. Coloreds have boyfriends, too." Iggy had all his bullets lined up on his bedside table, like little soldiers. I said, *Iggy, everyone will see.* He said, "So what, it'll keep 'em guessin'." He has thirteen bullets. He says that's not near enough. I asked him what he needs the bullets for, and he said for when the negroes riot. I asked him if he would shoot a colored person. I asked him if he would shoot William. He said that up in Boston it was the colored soldiers who caused all the trouble. He said, "If colored folk come into this neighborhood causin' trouble, I'll shoot 'em, sho'nuff." *Ping, ping,*

ping, ping. He flicked over the bullets, one by one. "I may be old," he said, "but I can still shoot straight."

I said, *Iggy, you're the one who shot the woodpecker, aren't you?* Tometta had told me about the woodpecker, and how she'd wrung its neck. Iggy said, "Jus' practicin'." Then he said, "That goddamn woodpecker damn near drove me mad. Got him on the first shot. *Pow!* Jus' like that, right out the window here." I said, *That woodpecker wasn't bothering anybody.* He said, "For Chrissake, Tootsie, it's only a goddamn woodpecker."

Iggy asked me to go see Billy Joe Alaska. He wants a whole box of bullets. I said, *I won't go to Billy Joe's house. Billy Joe is scary.* Iggy said, "There's nothin' to be a scared of. Billy Joe's a little daft, that's all." Today, I was swinging in the playground when I noticed Billy Joe sitting by the water fountain. He was picking his nose. I went up to him and said that Iggy wants more bullets for the rifle. A whole box. Billy Joe said, "Tell that old fart I'm all outta bullets."

Button:

I'm proud of Bitsy. I don't know how it came into her head to enter the Miss Chattanooga Pageant, but once she set her mind to do it, there was no stopping her. It's so unlike Bitsy. She has always been shy. But I guess she knows one thing – if we don't bust out and do something crazy then we'll be trapped in this boring old house all our lives.

It would not have occurred to anyone else in this family to enter the pageant. Certainly not to me. Of course, the whole idea of a beauty contest is silly, but who knows? If I had won the scholarship, I might have gone to college, and then – well, my whole life might have been different. Wanda puts up her nose at the very idea of a pageant, but it's not so much a matter of principle as that she doesn't want anyone to have a good time. Becca and Lynette used to poke fun at the photographs of contestants in the newspaper – until Bitsy entered. Now they're over the top with enthusiasm. I'll give this to Becca and Lynette, they are terrifically supportive of Bitsy. They're both so excited, you'd think they had entered the contest themselves.

I can't imagine Bitsy winning. She is certainly pretty enough, but she doesn't exactly have an outgoing personality. I'm afraid that when she gets up on the stage, she'll freeze, and really, I have no idea what she'll do in the talent competition, because, heavens knows, she has never shown any talent around here, unless it's a talent for staying out of sight. And she's terrified, apparently, of going to the dance for contestants at the Read House on Friday night. The pageant organizers have chosen an escort for each of the girls, and Bitsy is paired up with a fellow named Randy Sutherlin Wells. That's the way he gives his name – Randy Sutherlin Wells. He stopped by here today to introduce himself to Bitsy, and he was the sweetest boy – tall, with red hair, and a nice coat and tie. He wasn't required to come by and introduce himself, it's just something he said he felt like doing so as he wouldn't be a stranger when Bitsy met him on the night of the dance, and, I mean, it was a thoughtful thing to do, you know, it showed that Randy is a thoughtful person. He's only just graduated from McCallie Military Academy, and he will be going into the service in two weeks. I'd say the visit didn't go so well, because Bitsy just sat there like a bump on a log and didn't say a thing, and Randy had to make all the conversation – telling Bitsy all about himself and asking her what she was interested in and where she went to school and what were her plans for the future and things like that – and all the while Bitsy just *hmmming* and *uhhhing*. She looked really pretty though, in her new yellow sundress, so I hope Randy wasn't too disappointed. Finally, the poor boy just gave up and excused himself, but he was very polite and promised Bitsy that he'd see her at the dance on Friday night.

When he'd gone, I said, *Bitsy, what do you think of Randy?* She said, "He's OK."

I hope Bitsy won't be too disappointed. Becca and Lynette have gone to such lengths to build up her confidence that she's sure to have a fall. I can remember the only time I was chosen "queen" of anything. I was in the fifth grade, and I was supposed to be the child who would crown the Blessed Mother on May Day, because I had the best report card and the girl with the best report card always crowned the Blessed Mother. I would wear a pretty dress and a wreath of flowers in my hair and I would carry the crown in the procession and we would all sing, *O Mary, we crown thee with blossoms today, Queen of the Angels, Queen of the May.* All though April, I got more and more excited, and Mother made my dress, and you know, I must have made a hundred wreaths of flowers to try out, just out of flowers I found in the yard, clovers and dandelions and things like that, and I made a special novena to Mary that everything would turn out perfect, and then – I mean, three days before May Day the nuns chose Betty Hanafin to be the May queen, and everyone knew that her grades were not as good as mine. I was devastated. But I didn't show it. I just sat there at my desk in stony silence until the end of the schoolday. But when I got home, I cried and cried. There was no comforting me. Mother went to the convent and asked Sister Mary Agnes, the principal, why I wasn't chosen, and she said that it wasn't a hard and fast rule about the report cards, and besides, I had a "bad attitude." Mother accepted what Sister Mary Agnes said, and told me it was my fault that I wasn't the queen, that I should be nicer to the nuns, and all of that, but – really, I mean, it was unfair, and I never forgave my teachers for what they did. I had a May altar in the corner of my bedroom, a little table with a statue of Mary and flowers, and the first thing I did, you know, was toss the whole thing out in the trash, statue and all.

I guess I've been stubborn ever since. Buddy says I'm stubborn as a mule. Buddy says that if I wasn't so stubborn we'd get along better. What he means is, I suppose, is that I should stop being me. He can't bear the idea that there is part of me he doesn't control. But if I give that up, what would I have left? Since the business with the May crown, I've been determined to keep a part of me for myself. I've tried to explain this to Buddy. I've told him that it is better for both of us if I don't become a carbon copy of him, but he calls me "selfish." He says I'm holding back – in bed, I mean. What he really wants is someone who will fall down and worship his – his *thing*. No matter what I do, it's not enough. I've – you know, I've done everything he asks, or almost everything, but it's never enough. He says it's my "attitude." Just like the nuns.

It's too bad Buddy got wounded so early in the war. I think he was probably right to join the Navy. I didn't understand then, but I do now. If he hadn't been wounded so early in the war, the experience of being in the Navy might have been good for him. He would have had time to grow up, discover other interests in life. Buddy has a good mind. One of the things about Buddy that attracted me right away is that he's so smart. But he throws it all away. All he ever thinks about is that thing between his legs. If he applied himself, he might get a better education – go to night school, even college – and get a job where he can use his talent. But really, all he ever thinks about is sex. That's why I like Roger. At least Roger has other things on his mind. Birds might seem a trivial thing, but at least they occupy Roger's mind. When we went on the walk to Lula Lake, I asked him why he liked looking at birds. He said, "It's not just looking, it's learning. There's a hundred things to learn. What does the bird look like? What are its notes and song? Is it on the ground or in the trees? In thick grass or in the open? Does it walk or hop? What does it eat?" He rattled on like that, listing all the behaviors of birds. Such things don't interest me, but I can understand why Roger is interested. Since birds are everywhere, then everyplace is interesting for Roger. He said, "There's two things that make birdwatching exciting – the familiar and the unexpected."

Well, I guess you'd have to say that my life is mired in the familiar. Certainly, there's not much in my life that's unexpected. That's the one thing that's so exciting about Bitsy being in the Miss Chattanooga Pageant. It's the first unexpected thing that has happened around here in – I mean, I can't remember when. We have our tickets for the pageant. Everyone is going except Mother, Wanda, and Iggy. Even Emily Sue is going. I insisted that Becca and Lynette buy a ticket for Emily Sue. She may not understand what's happening, but after all, Bitsy is her sister, too.

I wish that Tometta could go to the pageant, but of course negroes are not allowed. It's so silly to exclude her. Up north, whites and coloreds go to public events together and nobody minds. It's just plain silly that Tometta can't come with us to the pageant. At the very least there should be a section of seats reserved for coloreds. When Silas Green and the all-colored New Orleans revue was at Memorial Auditorium, there was a section reserved for whites. Some of Becca's friends went to the show, and they said it was terrific. But the Miss Chattanooga Pageant is for whites only.

The big question is – will the beauty contest make a difference for Bitsy? It would be nice if she fell in love with Randy. He's not the kind of boy she would likely meet anywhere else. When he gets out of the service, he wants to go to a university and become a lawyer. He says he's interested in "international commerce." If Bitsy married Randy, she could travel all over the world, maybe live in Paris or London, and have adventures – the familiar and the unexpected. But maybe I'm just dreaming. Bitsy certainly didn't show much interest in Randy when he came to the house. I'm hoping for the best for Bitsy – in the contest I mean – I'm hoping she will win, but I'm afraid the whole affair is destined to be a big disappointment.

Roger:

The cuckoo is a bird you will hear but not see, somewhere a ways off, in a lone tree or at the edge of the woods – *c-c-c-c-cow! cow! cow!* – a raspy sort of sound, like the whetting of a scythe. "Raincrow" is what we call the bird in this part of the country. They say, when you hear the cry of the yellow-billed cuckoo on a sultry summer day, it will rain within the hour.

Today, I saw one. At the Ordnance Works. On my break. I took my binocs and went for a walk away from the laboratories, down toward the hickory woods. The Ordnance Works is a terrific place for birding. Thousands of acres of woods and meadows, with sparsely scattered factories or storage bunkers, and access is restricted to employees. No dogs except the animals used by the guards to patrol the perimeter, and those are kept on leashes. And no hunters. It's a birder's paradise. I heard the cuckoo before I saw him. I slipped up on him, and there he was, honing his scythe in the topmost branches of a hickory. A slim, streamlined bird, dusky olive brown with a pearly white breast, and bronze beauty-patches on each wing that you see only when the bird spreads its primaries. And tail feathers tipped with white circles, like a row of thumbprints.

The cuckoo is only with us for a few months of the year, May to September. It is curious that this bird should fly thousands of miles, all the way from South America, to seek out one particular treetop in a stand of hickories between two bunkers filled with explosives on a particular acre of land in Tennessee. I watched him for twenty minutes – and completely lost track of the time. When I looked at my watch, it was ten minutes past the end of my break. If I returned to my lab bench ten minutes late, Kelsen would rake me over the coals. So instead, I went to the testing range and called in from there, told Kelsen's secretary I was preparing a test. And I was. I'd been messing around with a new way of stabilizing TNT while giving it a more pourable consistency. The thing is, it is important to determine the melting point, so that the technicians will have a way to do the quality control. This is the sort of test we always do in a safety bunker. Not much danger, really, but it's standard practice to try things for the first time well away from the main laboratories.

Kelsen's secretary said, "It's a good thing you called in, Roger. The boss is gunning for you."

Each time we ship a new kind of ordnance, the engineers paint messages on the first few bombs, things like "To Uncle Adolph from the friendly folks at the Volunteer Ordnance Works," or "Tennessee TNT for Tojo." I painted a few of those slogans myself early in the war. But now the messages make me uneasy. The bombs we are making are not being delivered to Uncle Adolph or Tojo, but to women and children who are just as much victims of the war as we are. I told this to Kelsen. I said, *OK, we make bombs, but we don't have to revel in what we do.* He said, "Pull your socks up, Roger. If the brass in Washington thought you knew how to win the war, they'd make you a general." I said, *I have no objections to dropping bombs on our enemies. But if we don't reflect upon what we are doing, then we are no better than they are.* Kelsen said, "You think too damn much, Roger. Keep it up and you'll find yourself in a trench with a bayonet up your ass. You won't have time to be so self-righteous when the bullets are whizzing past your ears." Well, I don't take to that kind of threat, especially from a pompous ass like Mel, so I said, *Fuck off.* It's not the sort of thing I usually say. I don't like vulgarity, and Mel knows it. That's why he resents so much what I said. That's why he's gunning for me.

Sometimes I feel like saying the same thing to Buddy. At the dinner table last night he was railing against the Germans, telling the girls the damndest stories. According to Buddy, German soldiers use candy and soap as booby-traps. You wash your hands with the soap, and when it comes into contact with water – boom – it blows your hands off. The candy contains thermite. When the coating melts in your mouth, the candy flares up and scorches your insides, like a flamethrower down the throat. According to Buddy, as the Germans retreat in Italy and France, they are leaving behind these booby-traps for civilians – for the women and children. I asked him how he knew such stories were true. He said he read it in the newspaper. I told him that Nazi propagandists spread the same stories about American GI's, that the same rumors show up all over the world and there's probably not a word of truth to any of it. Buddy said, "Roger, it sounds to me like you are a Nazi sympathizer." I didn't answer him. I wanted to say "fuck off," but I wouldn't say something like that in front of the women. So I screwed up my mouth. I was trying to think of something appropriate to say when Button said to Buddy, "Roger is no Nazi sympathizer, and you know it. He's doing a lot more to win the war than you are."

That was the wrong thing to say. Buddy went flying off the handle. He snapped at Button, "Your boyfriend Roger didn't get a piece of Jap shrapnel in the leg. The only thing Roger has done for this war is damn near blow up his own family." Button said, "That's not fair." Buddy said, "I'll tell you what's fair. Fair's having a wife that's – fair's having a wife that gives her husband something besides criticism." Button said, "You always get around to that." She got up and went into the kitchen. I heard the backdoor slam. Becca said, "Come on, Buddy, take it easy." Buddy said, "Yeah, well, anyone can see what's going on around here – this little conspiracy between Button and Roger – and damned if I'll keep quiet about it." I said, *Buddy, that's malarkey. There's no conspiracy between "Button and Roger."* Well, now he was really pissed. He got up on his crutches and slammed down his fork on his plate, splattering peas all over the table. Wanda said, "For Christ sake, Buddy, stop acting like a fool." He was so mad, he could only stutter. He clumped over to where I was sitting and said, "I-I-I know you think I killed that woodpecker. Well, I did. And I-I-I'll kill every goddamn woodpecker that comes into our yard. I'll kill every goddamn thing with f-f-feathers that comes within a goddamn mile of this house. I'm the only one around here that's doing anything to protect this family, and you'd think someone would show appreciation."

In a small voice, Bitsy said, "I think Roger's right. German soldiers wouldn't leave booby-traps for children."

I helped Lynette and Bitsy clear the table and do the dishes. Becca went off to Warner Park for softball practice. Out in the backyard, Button and Tometta were swinging in the glider by the snowball bush. I don't know where Buddy went. After the dinner-table turmoil, I had to get out of the house, so I walked over to the park and sat in the bleachers watching Becca's team practice – not really paying attention exactly, just daydreaming and watching the girls have fun. At one point, Becca trotted over and sat down next to me. She said, "Roger, don't mind Buddy. He's in a bad frame of mind because everyone is paying more attention to Bitsy than to him right now."

When the Woolenettes had finished practice and gone home, I continued sitting there in the bleachers until the stars came out. The summer stars, the bird constellations. Vega, the swan. Aquila, the eagle. There's a raven in the sky, and a dove, a crane, a peacock, a toucan, and a bird of paradise. Except for the swan and the eagle, the only other avian constellation I would recognize is the raven. The others, I think, are in the southern sky. Still, that's a lot of birds to put among the stars. Eighty-eight constellations and eight of them are birds. If it was me, I'd have birds for all the constellations. I'd have a cuckoo, a painted bunting, a mocking bird, and a gnatcatcher. I'd have a red-headed woodpecker, a peewee, an oriole, and a brown creeper. I'd have eighty-eight kinds of birds in the sky. They'd be the same all over the globe, the same birds when you looked up at the stars, no matter where you lived. Just the same. As peaceful as can be.

Tootsie:

I like Randy Sutherlin Wells. If I were going to have a boyfriend, it would be Randy, not Horst. Horst is OK, but it's dumb to have a boyfriend who's in prison and who doesn't speak hardly any English at all. And who will go back to Germany when the war's over. All Bitsy thinks about is Horst. She goes down to the cemetery every chance she gets – whenever Horst is at the guardhouse. Iggy says that Horst is using Bitsy to figure out some way to escape, so he can do sabotage, like blowing up Chickamauga Dam or the TNT plant. He said, "If it was me, I'd keep my eye on Buddy's gun. The next thing you know, that Horst fellow will be askin' Bitsy to bring him a gun, and then, goddamn it, he'll shoot the guards, steal some dynamite, and – boom – there goes Chickamauga Dam." Iggy says that if the dam blew up it would flood the whole city, and wipe out war plants all the way to the Ohio River. He says that one German soldier on the loose in America can do more damage that a whole regiment in Europe.

Anyway, Horst is the reason why Bitsy isn't interested in Randy, but only me and Iggy know.

Becca and Lynette went to a lot of trouble getting Bitsy ready for the party at the Read House. They changed Lynette's graduation dress into a snazzy party dress by chopping off the top so that just two little violet ribbons went across Bitsy's shoulders, and adding a taffeta waistband and a sash the same color as the ribbons. When they were all done you would hardly have recognized the dress. Bitsy looked like a dreamboat.

We were waiting in the living room when Randy arrived to pick up Bitsy – even Mom was there, although Dad was in the basement. Bitsy was so nervous because we were all there to see her off. Randy showed up in a *tuxedo!* Bitsy was too nervous to open the door, so Becca let him in, and he came into the living room, and Becca was standing behind him jumping up and down and grinning, and Lynette was poking Bitsy in the side with her elbow to make her stand up, and Button said, "Hello, Randy" and then Button introduced everyone, including me. She called me Ellen instead of Tootsie, and it's the first time anyone called me Ellen in years, so I felt very grown up. Randy had eyes for no one but Bitsy. He said,

"Gosh, Eileen, you look sensational," and I think Bitsy felt very grown up too, 'cause hardly anyone calls her Eileen.

Anyway, Bitsy finally stood up, and Randy shook her hand, and they were standing there, and nobody was saying anything, and there was a boom from the basement, and the teacups rattled and the clock chimed, and Randy kind of looked around like he was thinking "What's that?", but no one said anything, so he said again, "Gosh, Eileen, you look sensational." Button said, "Randy, you look terrific, too" and he said, "It's my father's tuxedo, and I have his car too, and enough gasoline for – oh my gosh –" and he just ran right out the front door. We all sat there – except for Bitsy, Bitsy was standing – and wondered where Randy had gone, and Bitsy started crying, or almost crying, not because Randy had left, but because she was so nervous, and then he came back into the house with a corsage for Bitsy, and he said, "I almost forgot." Becca pinned the corsage onto Bitsy's taffeta waistband and gave her a kiss. There was another boom from the basement and the clock chimed again, and Randy looked around, puzzled, and Button said, "That's Roger," and Randy said, "Oh." Then he said, "Well, I think we'd better be going" and Lynette started nudging Bitsy out the door, and everyone said, "Have a good time."

Well, they weren't out of the house for two minutes when Bitsy came running back in and went right upstairs to her room. Becca said, "Oh, shit," and Lynette said, "I was afraid of that." The next thing you know, Randy was knocking on the door. He was very embarrassed. He said, "I'm sorry, I just opened the door to the car, and she ran away." Button said, "Don't worry, Randy. It's not your fault. Bitsy's nervous. This is the first time she's ever been in a beauty contest." He said, "What shall I tell Mrs. Bellwether?" – she's the lady who's in charge of the escorts – and Becca said, "Tell her that we locked Eileen in the rubber room and won't let her out."

I wanted to say what the real reason was – that Bitsy has a boyfriend that she is madly in love with, and that's why she didn't want to go to a party with another boy – but I couldn't say that because Bitsy's boyfriend is a secret.

Button said, "Randy, you are a very nice young man, and I'll give Mrs. Bellwether a call, and tell her that you were very polite, and that it's not your fault that Bitsy – Eileen – didn't come to the party." Randy said, "Will Eileen be in the pageant tomorrow night? I'd sure like to see her again." Button shrugged. She said, "We all hope so." Just then, there was another boom, and Randy said, "Roger?" and everybody nodded.

Tometta:

You might wanna hol' on to yoah hat. Say hullo to *Missus Tometta Jackson!* Yep, William come home on leave an' we done snuck off an' got married. I ain't tol' no one here at the house, 'cept course Nana. I jest wanna be left alone by this lot, an' enjoy it fer a spell. Course, I be wantin' to tell Button soon, fore she finds out on her own. Seems ever'body know ever'one else's business in this house, but I s'pect Button could keep a secret.

William be shippin' out soon. He got two weeks leave 'fore he gotta go. He got here las' Friday. Gave me such a start, I be ready to kill him! I knew he be comin' soon, but didn't s'pect him to jest show up on the doorstep. But he say they get tol' ever'thing las' minute. They still ain't tol' 'em they be shipping out, but William says it be clear as day to ever'one at the camp.

Well, come Friday night William took me downtown fer dinner an' dancin'. An' to see William in his uniform – well, let me tell ya, all the girls be starin'. We danced till near 'bout one o'clock. On the walk home, we stopped under an ole elm tree an' started kissin'. Bold as can be, I look him in the eyes an' says to him, *William, I ain't gonna let you go off to war without makin' love to you.* He gave me one of his looks, one eyebrow raised, a half-grin on his face, lips pressed tight together, an' says, "Well sometimes desp'rate times call fer desp'rate measures, I wanted to give yoah a proper weddin', but let's git hitched this weekend?" *Yes, yes*, I cried. He gave me a huge kiss on the lips, an' says, "Tomorrow mornin' I'll ask yoah mama, she say it be ok, we'll go on down the town hall an' get married." We talked excitedly the rest of the walk home on all the things we'd do after the war. With a kiss, he left me quickly at the door, an' says, "Sleep tight Sugah, we's got a big day ahead a us." I didn't sleep a wink.

Sho' Mama gave her blessin', an' we headed on downtown. The ceremony wasn't much more then signin' papers, but I couldn't a been more happy. Once the justice of the peace finished his speech, William gently kissed me an' says, "I love you, Tometta. I been reborn, an' owe it all to you."

William's stayin' with his uncle. He sold his house once he gone into the army. I think he wanted to leave the memories behind an' start new. So he got us a room fer the night at one of the colored hotels downtown. We checked into the hotel as Mr. an' Mrs. Jackson, which made me feel mighty proud, though the man at the desk put a slight smirk on his face, like he didn't think it to be true. William carried me into the room like you see in the movies. As he placed me down, my legs trembled to feel the floor. Here's what I'd dreamt an' wished for, an' I be so nervous, I was shakin' like a leaf in the wind. My eyes was filled with tears of fright an' joy. I dunno if William mistook me to be sad, cause he says, "I's sorry I couldn't give you a proper weddin' Tometta, I'll make it all up to you once this war be ovah." I says, *That was the best wedding I could evah hope fer*, as I pushed the shoes off my feet, unbuttoned my dress, an' let it slide to the ground. He look at me fer a moment, an' says in a whisper, "Tometta, you's more beautiful than I evah could imagine."

Truth be tol', that first time was exciting an' all, but it barely gave me a hint of what was to come. This pas' week be the best of my life. We make love whenever we can, wherever we can. It be like all my troubles been washed away.

The only thing that worries me is Buddy. He be watchin' William an' I like a hawk. Even William done notice. William says to me, "That man don't bother you none does he?" *No, no*, I says, *he jest nosey is all*. I could tell my lie didn't hold much water, on account of the look on William's face, but he said nothin' more.

Buddy:

Everything is so topsy-turvy around here that no one notices what's going on in Eva's shack. *It's Bitsy this, and Bitsy that. Why didn't Bitsy go to the party? Will Bitsy go to the pageant? What's Bitsy going to do in the talent contest?* Meanwhile, Tometta is getting it on with that man of hers, right under our noses.

I suppose she thinks no one notices, but it's clear as day what's going on. Whenever that William fellow shows up, Tometta helps Eva out to the glider, then her and the boyfriend disappear into the shack. Twenty minutes later they come shambling out with big grins on their faces, and him jacking up his trousers, and her glowing like a hot stove. You'd have to be blind not to know what's going on.

Wanda was out in the sideyard taking the sun, and I'm out there too just messing around, so I said to her, *Have you noticed what Tometta's up to?* She said, "Buddy, you've got better things to think about than what Tometta's up to." And I know what she meant, but right then I wasn't interested in Wanda. I couldn't stop thinking about what was going on in Eva's shack. It boggles the imagination to think of that nigger soldier getting into a girl as young as Tometta. Why, he's older than me. *Poontang.* That's what they call it. Nigger pussy. They say there's nothing hotter than a colored girl in summertime, and, let me tell you, July has been hotter than the hinges of hell. When that girl walks around the kitchen in her cotton dress, with the damp cloth sticking to her tits and ass, and the sweat glistening on her arms, well – it makes a man think. The trouble is, you can be damn sure you'd catch a mess of diseases. It's not hard to imagine the women old Willy the Wonker has been diddling, him being in the army and all – and anything he's picked up he's bound to have given to Tometta, that's for sure. Or maybe it's the other way round. That girl didn't just fall off the turnip truck herself. Still, that Tometta is really something. It would almost be worth your dick falling off just to get into her honeypot.

She was in the kitchen fixing chicken salad for lunch. I asked, *How old is that William fellow of yours, Tometta?* She said, "Old nuff an' not too old." I said, *He's old enough to be your daddy. He's not your daddy, is he?* She said, "Mista Cioffi, if yoah keep talkin' like that, I jest might tell William what you done said, an' I don't s'pose he'd like you talkin' to me like that." I said, *I'm just trying to be friendly, Tometta. I think you're swell. I think you and I should be friends.* She said, "I reckon I's got all the friends I need."

Well, I'll tell you this, Tometta may have a sassy mouth, but she sure makes an A-OK chicken salad. Tometta's chicken salad on a piece of white bread is a feast fit for a king. I was sitting on the back steps chowin' down a chicken-salad sandwich when Becca came home from softball practice. I said, *Becca, When are we going to have some more target practice?* She said, "I'm not going back into that cave with a gun. The way bullets ricochet around in there, a person could get killed." I said, *We'll go down to the railroad tracks behind the cemetery. Nobody would hear us there. Come on, Becca, I know you like shooting the damn thing. You're a pistol-packin' mama.* She liked that. She liked being called a pistol-packin' mama. She said, "OK Buddy, I'll meet you on the viaduct at one o'clock."

That sounded fine to me. I like Becca's spunk. She's not afraid of nuthin.' So, while Becca was eating lunch, I went upstairs to get the thirty-eight.

I met Becca on the viaduct. It took me twice as long to get there because of my busted leg, having to hobble along on crutches and all. We went down Bailey Avenue past where they keep those Nazi POW's locked up at night, and then cut through the cemetery to the railroad yard. Wasn't nobody within half-a-mile, except for the inhabitants of the cemetery, and they've heard the last gunshots they'll ever hear. We had a heck of a time finding something to shoot at. Because of the war, the coloreds go along the tracks picking up every tin can and bottle they can find, and sell them to the trash man. Finally, Becca managed to scrounge up a couple of Dr. Pepper bottles and we set 'em up on the rails.

I put the thirty-eight in Becca's hand, and she patted it back and forth from hand to hand like she was making corn bread. I said, *Becca, you look like heaven.* She said, "You'd better shut up, Buddy, or I'll use the gun on you." We laughed. I'll tell you, she did look like heaven, in her shorts and halter, with lipstick redder than a ripe tomato, and all those painted toenails peeking out of her sandals. I gave her six bullets and said, *OK, Becca-Boo, blast away.*

It wasn't so easy to help her this time, me being on crutches and all, but I snuggled up as close as I could get and when she squeezed the trigger the recoil threw her against me. She got off three shots without hitting a bottle, so she went down the tracks and moved the bottles closer to where we were standing. Two more shots and she still didn't hit anything. I said, *I think you need me to steady your hands.* She said, "I know what you've got in mind, Buddy." But she let me put my arms around her to steady the gun, and she leaned against me, and I was leaning back on the crutches, and I know for sure she must have felt the bulge in my pants. I said, *Easy does it.*

That's when we noticed the niggers.

There were three mean-looking boys – maybe eighteen, nineteen years old – walking down the tracks towards us. I said to Becca, *Just act casual. There's nothing to be afraid of.* Anyway, the colored boys stopped, just by us, and leaned against the cemetery wall, and watched what we were doing. Becca got off a shot. She was so nervous, and the gun was shaking so bad, that damned if she didn't hit a bottle, and glass went flying all over creation. The biggest and meanest looking of the colored boys said, "Missy, you'd better give me the gun afore you hurt yerself." Before I knew what was happening, he stepped away from the wall, took hold of the gun, and the other two guys started running like bats out of hell.

But the fucker wasn't quick enough. Becca held onto the thirty-eight just long enough for me to swing a crutch. I caught the big guy's foot as he started to run. He tumbled down between the tracks and the gun flew out of his hand. I hopped over there on my gimpy leg – like a goddamn one-legged jackrabbit – and as he tried to get up I gave him a whack with the crutch, swung it as hard as I could and caught him right in the belly and knocked the wind out of him. The other boys stopped running and turned around to help their pal, but by then I had managed to pick up the thirty-eight. I pointed it square at the big boy's eyes and said, *Clear out now with your pals or I'll blow those shiny teeth right out of your mouth.*

I'll tell you this, they cleared out. All the while I was wondering if there were any bullets in the chamber, 'cause I was too scared to remember how many shots Becca had fired, so when the niggers were gone off down the tracks, I flipped open the cylinder and damned if it wasn't empty. I showed the empty cylinder to Becca, and she laughed. She said, "Buddy, you were brave as all get out. I never thought you had it in you." I said, *How about a little kiss as a reward?* I was only joking. Well, Becca put her hand behind my neck and gave me a kiss on the mouth – I mean, a real, honest-to-god, slobbery kiss. I couldn't believe it. I just looked at her with my eyes popping out of my head. She said, "Buddy, don't you go getting any ideas. That's just for what you did to those niggers." Well, maybe I wasn't getting any ideas, but I'll tell you this, I was as happy as a fly on shit. I slipped one last bullet into the thirty-eight and blew that other Dr. Pepper bottle to kingdom come.

To tell the truth, the whole business with those colored boys surprised me too. When it was over, I couldn't even remember how it happened – it was like some kind of automatic reflex. I can't even remember whether it was Becca or the gun that was uppermost in my mind when I tripped up that fella. I suspect it was the gun, but there's no harm in letting Becca think I did what I did to save her skin. The trouble is, when we got home there was no one we could tell about what had happened because Becca didn't want anyone to know about us going to the tracks. I suppose eventually Becca will tell Lynette – those two girls tell each other everything – but Button's the one I'd like to know what happened. I wish Becca would tell Button how I handled those three colored boys. Button thinks I'm such a mamby-pamby; she should have seen me handle those spades. But of course, if Button knew what I was doing on the tracks – with Becca, I mean – well, that wouldn't be any help at all. Anyway, instead of everyone hearing about what I'd done, all we heard about was Bitsy. *Bitsy's big night. What's Bitsy going to wear? How will we fix Bitsy's hair? Who gets to go backstage with Bitsy? Bitsy, Bitsy, Bitsy.* And meanwhile, I'm just sitting there, and no one knows how I managed to keep one more gun out of the hands of the coloreds, and how what happened on the tracks proves everything I've been saying about the spooks gathering up guns for the big riot.

Button:

Buddy refused to attend the Miss Chattanooga pageant. Of course, he was just being stubborn. He can't bear it that he's not the center of attention. So we let him stay at home and pout. We managed to talk Mother into using Buddy's ticket. She finally came around to the idea of Bitsy being in the pageant.

Buddy and Wanda are our prima donnas. I can accept that Buddy didn't go to the pageant – somehow, I expected it, but I'm terribly disappointed that Wanda didn't see fit to attend. After all, she is Bitsy's sister, and Bitsy needed all the support she could get. It was brave of Bitsy to get up there on the stage with all those other girls and address an audience. An audience of *five thousand people!* I never thought it possible that Bitsy could be so brave. The eight of us clapped and cheered like crazy, but Wanda and Buddy should have been there too.

Buddy is in one of his terrible moods. He was down on the tracks with Becca and that gun of his. He thinks I don't know what's going on, but everything becomes public knowledge around here sooner or later. I heard Becca telling Lynette all about what happened as they were primping for the pageant. They were in the bathroom and I was waiting my turn. I didn't hear everything she said, but there was something about colored boys and Buddy scaring them off. Becca said, "I kissed him." Lynette said, "What do you mean 'I kissed him'?" Becca said, "Just what I said." "On the mouth?" asked Lynette. "Yeah," said Becca. "Jesus," said Lynette, "what was it like?" Becca said, "Oh, OK, I guess." Lynette said, "I think I'd rather kiss Billy Joe Alaska." Becca said, "Buddy's not so bad." Lynette said, "What about Button? What would Button say?"

Well, Button doesn't give a hoot who Buddy kisses, although it's a bit disappointing when your own sisters start fooling around with your husband. Becca is just toying with Buddy. She's got way too much sense to get seriously involved. Wanda's the one I'm worried about. She could very easily get into bed with Buddy, if she hasn't done so already. The two of them were alone in the house while the rest of us were at the pageant, and Buddy was in one of his horny moods because of Becca's kiss, and – well, God knows what happened. I'm absolutely certain that something did happen, because when we got home from the pageant Buddy was nowhere to be seen, and he didn't get home until just before dawn, drunk as a coot, and Buddy hardly ever drinks, and he almost never goes out to bars.

The pageant was wonderful. Ellis Goodloe's orchestra played, and Pierre Dale was the MC, and twenty-three girls competed for the title and the chance to go to the Miss Tennessee contest in Nashville – and then of course on to Atlantic City. First of all, the girls came out in their evening dresses, and Pierre Dale introduced them one by one, and when he said "Eileen Buffon, nineteen years old, a recent graduate of Notre Dame High School," we could see Bitsy's knees shaking even from where we sat, which was six rows back from the front, and Mother was almost as nervous as Bitsy, especially when Pierre Dale said "Notre Dame High School," because she imagined that all the Catholics in the audience would think Bitsy was tacky. Thank goodness Wanda wasn't there, because if she had seen Bitsy's evening dress she might have gone flying off the handle and shouted a protest or something, but Bitsy looked as pretty as any of the girls, although the other girls' dresses were mostly black, or at least dark, and very sophisticated, and Bitsy's dress was pink, with a bow at the waist, and she didn't look sophisticated at all, in fact, she looked like she was ready for a high school dance.

The girls performed the talent competition in alphabetical order, which meant that Bitsy came second, after Susan Applegate, a girl from Soddy-Daisy. Susan played the violin, something by Mozart I think, a piano concerto or something like that, arranged for the violin, and the Ellis Goodloe Orchestra played along with her, and she was pretty good, but not terrific, because she missed a bunch of notes, and Alma leaned over to me and said, "She's squeaky." We were all on pins and needles, because we didn't have the slightest idea what Bitsy was going to do, at least not until Pierre Dale made the announcement, "Ladies and gentlemen, here is Eileen Buffon, in a very pretty pink dress, who will recite a poem, 'Trees' by Joyce Kilmer." Well, my goodness, I thought I would die. We were sitting on the edges of our seats, and Bitsy walked to the front of the stage, right up to the microphone, and the Ellis Goodloe orchestra played a little introduction, and Bitsy just stood there, saying nothing, with her eyes closed, for what seemed like ages, and the orchestra played another little introduction, and still Bitsy didn't say anything, and

Becca whispered "Shit" loud enough for everyone around us to hear, and Mother slumped down in her seat and I thought she was going to die of embarrassment, and then Pierre Dale came over to Bitsy and put his arm around her shoulders, and said, "Eileen is just a little nervous folks, the cat has got her tongue," and he nodded to Ellis Goodloe, and the orchestra played another few notes, and Bitsy said, "I think that I shall never...," then stopped dead.

Well, the audience broke out laughing, because they thought it was part of Bitsy's act. It was friendly laughter, so it made Bitsy less nervous. She opened her eyes for the first time and said, "...see," and the audience laughed again because they thought it was some sort of comedy routine. The orchestra got into the spirit and added a little goofy background music, which helped Bitsy along, and she said, "A poem so lovely as a summer wears," and Becca whispered, "Double shit," and Lynette cracked up laughing, and Mother had her eyes closed, and Alma was fingering her rosary beads, which at that moment may have been just what Bitsy needed – a little help from heaven, I mean – but the audience was in stitches.

"A nest of flowers on her flowing breast," said Bitsy, and the orchestra was cutting up, with horns making little toots and saxes swooning, because everyone thought it was all an act, and to tell the truth, it was so funny I would have thought so too if I hadn't known better. Somehow Bitsy got to the end of the poem, and recited, "Poems are writ by fools like me, but only God can make a...," and she stopped one word short from the end, and there was another long silence, and the audience was in hysterics, and the orchestra played a little fanfare, and Pierre Dale didn't know whether to come forward or not, I mean, he was teetering back and forth and winking to the audience, and I'm saying a prayer, "Dear God, let her finish," and Becca's whispering "Shit, shit, triple-shit," and Lynette is jabbing Becca in the ribs to make her stop, and all of a sudden, right out of the blue, Bitsy blurts out, "...tree."

Poor Bitsy didn't know what was going on. She understood that the audience liked her performance, but she didn't know why. Pierre Dale came forward, put his arm around her pretty bare shoulders, and said into the microphone, "Wasn't that just super-dooper, folks? Just what we needed to get the show off to a great start." He winked at the orchestra and said, "Took me by surprise, too. Let's have a big hand for our lovely comedienne," and the audience clapped like crazy, and Susan Applegate looked a bit miffed that she had been upstaged by Bitsy.

Mother refused to stay for the bathing suit competition, and asked Alma to take her home at the intermission. It was just as well that Mother wasn't there when the girls came out in their bathing costumes, because Becca and Lynette had stitched some padding into the top of Bitsy's suit and she looked much bustier than usual. Bitsy paraded up and down the runway with the other girls, and then took a turn by herself, and the audience clapped hard for Bitsy because they had had more fun with Bitsy's poem than all the other acts in the talent competition. By now Bitsy seemed fairly relaxed, and appeared to be having fun, and she managed to smile at the judges, but her bathing suit was kind of dowdy compared to the stylish suits the other girls wore, and you could just see a bit of the padding peeking out of her bodice, but Bitsy seemed not to notice. She was as pretty as any of them.

The astonishing thing is – when all was said and done – Bitsy won third place. When Pierre Dale said, "In third place, the hilarious 'Trees' girl, Eileen Buffon," Becca, Lynette, and Tootsie jumped out of their chairs and cheered and cheered, and even Emily Sue seemed to know that something exciting had happened because she was bouncing up and down in her seat, and Roger gave my hand squeeze and said, "Wow! How about that?"

Bitsy's prize is a two-hundred-dollar shopping spree at Loveman's Department Store.

Iggy:

Lawdy, you shoulda seen all the excitement. Turns out Bitsy won third prize in the Miss Chattanooga Pageant. If I was a bettin' man I'd of given 10-1 odds that Bitsy would come in dead last. I'll admit she's a nice lookin' girl, but she ain't exactly the type of gal you'd expect to be waltzin' round a stage in a bathin' suit. I'll tell ya what. I'd say as it's that Kraut boyfriend of hers. He's bringin' her right out of her shell. Makin' "pin-up" photographs, she is. Sashayin' round like Betty Grable. I'd say as that girl has undergone a *trans-for-may-shun*.

She won a two-hundred-dollar shoppin' spree at Loveman's. That's her prize. Well, the other girls wanted in on that. Becca an' Lynette, they was right quick to volunteer. So did Tootsie. Not to spend the money on themselves, but to help Bitsy spend the money. Poor Bitsy. There's nothin' worse than havin' money in your pocket fer the first time, an' too much advice on how to spend it.

Anyways, they come waltzin' in here to show me what they bought, their arms full of shoppin' bags an' big smiles plastered all ovah their faces, talkin' jitterbug talk. "Look, Uncle Iggy, wait'll you see – lovey-lovey – oodles of goodies – umpteen percent – gee eyes – killeroos." I never saw such things. Trikshorts. Halter tops. Pedal pushers. Peasant blouses. "Look – just look at these, Uncle Iggy. Aren't they just too good-looking for words." I says, *She'll look like Floosie Belle in those, that's sho'*. "Snazzy," says Tootsie. "Jazzy," says Lynette. Lawdy me, the underwear they had in those bags. I never seen such skimpy bits of nothin' since I was at the striptease in New Orleans. "Everybody's going crazy over these," says Becca. "Panties and bras in sherbet shades," says Lynette. Tootsie reads the tags: "Lemon yellow – ice blue – pink raspberry – French vanilla." "And wait'll you see her yummy nightie," says Lynette. "A pink satin spasm," says Becca, "with a fab lace top." "Like Rita Hayworth," says Lynette. "Sensational," says Tootsie. *Ducky*, says I.

Well, I'd say as those girls was havin' the time of their lives. Off they went to Becca an' Lynette's room to try things on, an' I could hear em laughin' an' gigglin' all the way down the hall. "Wow!" shouted Becca. "Glamorous!" shouted Lynette. The next afternoon, Tootsie came by to see me – to give me my report, so to speak. "You should of seen Bitsy in her Rita Hayworth nightgown," said Tootsie, "ooo-la-la." *Not me*, I says, *I'm too ole fer that.* "Bitsy showed the nightgown to Horst," said Tootsie. Hell's bells, I couldn't believe my ears. Accordin' to Tootsie, Bitsy took the nightgown with her when she went to talk to Horst this mornin'. Carried it in a shoppin' bag. An' took it out to show him. Right there on Bailey Av'nue. So Tootsie says. Bitsy says to Horst, "Tell the others to go away and I'll show you something." An' he does. An' the other POWs go away. An' Bitsy shows him the nightie. Well, mark my word, there's gonna be trouble there. It's one thing to have a pin-up hangin' on the wall. It's sumthin' else all together to be imaginin' the real thing. That Horst fellow may be a Kraut, but he's a man jus' like the rest of us, an' he's been locked up now for more'n six months without a woman, 'cept fer pretty little Bitsy chattin' ovah the wall showin' him a satin nightgown – with a black lace top. I'd say, if Mamie knew what was goin' on, she'd be fit to be tied. If Nelson knew what his youngest daughter was up to, he'd turn ovah in the grave.

Kids these days have less in'ibitions than in my time. I can't imagine Kathleen Fitzgibbons showin' me a satin nightie with a lace top. Sho' in those days a fella had to use his imagination. I'm not sayin' that I didn't conjure up such things myself. When I was layin' in that mosquito-ridden tent down in Cuba, an' in that crab-infested hospital in Tampa, I dreamt up plenty of images of Kathleen in her nightie, an' sometimes in nothin' at all. Them dreams was the only thing that kept me goin' when I damned near died of yella fever, or dysentery, or whatever it was. Course, when I finally did get home, Kathleen had up an' gone somewhere else, without so much as a goodbye.

Oh, I was a dreamer, all right. You've gotta be a dreamer when women won't pay you a bit of mind. With all my coughin' an' wheezin', they wouldn't give me the time of day. Closest I ever came to havin' a lady friend was when I was workin' fer Southern Mutual. There was a gal in the office named Myrtle Serene. Now, I know as "Myrtle" is an old-fashioned name, the sort of name that you'd expect to go with a school marm or a Sunday school teacher, but my Myrtle was built like a brick shithouse, with flamin' red hair an' a temper to match. I asked her out on a date, an' when I showed up at her apartment she met me at the door in a flimsy little housecoat with – well, what I saw peekin' out of the top of that housecoat would give the Grand Canyon a run fer its money. She done ask me in, an' she says, "Make yourself comfy, Ignatius." She says, "I'll be only a minute. Just want to dab on a little perfume." So I's sittin' there in my chair, an' next thing I know she comes tippy-toein' out of her bedroom in nothin' but her slip an' undies, holdin' up a dress in each hand. "Which one would you say as I should wear, Ignatius?" she asks. Well, I got so excited tryin' to spit out an answer, I started wheezin', an' the next thing you know I was coughin' to beat the band – an' I couldn't stop fer the life of me. Myrtle, she didn't know what to do. She stood there holdin' the dresses, with her mouth hangin' open. "Sweet baby Jesus," she yells, "are you dyin' or what?" By this time, I'm gettin' red in the face, I'm doubled over, an' hackin away, an' Myrtle says, "Christ, Ignatius, that's no way for a gentleman to behave."

I'd say as that was the last time I ever asked a lady-friend out on a date. Not that I didn't want to. Jus' didn't have the chest fer it. Those goddamn Cuban skeeters, that's what it was, an' the humidity, an' – well, I jus' didn't have the chest fer it. So, dreamin' it was. Dreamin' was all I had. An lawdy, I could dream with the best of 'em.

Well, not any more. I'm too old fer that now – an' thank Heaven fer it. If there's one good thing about gettin' old, it's not havin' your pecker leadin' you around like a pup on a leash. I may have damn near every malady known to man – bad chest, piles, constipation, rash, bad teeth, gout, dyspepsia, stiff joints, an' varicose veins – but one problem I don't have to worry on no more is bein' horny. I'll tell you this, when you're livin' in a house full of women who buy Trikshorts an' sherbet underwear – well, it's jus' as well that the troublesome ole wanker has finally been laid to rest.

Tootsie:

Chattanooga is having a heat wave. The temperature has been over a hundred degrees for three days in a row. We're doing everything just to stay cool. Today, Buddy was spraying me with the hose. Becca and Lynette came outside in their sunsuits, and Buddy sprayed them too, and pretty soon we were all were running around under the spray, soaking wet. Except for Buddy, who wouldn't let us have a turn at the hose. Mom was laying in the deck chair in the side yard, and Buddy gave her a squirt and she got mad and said, "Buddy, you do that again and I'll wring your neck," and she stomped off into the house to put on dry clothes. Buddy said, "What a spoilsport." Then he squirted the hose down the back of Becca's shorts, and Becca squeaked, "Buddy, you do that again and I'll wring your neck."

In the afternoon, Buddy, Becca and Lynette went to the movies at the Capitol, which is refrigerated – the only refrigerated movie theater in Chattanooga – but Mom wouldn't let me go. She said the films were rated "Objectionable in Part" and weren't suitable for kids. I wanted to see them anyway, because of the ad in the newspaper: "*Must see sensations! All guards down, all brakes off, youth on a rampage, TEENAGERS making their own rules for a lost generation.*" The movies were "Crime School," with Humphrey Bogart, and "Girls on Probation," with Ronald Reagan, and I don't see why I shouldn't be allowed to see them. I'm almost a teenager, and Buddy says I act like a teenager, and Tometta saw "Girls on Probation" at the Harlem and she's only seventeen. I asked Dad if I could go, and he said, "Sure," and when I told Mom, she came storming into the house and said to Dad, "It's just like you to undermine everything I do," and he said, "Sorry, Tootsie, but your Mom knows best."

When Buddy and the girls got home from the movies, I asked 'em if the films were any good. "Cool as a cucumber," said Lynette. "Freezy-breezy" said Becca. "The movies – well I think you're mom was probably right, those movies were hot," said Uncle Buddy. After supper, Mamie made a pitcher of iced lemonade and we all sat out on the front porch. The only one who doesn't seem to mind the heat is Emily Sue, who just sat there smiling like she was at the North

Pole, and all the while the rest of us were sweating away, and Dad said, "A few more days like this and we'll have to shut down the plant. It's getting too hot to pour the TNT." Button said, "I can see it in the papers: *War called off on account of the heat*." Becca said, "Whew-ie," and she wrang the water out of her kerchief. June bugs were banging their heads against the porch light, and Buddy said, "Watch this," and he went into the house and got a piece of thread, and he caught a june bug and tied the thread to one of its legs, and the June bug went flying round and round in circles at the end of the thread, buzzin' like a dive bomber, and Buddy made it zoom close to Becca and Lynette, and they ducked and squealed. "Iki, waki, konki, sookekki," said Buddy, and we all looked at him like he was crazy, and he said it's a Jap war cry that he read about it in the newspaper, and Becca said it sounds like the name of a new song. Aunt Button said, "Buddy, you'd think you'd leave that poor insect alone," and Buddy said, "Jeez Louise, Button, it's only a goddamn June bug." Somewhere away off there was heat lightning, and Dad said, "Unless you can hear the thunder, there's no hope of rain." So we just sat there in the sweltering heat wishing it would rain, all except Bitsy, who went off somewhere on her own, and Alma, who hasn't come out of her room since the night of the Miss Chattanooga Pageant.

Buddy:

So what's the big deal? She only won third place. From what I hear, it was a fluke, anyway. Imagine, reciting Joyce Kilmer's "Trees." That must be the dumbest poem ever written. The only reason Bitsy ever heard of the poem is because Kilmer was a Catholic. It's the only poem the nuns let Catholic girls read. No wonder Catholic women are screwed up. The only poem they're allowed to read is about trees. That's why they lay there like bumps on a log when they're having sex.

Thank God my parents had the good sense to send me to a public school. That's one advantage to being from New York; in New York it's OK for a Catholic kid to go to public school. Not that my folks were such good Catholics anyway. They went to church on Sunday, but that's about it. There wasn't any "sex-is-a-sin" stuff at our house. And none of it at school, either. At public school, we learned about sex in the playground, where kids should learn about sex. A little hanky-panky with the girls – pulling pigtails, snapping bra straps, copping a feel – basically a good, healthy, American introduction to sex. Give me a public-school girl any day. The girls that went to Catholic schools in New York were screwed up from day one. Just looking at a boy was a venial sin. If you looked for more than a second, that was a mortal sin. You had to be an accountant to keep track of whether or not you'll go to heaven. A kiss on the cheek was – well, let's say – a number-one sin. A kiss on the lips was a number two. Open your mouth, that's a three. Tongue, a four. Wiggle your tongue when it's in his mouth and you go straight to hell, sure as shootin,' do not pass GO, do not collect two hundred dollars.

The Catholic Church has a lot to answer for when it comes to sex. Look at that Tometta girl. Now there's a woman who is comfortable with her body – and with sex, too, as far as I can see. Those negro girls go to Protestant churches, but their real religion is some sort of voodoo from Africa. What they do in church is like nothing I ever saw in any white Protestant church – all that singing and clapping and swaying and AMENing and PRAISE-THE-LORDing. Let me tell you, there's a devil loose in those negro churches, and I say, more power to him. Better all that swinging and clapping than "Bless me, Father, for I have sinned." The women around this house would have been better off as Holy Rollers. They might have had a healthier attitude toward sex.

And that goes for Wanda, too.

Especially, Wanda.

That woman's got some kind of perverse streak in her. Anyone who can figure out what she's up to should get a Ph.D. in fuckology. No wonder Roger is always out looking at birds – Wanda would drive anyone a little chirpy. She's the sexual equivalent of a school of piranhas – she nibbles you to death with little bites.

My mistake was staying home alone with Wanda on the night of the Miss Chattanooga Pageant. I'll tell you this, that lady needs a full time chaperone, someone to follow her around with a bucket of cold water. I knew she was kinky – the way she prances around in her underwear, posing in front of the mirror, that sort of thing – but I sure as hell wasn't ready for Wanda's hormonal blitzkrieg. She flipped out. Loony tunes. Guards down, brakes off, a thirty-two-year-old sexpot on a rampage.

I sure as hell wasn't expecting it. I knew the lady had a flair for provocation, but I never guessed she'd be quite so blatant about it coming on like D-Day. It's not exactly the kind of behavior you'd expect from someone married to Roger. Mister Jekyll and Missus Hyde, that's them. Barney Google and Betty Boop. But who knows? Maybe any woman who was married to Roger would turn out like Wanda.

I'm sitting in the living room, listening to "Inner Sanctum," with my busted leg propped up on the hassock, and in she walks in her terrylene robe with ric-rac hems and her fluffy slippers, and she's holding the robe shut with her arms, and she sprawls on the sofa, and kicks off the slippers, and says, "Would you mind if I put on the fan?" Well, jeez Louise, I did mind, because the fan makes a hell of a racket and I was trying to listen to the radio, but I said, *Sure, Sugar, put on the fan.* So the fan is right there on the table behind the sofa, and she turns it on, and it oscillates back and forth, and she adjusts it so as it sweeps from her red-painted toenails up to her penciled eyebrows and back again, and her robe is jacked up so I can see – well, I could see her panties. I was trying to listen to "Inner Sanctum," but I'm distracted, so I say to her, *Hot enough for you?* It wasn't exactly stimulating conversation, but it's not like the lady was expecting to discuss Roosevelt and Dewey. She says, "So how come you didn't go to see Bitsy make a fool of herself?" I said, *As far as I'm concerned, everyone's making far too much of Bitsy's little escapade. It's all just a play for attention.* And Wanda says, "They won't be back until at least midnight."

Well, that's when I began to get the drift – that Wanda's on the make, I mean, seriously on the make this time. So I say, *Wanda, is it just my imagination, or are you giving me the come on?* She says, "I'm not giving anyone the *come on*." So, I go back to listening to "Inner Sanctum," and she jacks up her robe a bit more and starts nibbling on her fingernails, and pretty soon I can't concentrate on the program, and I say, *Those are pretty undies you're wearing.* She tugs down her ric-rac hem a bit so I can't see her panties anymore, but at the same time she lets the top of her robe fall open just enough for me to see that she's not wearing a bra, and I say, *Those sure are pretty freckles you've got on your tits.*

Damned if she doesn't say, "Would you like to rub freckle cream on them?" Can you believe it? *Would you like to rub freckle cream on my tits.* I've heard a lot of lines in my day, but that was the best. So I said, *I'm always glad to help out a gal in need.*

Without so much as a fair-thee-well, she gets up and sashays out of the room and up the stairs. My dick's so hard I can hardly get out of my chair, and when I stand up it's poking out like a robot rocket. I push it down, so I won't be embarrassed, and hobble upstairs on my crutches, and Wanda's standing at the top of the stairs with a bottle of Stillman's Freckle Cream in her hand, and she puts her finger to her lips and says, "Shhhh," and points to Iggy's room. Then she whispers, "Not in my room. Roger's sense of smell is like a bloodhound's." So off we go down the hall to Bitsy's and Alma's room, with the big double bed, and we close the door, and I whisper, *Alma's bed is probably full of cinders and ashes*, and Wanda whispers, "Christ Buddy, no one's taking you to bed."

She sits down on the edge of the bed and gives me the bottle of freckle cream. Then she opens her robe so most of her tits are exposed, with just the – well, just the nipples covered, and I dab a bit of cream on my hand and go to town. I rub the cream round and round, and I'm letting my fingers slip under the robe, so as to rub the cream over more and more of her breasts, and she doesn't stop me at all, and pretty soon I've got her tit in my hand, and she's got her eyes closed and she's moaning, and I whisper, *Keep it low, will ya, or Iggy will hear.* Wanda whispers, "Rub it on my thighs," and she lets her robe slip completely off, and she spreads her legs, and I hardly knew whether to look at her boobs or at what I could see through her black lace panties. When I got over my shock, I said, *There aren't any freckles on your thighs*, and she says, "For Christ sakes, Buddy, just rub."

I could hardly tell you what happened next. Wanda had my clothes off and she dropped her panties, and we were stark naked on the bed, and she was on top of me, and damned if there wasn't cinders in the sheets – I could feel them scratching my back, and Wanda's trying to guide my dick into her pussy, and she says, "Make sure you pull it out before you come." *Pull it out?* Hell, I couldn't even get it in. My dick was as limp as cooked spaghetti. I didn't know what the trouble was, so I said, *Just touch it a bit,* and she does but nothing happens, so she rubs freckle cream on it, but that doesn't do any good either. And just then, when Wanda's rubbing freckle cream on my pecker, the door opens and Alma looks into the room. Jeez Louise, I thought I would die. But Wanda gets up as cool as a cucumber and says to Alma, "Close the door, Alma. Can't you see we're busy," and Alma closes the door.

Wanda says, "Buddy, you're good for nothing." And I said, *I don't know what's wrong.* She says, "I'll tell you what's wrong. You're all talk and a limp dick." She puts on her robe, picks up her bottle of Stillman's Freckle Cream, and marches out of the room.

Limp Dick. She's got a lot of nerve. The only thing that's wrong with me is all these crazy women. Wanda is coming on like some kind of sex maniac, there's cinders on the sheets and the religious fanatic who put them there pops out of nowhere, my leg's in a cast, and somehow I'm supposed to have a boner. To tell the truth, I don't exactly know why I couldn't get it up. All I know is, it wasn't my fault. My equipment was A-OK in the living room, ready for action, and then – well, if Wanda hadn't been so aggressive. God, it was embarrassing. Not just that I couldn't get it up, *but Alma coming in and finding us* – well, heaven knows what will come of that. I was so flustered, I put on my clothes and hightailed it out of the house. What I needed was a good stiff drink.

I'll steer clear of Wanda from now on, that's for sure. And I'll tell you this – I'll never have to worry about freckles on my pecker.

Roger:

I didn't mean to take hold of Button's hand. When Pierre Dale announced, "In third place, the hilarious 'Trees' girl, Eileen Buffon," it just seemed the thing to do. I took her hand and gave it a squeeze, and said, *Wow, how about that?* And Button gave me a little squeeze back, and smiled. It was all over in a second.

The more I think about Button, the nicer she seems. I'd like to ask her to go for another walk on the mountain, or down to Chattanooga Valley, but it's too complicated. Too many other people would be upset. It's like my grandmother used to say, "You've made your bed, Roggie-boy, now lie in it." I made my bed twelve years ago and I've been laying in it ever since. As a marriage bed, there's not much to be said for it. It's been years and years since there was any real physical contact between Wanda and myself. I don't know what happened. Somewhere along the line she started turning me away. There's no point trying to make up with her now. She's got her mind set against me, and once Wanda sets her mind to anything there's no turning back. Like Granny said, I made my bed. Button made her bed, too. What I've been thinking lately is – it's too bad they're not the same bed.

Right now, what Button has on her mind is Alma. Button and Mamie are running around like chickens with their heads cut off trying to figure out what's wrong with Alma. The girl won't come out of her room. She won't touch her food. She's wasting away. Button wants a doctor, but Mamie insisted on calling Father Sayers. Sayers wouldn't come, because the last time he was here Button said something about needing a doctor rather than a priest, so the assistant pastor, a fellow named O'Neil, came instead. O'Neil is a young priest, not much older than Alma, fresh off the boat from Ireland. He went upstairs and locked himself away with Alma for an hour and a half, and when he came downstairs he said, "She's had a shock to her system." Button asked, "What sort of shock?" O'Neil said, "I can't exactly say, but it'd be as well if Alma was away from the house for awhile." He suggested admitting Alma to the hospital, so that she can be fed – intravenously, if necessary – to get her strength back. He said he will counsel her there, help her get things sorted out. Button asked again, "What sort of shock?" O'Neil said,

"I'm not exactly sure of the details. Let's just say it was a shock of a – of a serious nature, and let it rest at that." Button didn't want to let it rest, but Mamie had heard enough. It's typical of Mamie that she didn't want to know. She thanked Father O'Neil and shooed him out of the house. Mamie's powers of denial are absolute. The priest was hardly out the door when she was in the kitchen chopping okra as if nothing had happened at all. An hour later O'Neil rang up, saying he had made arrangements at Erlanger Hospital and we should bring Alma over. Mamie went right on fussing about the kitchen, avoiding any decision, so Button took charge. She was pleased that Alma would get professional help, so we bundled Alma into my car and drove her to hospital. She wept like a baby all the while.

I must say, I have more confidence in Father O'Neil than in Father Sayers. Sayers' attitude toward Alma was condescending. According to him, Alma is a typical female hysteric – "religious, but without the proper rationality to keep her spirituality in balance." O'Neil seems to have a more sympathetic understanding of human nature. He knows more than what he's telling us, that's sure, but he seems warmly disposed toward Alma and confident that her problem has a reasonable solution. I suspect he wants her in the hospital for psychological, as well as physical, observation.

Alma's been moody and introverted for as long as I have know her – which, come to think of it, is since the day she was born. Her moodiness became morbid at adolescence, and I'd say it almost certainly has a sexual component. Adolescence is a hard time for any kid, especially these days with all the explicit provocation in the movies and music – and for a girl like Alma, going to a Catholic school where the emphasis is on sin and hell and all that stuff, well, it's easy to see how she might have a hard time putting it all together. She went nuts on religion, that's all. Most kids grow out of if but Alma seems to be taking longer than most. She's what? – twenty-two years old now. It's time for her to shake it off and grow up.

And speaking of adolescence, it's time I should start keeping an eye on Tootsie. Her breasts are budding. She's getting to the age where she'll take an interest in – you know, boy-girl things, and, well, frankly, I wish she were growing up in a better environment. It's not that I don't love Mamie's family – they're as dear to me as if they were my own. But too many adult things are going on around this house for a young girl to handle. Tootsie should have a home of her own, a mother and father who can provide her with some kind of normal family life, and a neighborhood with kids her own age to play with. Instead, she pals around with the likes of Becca, Lynette, and Buddy, and thinks she should go to the same movies as the grown-ups, and – to top it all off, she sees Alma going slightly cuckoo. To make matters worse, her mother and father barely get along.

It's hard to know where my responsibilities lie, and how I should carry them off. If I left Wanda, and moved out of this house – maybe got a divorce and married someone, say, *more like Button* – well, it's hard to know how the rest of this family would survive. Oh, I suppose they would get along somehow. Buddy might even get a job if his back was against the wall. Becca and Lynette might finally decide to grow up. The Buffons are a resourceful lot. Perhaps I overestimate my importance around here. The thing is, if I left, I doubt if I could take Tootsie with me. If there was a separation or divorce, the court would almost certainly award Tootsie to Wanda – if that's what Wanda wanted. Come to think of it, I doubt that Wanda would insist on custody of Tootsie. She doesn't show much interest in her daughter now. But, believe you me, I don't underestimate Wanda's capacity to be perverse, plain and simple. She might ask for Tootsie just to get at me, confident that around this house a girl can grow up without a lick of help from her mother.

The trouble is, I don't know what I want, or how I would get it if I knew what I wanted. What I would *really* like, I think, is to buy – oh, say, fifty acres of land down in Chattanooga Valley, something with a little house on it – a tin-roofed shack would be fine, something I could fix up – and organize a bird sanctuary. Open it to the public for a modest charge, and give lessons in ornithology. Maybe write a guidebook on the birds of the southern Appalachians. We need such a guide. A lady named Emma Bell Miles did a book back at the turn of the century, but it's out of print and out of date. With the entrance fees to my sanctuary, and the ornithology lessons, and the guidebook, I just might make a go of it. It wouldn't take much to live in the country, especially if I had a garden, maybe a few chickens and a goat or two. Certainly, it'd be a better place for

Tootsie to grow up, in the outdoors with nature all about her. Of course, it would be nice to have someone to share it with. A woman, I mean. Someone besides Wanda.

A place in the country might be just the ticket. Better for me, too. My life has drifted willy-nilly into the business of killing people. God knows how many thousands of men, women, and children have been blown to smithereens by the explosives I've provided. Sometimes I dream of them. The victims of the bombs, I mean. With crusty skin as black as roast pigs. White eyes starring out of faceless skulls. Holding their body parts in their hands. And I wake up in a sweat. It's a bizarre way to kill people, when you think about it – beavering away in a spic-'n-span laboratory in a bird-filled forest in Tennessee. I'm like a chef in a kitchen. Mixing up my recipes – a cup of nitrate, a tablespoon of ammonia, a pinch of formaldehyde. Stir, melt, pour. Bombs go out the door of the plant like loaves of bread from a bakery. Convoyed across the Atlantic, and now the Pacific too. Loaded into airplanes. Dropped onto cities. I'm not a politician, or a philosopher, or a moral theologian. I can't balance the accounts of good and evil. I have no idea whether what I'm doing for the war effort adds or subtracts from the sum total of human suffering. All I know is, I'm good at it. And I love what I'm doing.

And I hate it.

That's why I want the place in the country.

As Button and I were driving back from the hospital, I said, *Button, my grandmother always used to say, "Roggie-boy, you've made your bed, now you must lie in it." I asked Button, Do you think that's so? Do you think the decisions you make are made forever?* She was very quiet. I suppose that Alma was still very much on her mind. Button's like that. Button assumes the cares and woes of others. That's what's truly fine about Button. Finally, she asked, "What did you say?" I said, *Do you think that once we've made our beds, we must lie in them forever?* She laughed. I don't know what she was thinking, but she thought it was funny.

Button:

There's an amazing story in the News-Free Press this evening. An American soldier killed a Jap somewhere in New Guinea. On the Jap's body was a newspaper photograph of a Chattanooga girl named Betty Gae Peek, a sort of glamour photograph of Betty Gae in a bathing suit that was taken by a News-Free Press photographer at Lake Winnepesaukah months and months ago. Actually, the photo was in the newspaper last summer. The American soldier had no idea how the Jap got the photo – nor does anyone else, apparently. But there it was, folded in a pocket next to the Jap's heart, in the jungles of New Guinea. The story was titled, "Girl's pin-up found on dead Nip." And the funny thing is, the soldier sent the newspaper photo to Betty Gae Peek so she could see what he found – *and he asked her to mail it back to him.*

I don't know what it was about the story that caught my interest. I don't even know if the story made me happy or sad. It's romantic in a way, I guess, I mean – the way the American soldier asked Betty Gae Peek to mail the photo back to him – but the business about the Japanese soldier having the white girl's picture in the first place is a little scary. I don't know why it's scary. I'm ashamed of Buddy when he treats people of other races as if they are somehow less than human. He always refers to the Japanese people he met in Hawaii with utter contempt, especially the women, and his way of talking makes me cringe. But if the story in the newspaper scares me, then maybe it's because I'm prejudiced too. I mean, why should it be OK for the American soldier to ask for the return of the photo, but not for the Japanese soldier to have it in the first place? Oh dear, does any of this make any sense? I don't know. Sometimes I think we inherit our prejudices – like they are in our genes or something – and no matter how hard we try to be unprejudiced, the old feelings keep popping up. But you know, I'll tell you something I've observed: prejudice is stronger in men than in women. As far as I'm concerned, it's one more part of their maleness. I suppose it makes them feel more "manly" if they can look down on someone else.

The other story I read today came from Tometta. It's a story of her own, written out by hand in a ruled notebook, a story about a colored girl's first day of school. You know, I never thought

Tometta would take me up on my suggestion, but she did, and her story is good. I must have read it five times. I said to her, *Tometta, your story is wonderful. It's like I was in that little girl's head, thinking her thoughts.* She said, "I'm 'fraid the grammar and spellin' ain't right, but I did what you tol' me and jest wrote exactly what come into my head." I said, *It's perfect. You shouldn't worry about grammar and spelling. You should write just the way you think. That's what makes the story so good.* She said, "Missus Cioffi, to tell the –" I reminded her to call me Button. "Button," she said, "to tell the truth, the story was easy to write. It jest came pourin' out." I said, *That means you're a natural writer, Tometta. Will you write more? I'd love to read more of your stories.* She said, "I'm 'fraid that if I start, I won't be able to stop."

I wish I could do what Tometta has done. It's ironic that I encourage her to write stories, but I can't do it myself. I don't have the gift – or the courage. I think that if I saw my thoughts on paper, I'd die. I'd be embarrassed to let anyone read them. That's why I could never be a writer. That's why I so admire Tometta. She has a kind of fierce honesty. There was a part in her story about her father, who wasn't part of her life, and – well, to tell the truth, it wasn't a flattering description, and conveyed a lot of anger. Clearly, Tometta was working through a lot of animosity. It must have taken courage to write that story – the kind of courage I don't have. I think if I started writing my own story, especially the part involving Buddy, that I – no, you know, it doesn't even bear thinking on.

Alma's the one who should write down her stories – to get them out of her system. That's what psychiatrists do, I suppose – help patients tell their stories, so they won't keep them bottled up inside. Sometimes when I look at Alma, I think she is going to bust wide open, like – you know, like everything goes into her head and nothing comes out. I don't know what she told Father O'Neil, but I suspect it has something to do with Buddy. I don't know why, just call it a woman's intuition, but I'm sure that Buddy is somehow involved. When Roger and I got home from taking Alma to the hospital, I asked Buddy, *Have you been pestering Alma?* He exploded, "What do you mean, pestering?" I said, *You know what I mean. Flirting. Messing around.* I knew he would deny it, but I felt I had to ask. He said, "You're out of your mind. That girl is as loony-tunes as Elmer Fudd."

Coming home from the hospital, Roger asked me if I thought the decisions we make are forever. *You've made your bed, now you must lie in it.* That's the expression he mentioned – I think he said his grandmother used it. To tell the truth, I agree with his grandmother. I mean, it's got something to do with accepting the consequences of our decisions, and living out our responsibilities, no matter what. Otherwise, what's there to live for – that's *worth* living for, I mean? That's another thing I admire about Tometta. I'm sure she would rather be somewhere else than taking care of her great-grandmother and cooking for white people, but she knows where her responsibilities lie and she does what she has to do. She stays in the bed that was made for her. I know it sounds corny – you know, just the sort of thing a grandmother would say – but I don't know what the alternative is. Heavens knows, I'd like to be away from here, somewhere on my own, with no one to worry about but myself. But what about Alma? Mother's too old to deal with Alma, and, you know, Mother refuses to admit there's even a problem. And there's Iggy. And Emily Sue. Roger can't be asked to shoulder all the responsibilities. He's a good man, but he has problems of his own. And, you know, where would Buddy be without me? I know it sounds silly, but with no one to rail against, Buddy would be even more miserable than he is already. Buddy is my responsibility, too.

So I guess that maybe Roger's grandmother is right. I made my bed, and now I'll lie in it – no matter what.

Iggy:

Hell's bells, it's hotter'n hell. You could fry a egg on the windowsill. Lyin' here in bed is like bakin' in a oven. Worse'n hell, it is. An' nobody gives a rat's ass. Nobody says, *Iggy, can I bring you a glass of iced lemonade.* Nobody says, *Iggy, why don't you take the electric fan, you need it worse than the rest of us.* I lie here bakin' in the heat, doin nothin', an' nobody gives a blue damn.

Look at that old dog out in Missouri, the one they was talkin' about on the radio. Old Drive, its name is. Got itself trapped in a cave. Squeezed 'tween the rocks an' couldn't get out. Did they leave it there to die? Hell, no! First thing ya know, the whole country is in a dither. The story's been on the radio fer days, pushin' the war news to second place. It's a regular circus out there in Missouri, as near as I can tell, with a whole army of engineers blastin' away through the limestone, cuttin' a tunnel to save the dog, an' him jus' a old hound dog, a plain ole coon dog.

That goddamn dog gets more attention than me. Lawd knows, I'm trapped in this cave of a room, in this here bed, worse than any ole dog. Can't go nowheres. Jus' lyin' here swelterin' in the heat, an' listenin' on the radio to how the whole state of Missouri is tryin' to get Old Drive outta a hole. Sometimes I figure I'll jus' go ahead an' die, an' then, when the nigras come, there won't be no one aroun' here to provide this family with any protection at all. Buddy's got a gun, sho' nuff, but Buddy couldn't hit the side of a barn if he was inside shootin' out. I'm the only one aroun' here that's a sharpshooter. Got my badge to prove it. Didn't I croak that goddamn woodpecker with one shot? *One shot.* But why should I take care of this family when they don't give two hoots fer me? It'd serve 'em right to be left on their own. Only Tootsie pays any mind to me at all, an' evah since Bitsy took up with that Kraut fella, Tootsie's been payin' more attention to Bitsy than she does me. I'd say that Tootsie likes the Kraut, too. I'd say that Tootsie has a crush on Bitsy's fella.

I said to Tootsie, *Tell Bitsy to ask her German boyfriend how many American G.I.s he killed before he was taken prisoner. That German fella may have killed half-a-dozen American boys.* She says, "It's not his fault, Uncle Iggy. A soldier has to do what he's ordered to do." I said, *That don't make no difference. It's the Krauts that started the damn war.* She said, "You have a gun, Uncle Iggy, and you're gonna shoot people, too. So you're just the same as Horst." Well, I'd say as it's not the same thing at all. If the colored folk want trouble, then we's got to protect ourselves. Almost every night now there's trouble in the nigra neighborhoods. Knife fights. Gunshots. People breakin' inta stores. Stealin' liquor an' stealin' guns. An' you can't jus' blame it on the hot weather. The same things been happenin' all ovah the country. The trouble is, you give a colored person a inch an' he'll take a mile. Look what's happenin' up in Philadelphia. They started hirin' colored folk to run the trolleys. Well, next thing you know the white workers go on strike an' shut the whole system down – as well they should. Let nigras have some of the trolley jobs, an' pretty soon they'll be wantin' 'em all. Those nigras will work for peanuts. They live in tarpaper shacks, catch fish in drainage ditches, eat dandelions from the white folk's yards – so what do they need money fer? Meanwhile, the white man who requires a decent wage to provide his family with a civilized house an' three square meals a day gets dumped into the street. So what does Roosevelt do? He seizes the Philadelphia transport system, that's what he does. Takes over the trolleys an' the trains. Like a goddamn dictator. Worse'n Hitler or Mussolini. *Social equality.* That's what FDR calls it – *social equality.* Social destruction is more like it. Give the nigras a foot in the door an' purdy soon the whole country will go to hell in a handbasket. We'll all be eatin' catfish an' dandelions. No need fer it, either. The coloreds are happy jus' as they are. Put 'em in a fancy house an' they wouldn't know what to do with it. Next thing you know, Pres-ee-dint Roosevelt will be invitin' colored folk to the White House, an' they'll be eatin' catfish in Lincoln's bedroom. An' I wouldn't expect anything better from that Dewey fella, either. Him an' Roosevelt are two peas in a pod as far as "social equality" is concerned. The only person this country can count on is Senator Harry Byrd. Harry knows what's best fer the white man – an' what's best fer the nigras, too.

If Harry Byrd don't sort things out, then I got my little soldiers lined up right here. Thirteen little steel soldiers. Thirteen dead nigras, if they's bold enough to try somethin'. One li'l soldier per nigra, jus' like fer the woodpecker. *Ping. Ping. Ping. Ping. Ping. Ping. Ping. Ping. Ping. Ping. Ping. Ping. Ping.*

Tootsie:

I've got a really, really, really big secret. This secret's too big even for Iggy. I can't tell secrets to Iggy anymore. He's been acting crazy lately. His eyes roll around in his head, and he talks even when no one is in the room. He keeps his thirteen bullets lined up on his bedside table and calls them his "little soldiers." I can't trust Iggy with secrets anymore.

Especially not *this* secret.

This secret is about Horst. Horst has escaped from the guard house at the cemetery. That's not the secret, of course. About Horst escaping, I mean. Everybody knows that. It was in the papers and on the radio. *A German soldier, blonde, with a mustache, believed to be wearing a gray prisoner's uniform with "P.O.W." on the back, escaped yesterday from a work detail at the National Cemetery.* Horst slipped over the wall while the prisoners were mowing grass and ran away down the railroad tracks. One of the other prisoners distracted the guard and gave Horst a chance to get away. The Chattanooga police and the M.P.'s are looking everywhere. The really big secret is – I know where Horst is hiding.

Buddy is upset about the escape. Buddy said to Dad, "See, Roger, I told you my gun was a good idea." Buddy said to Becca, "I hope you don't mind me going into your room so much, but I want to keep checking on the thirty-eight." Buddy said to Tometta, "You'd better watch out, girl, or the Nazi'll get you." But Horst isn't dangerous. Horst is nice. The only reason Horst escaped is so he can be with Bitsy.

I was coming up the alley from the playground when I heard Horst whisper "Tootzee." He was hiding in our garage. I couldn't believe my ears. I thought maybe the war was over and they'd let Horst go. Then I figured he must have escaped. He said, "Bit-zee," and I knew that he wanted to see Bitsy. That's why he escaped. He's not dangerous at all.

Horst is hiding in the playhouse Dad made for me in the loft of the garage. It's a good hiding place. No one ever goes up there but me. To get to the playhouse you have to climb a ladder. There are cushions for Horst to sleep on. Bitsy and I sneak him things to eat. Bitsy's so excited she can hardly see straight. But I think she's scared too. She loves Horst so much, and now she can be with him. She goes to see him in the playhouse. Last night she stayed with him all night. She wore her new nightgown. Bitsy said Horst asked her to wear her Lana Turner nightgown.

Bitsy *did it*. Bitsy did it with Horst. Bitsy said she wants to get married to Horst, and that's why she did it. She said she doesn't care if she has a baby, that it'll be Horst's baby, and Horst will want to stay in America when the war's over so he can be with his baby. Bitsy is lucky. Horst is nice, and he loves Bitsy. They sleep in my playhouse, on the cushions, with Horst's little carvings lined up overhead. When Bitsy is at work, I sneak up to the playhouse and talk to Horst. He knows a bit of English, and I know eek-leeba-dick. I told Horst, *eek-leeba-dick*. It means "I love you." But I know that Horst is Bitsy's boyfriend.

I asked Dad how long it will be till the war is over. He says if the Germans haven't surrendered by Thanksgiving, there won't be anything left to surrender. I don't know if we can hide Horst till Thanksgiving. The police are looking everywhere. Buddy says, "If that Nazi S.O.B. shows up here, I'll make him sorry he ever left his frau-maw and herr-paw." Buddy said, "That chicken-shit must be around here somewhere. He can't go far in his P.O.W. uniform."

Tometta's suspicious. Tometta said, "You sho' goin' up to the playhouse a lot." If Tometta found out that Horst is in the playhouse, she might tell her boyfriend William. If William finds out about Horst, he will do something for sure. Tometta said, "It mus' be scorchin' hot up there in the playhouse. You think you'd be playin' outdoors where it be cool." And it is hot in the playhouse, all right. Poor Horst is burning up. He lays there on the cushions in his underwear. He asked me if I mind – him being in his underwear – but I don't mind. I brought him some Life magazines so he wouldn't be bored. I think it was a mistake to bring him the magazines. When Horst saw the pictures of bombs falling on German cities, he got really upset. Horst's family is in a city called Essen. Dad says that lots of bombs have been dropped on Essen. No wonder Horst is worried about his family.

I'm worried about my family. Especially Bitsy. Bitsy's acting really strange, almost as strange as Alma and Iggy. Her eyes go round and round, and her mouth moves even when she's talking to no one at all. I think it has something to do with "doing it." Dad took the whole family to Lake Winnepesaukah today – Buddy, Button, Emily Sue, Becca, and Lynette. And me. We all piled into Dad's car and drove to Lake Winnepesaukah. But Bitsy didn't go. Bitsy spent the day in the playhouse with Horst. *Doing it.*

Buddy:

I don't particularly like the idea of riding in Roger's car, but I'll be damned if I was going to stay home with Wanda. Besides, it turned out to be not so bad after all. We were jammed into the car like sardines, and Emily Sue was sitting on my lap. She wiggled all the way to the lake, and it was all I could do to keep my pecker from lifting her right up in the air. I can't for the life of me figure out why God put such a simple mind into such a terrific body. If you caught a glimpse of Emily Sue, you'd say, *Wow, there's one sensational doll.* Then after a minute you think, *Uh, oh.* And the other thing you notice is – she can't sit still.

Lynette was squeezed in next to me in her sunsuit, and Becca was looking back from the front seat of the car, with her chin resting on her bare shoulder, winking, and saying, "How'ya doin', Buddy." Let me tell you, by the time we got to the lake I was worn out – and the day hadn't even started. I don't know what it is, but women drive me nuts. I think about them all the time. I can't keep my eyes off them. I dream about them. There's not twenty seconds during the day when they're not on my mind. Button says I'm crazy. Button says that being so preoccupied with women isn't normal, that it's "adolescent." Well, to me it's as normal as all get out. I'd say *most* men think about women all the time; least ways, most of the men I know. Not Roger, maybe. If a good-lookin' woman was to walk by, Roger wouldn't even notice. He can spot a pie-eyed warbler twenty miles away, but if Barbara Stanwyck was to blow in his ear he'd think it was the wind. That's why Button likes him, of course. She think's he's "normal." Button and Roger are two un-normal peas in a pod, if you ask me. Jeez Louise, if men and women weren't supposed to take notice of each other, then why are there two sexes. Sex is what makes the world go round. It's not just me, it's everybody. It's everywhere, like the static electricity that builds up before a summer storm. And, I'll tell you this, the electricity sure was crackling in Roger's car on the way to the lake. Every time Emily Sue wiggled her sweet little ass, she threw off sparks – and she didn't even know what she was doing. Sex is just there, that's what. It's part of the world – as normal as sweet potato pie. OK, so I do a bit of flirting, cop a feel now and then, steal a kiss. I'm no different than anyone else. If Button didn't want a man with a normal sexual appetite, then why the hell did she marry me?

If you want to check out chicks, there's no better place to do it than the pool at Lake Winnepesaukah, much better than the pool at Warner Park. There's no one but city girls at Warner Park – prissified city girls, sitting around the pool with their shoulders hunched over so you won't notice they have tits. At Lake Winnepesaukah you get the country girls – those North Georgia peaches who lost their virginity in the sixth grade and still have hay in their hair. When you're changing in the men's locker room you can hear them on the other side of the partition, giggling and snickering and talking about guys. God, what I wouldn't give for x-ray vision so I could see right through the wall, and watch all those sweetie-pies from Ootewah and Ringgold and Graysville wrigglin' into their bathing suits. When they come out to the pool, they *parade* out, with their tits stuck out to here, and their asses swinging in time, and their locker keys jingle-jangling on their ankles announcing "Hey guys, here I am." The only thing missing is a marching band. Thirty seconds later, they've got every guy in the pool sized up and checked out.

I hate to say it, but those country girls make Lynette and Becca look like – well, like what they are, Catholic schoolgirls. Put Becca by herself and you'd say she was pretty sexy, but stick her next to the Georgia girls at Lake Winnepesaukah and she looks like she's ready for her First Comnunion. The only woman in this family who's near half as sexy as a Georgia girl in a bathing suit is Emily Sue. With cotton candy stuck on her face she looks good enough to eat. I've seen guys swim up to Emily Sue and start flirting – it takes 'em about a minute to notice something's wrong, and then they swim away. She's a sexual booby-trap, that's what, sitting there at the side of the pool, splashing her feet in the water and looking like God gave her more chest than was good for her. All that lovely peachfuzz curling out from the crotch of her bathing suit. I'll tell you, I feel sorry for her. At the pool, Becca and Lynette stay miles away from Emily Sue, 'cause they don't want the guys to know she's their sister. But I keep an eye on her. I splash her now and then, make her laugh, help her have a little bit of fun. It's not her fault that God gave her more boobs than brains.

The pool was jammed. The temperature must have been one-hundred-and-ten, and everybody and his brother was trying to cool off. Even Roger took a dip. Button didn't come to the pool, of course. That's just like her. Doesn't know how to have fun. Preferred to sit by herself under the trees by the lake licking a cherry snowball. Button's only five years older than Lynette, but you'd think she was Lynette's mother. Lynette and Becca get a kick outta life, but Button – hell, Button's middle-aged. I don't know how it happened. One day she was a nifty tomato making out in the back row of the Tivoli Theater, and the next day she's middle-aged. I'll tell you this, it won't happen to me – not if I can help it. I'm thirty years old and I'm not ready yet to sit under goddamn pine trees licking snowballs. I've got a few good kicks in me yet and I intend to have some fun.

We stayed in the pool all afternoon. Except for Roger; he was in and out in a minute. Off to sit with Button, I suppose – pointing out the pinkdicked dippers and yellow-breasted gooney-floppers. And the swans. I suppose Roger spent the afternoon giving Button a lecture on the mating habits of swans. *You see, Button, there's a boy swan, and a girl swan, and they swim around and around the lake with their eyes closed, and then the stork comes and brings a baby swan. "And where do baby storks come from, Roger?" Ah, well, you see, Button, ah, ah...* Fuck 'em. The pool is where the action is. I'll tell you this, it's not like the babes ignored me. With my good leg in a cast, my gimpy leg ain't so noticeable. I must have flirted with twenty women. Chatted up two of 'em. Just sat there in a pool chair, with my busted ankle propped up on another chair, and waited for the women to come to me – like flies to honey, you might say. Button says I ask for it, that I radiate a signal that says "I'm available." That's baloney. I just sit there and they come to me. It's not my fault if I'm still attractive.

After the swim we had a bite to eat, then we fooled around until nightfall – played some miniature golf, shot some SkeeBalls, went to the penny arcade. I gave Becca and Lynette some target practice at the shooting gallery. The girls were awful shots – until I let 'em in on the secret. The sights on those shooting-gallery rifles are deliberately misaligned. If you aim directly at a duck, you'll always miss. What you've got to do is see where the bullets hit compared to where you're aiming, then make the adjustment in your mind. Once you have the trick, it's easy to hit the target. I was knocking over ducks like dominoes. *Bang. Flop. Bang. Flop.* With the rifle I was using, you had to aim one duck-width to the left. *Pretend the duck is the Nazi P.O.W,* I said to Becca. I whispered into her ear, *One duck-width to the left.* She aimed. *Here he comes,* I shouted. *Bang. Flop.* She picked him off. *One dead Nazi,* I said. Tootsie said, "You shouldn't be pretending to shoot people. The German soldier is probably a nice man. Maybe he had a good reason to escape." *He's still a Nazi,* I said. Becca aimed again. *Bang. Flop.*

Best of all was the boat shute. God, how I wanted to get Becca into the boat shute. To make it even better, we had the front seat of the boat, with Lynette and Tootsie sitting behind. First, the boat went through the Tunnel of Love, and let me tell you, it was dark. I was giving Becca little grabs, under her arm, and on her tummy. She screeched, "Stop that, Buddy." But I could tell she liked it. I let the back of my hand brush across her tits. She screamed. Lynette said, "Buddy, behave yourself." I put my hand on Becca's tummy, between her halter and her shorts, and left it there. "Jesus, Buddy" she whispered at the top of her voice, "Tootsie's here." *Tootsie can't see a thing,* I said. I let my fingers slip ever so slightly under her halter top. She squealed, "Stop that, Buddy, or I'll do it to you." *Go ahead,* I said, and I grabbed her hand and put it in my lap. I don't think she realized what I'd done, 'cause she left her hand there for half-a-second. Then she hollered, "Buddy Cioffi" and yanked her hand away. Lynette yelled, "What's going on up there." Tootsie said, "Buddy's a sex maniac." Becca said, "Jesus, Buddy, you're incorrigible." The boat came out of the Tunnel of Love and started up the incline. Everyone was screaming. We went over the top and plummeted down the slide into the water. Spray went everywhere. I'll tell you this, Becca may have played hard to get in the dark, but when we started down that slide, she threw her arms around my neck and held on for dear life.

Incorrigible. Is that so bad?

Button:

On the way back from Lake Winnepesaukah, I somehow ended up sitting on Buddy's lap. I suppose he was disappointed. He would have preferred Becca or Lynette, or even Emily Sue, but he got me instead. Of course, he made some little joke about it, some snitty remark about "wasting a lap on a wife." He can't resist the inclination to humiliate me. But once we were on the way home he settled down. He rested his cheek against my shoulder, and it was easy to remember why I fell in love with him, I mean, Buddy can be very tender and affectionate when he wants to be, and it reminded me of how we used to go to the movies when we first got married and sit in the balcony, and Buddy would snuggle against my neck, and then we would go home and try and make a baby, and it's hard to imagine that anyone could be sweeter than he was then. He was always like that before he went into the Navy.

When we got home from the lake, he was actually in a romantic mood. He held my hand as we got out of the car. I knew he wanted to make love, and I had a feeling that we might do it the way we used to when we first got married, without Buddy trying to turn everything into a big production. He was – he was sweet. He crawled into bed and snuggled up against me, and he looked kind of cute in his shorts and his cast, and I thought, *Why not?* because he was sweet, and he wasn't trying to jam his head between my legs, or sticking his finger up my bum, or any of his usual tricks. He was affectionate, and he seemed to want me to have a good time, so I thought, *Why not?* and I touched his thing and made it hard, and I got on top of him, and we made love with him laying there on his back as happy as can be, and afterwards he closed his eyes and went to sleep.

I lay there for hours, thinking about what had happened, and wondering if maybe Buddy and I could get things going again, maybe get a place of our own, like the apartment we had on Cameron Hill – it was the tiniest little apartment but it was ours, and sometimes I wonder if the problem with our marriage is that we don't have a place of our own, like around here Buddy has so many women to show off for that he doesn't often think of me. By morning, I had almost convinced myself that we could make our marriage work again.

After breakfast I went looking for Tometta's story, so I could return it to her. I had left the notebook on the bureau in our room, and when I went to get it it was gone. I said to Buddy, *Have you seen a blue notebook that I left in our room?* He said, "I threw it out." I said, *What do you mean 'I threw it out'?* He said, "Just what I said. I was tidying up the room and I tossed it." I said, *Buddy, you never tidy up the room.* He said "You never notice anything I do." I asked, *Where did you put the notebook?* He said, "I tossed it in the stove."

Really, I couldn't believe it. I mean, it was like the love birds all over again, except this time what he threw out wasn't mine – and it was irreplaceable. I couldn't imagine what Tometta would say when she found out her story was gone. I said, *Buddy, do you know what was in the notebook?* He said, "Yeah, it was something Tometta wrote. It had her name on it." I said, *It was a story she wrote. It was the only copy.* He said, "It was chicken-scratch."

Chicken-scratch! I was fit to be tied. I said, *Buddy, That's the awfullest thing you've ever done. Why did you do it?* He said, "If you keep coddling up to that colored girl, she's going to start thinking she owns this place." I said, *It was her story, Buddy. It was a story she wrote. It was a wonderful story.* He said, "For Christsake, Button, it was gibberish. The girl can't even spell." I started crying. I mean, I haven't cried for years, but I started crying. Buddy said, "If you paid half as much attention to me as you do that colored girl, we' be a lot better off." I looked at him and the tears were streaming down my cheeks. He said, "I don't know what you see in her anyways, she's just a black slut." I was speechless. I shook my head, and cried and cried. He said, "On second thought, maybe there is something you could learn from her. Like how to have fun in bed."

It's hopeless. Buddy always brings things around to that. I marched upstairs to our room and threw everything of mine into a laundry basket – everything that would fit, I mean – and hauled it through Iggy's room to the sleeping porch. Bed linen and a pillow, too. Iggy said, "I knew it would come to his." I said, *You were right, Uncle Iggy.* Buddy watched me lugging all the stuff down the hall, and said, "I can't believe you're so upset about a little bit of scribble. I was only tidying up the room. It's not my fault you left the notebook laying around." It's hopeless, it's utterly hopeless. I can't believe I wasted a whole night thinking good thoughts about Buddy. If he won't leave this house, then I will. I'll never go back to his bed. *Ever*. I forgave him for breaking the lovebirds, but I'll never forgive him for destroying Tometta's story. He did it for spite, of course, because he's jealous – jealous of Tometta. He can't bear to think that a colored girl is smarter and nicer than he'll ever be. He's petty, and spiteful, and hopeless – utterly hopeless.

I went to Tometta and told her what happened. I told her how sorry I was, and how I knew the story couldn't be replaced. She was sitting in the glider with Eva. She said, "Oh, don't you fret, Missus Cioffi, it was jest an ole story." I said, *Oh no, Tometta. It was a wonderful story.* She said, "Mister Cioffi, he jest weren't thinkin'." I said, *Mister Cioffi is a bastard.* I couldn't believe I said it. I've never used a word like that before, but it sounded right. I said it again, *Mister Cioffi is a bastard.* She said, "He jest got a mean streak." Then she added, "I can write that ole story ag'in."

I felt so ashamed. Ashamed that Tometta was making excuses for Buddy. Ashamed that she felt it was necessary to excuse Buddy. He thinks the negroes are about to have a revolution, or a riot, or something. Well, they should. Negroes have every right to riot against the likes of Buddy. I said to Eva, *I'm so sorry about what happened to your great-granddaughter's story.* She said, "I s'pect it was jest an ole story." She tapped her temple: "The only stories that matters is in here."

I know that Tometta won't rewrite the story that Buddy destroyed, but if she doesn't write other stories, I'll never forgive myself. And I'll never forgive Buddy.

Roger:

It was the best afternoon ever. Buddy and the girls hung out at the pool. I took a short swim and then went to look for Button. I found her by the lake, all by herself, in the grass under the trees. She seemed content to be by herself. I said, Would *you mind if I join you?* She said, "Suit yourself." I said, *Would you like to do anything? The ferris wheel? The bumper cars?* She said, "I'd rather just sit."

That's what I like about Button. She has a knack for solitude. It doesn't take much to make her happy. She's never bored. I sat down nearby, with my back against a tree, and we just sat there for half-a-hour saying nothing at all, trying to keep cool, and watching the swans glide on the lake.

Then the most amazing thing happened. I was sitting there, thinking about nothing at all, watching the swans and watching Button, when it dawned on me that I was in love. It's like – *click* – some little light came on. I suddenly realized that of all the people in the world, Button was the only person I cared about, the only person I enjoyed being with. Moreover, I had this sudden compulsion to – well, to take her in my arms. *Click*. It came out of nowhere. I had thought all of that was past. I had thought I'd gotten that sort of thing out of my system. I haven't looked at a woman in that way for years, not even Wanda. Come to think of it, I'm not sure I've ever looked at a woman in quite that way. I don't remember ever actually being in love. I guess when I married Wanda I did it because it was the thing to do. She had always been a part of my life, ever since I was a kid. She was the oldest of the Buffon girls, the closest to my own age, so it seemed natural that she was the one I'd marry. But it's not like we were in love. There was never anything like romance. Or courtship. One day we were sitting on the front porch, and I said, *Let's get married*, or something as simple as that, and she said, "OK ," or something equally trite, and that's how it happened. Before that moment, I don't think I had touched her, except maybe playing around as kids. There was a bit of kissing, I suppose, sitting on the basement steps when we were really young, the kind of thing kids do because it's the thing to do, but never later, never when we were old enough to know what we were doing, never any serious lovemaking.

I don't remember ever feeling for Wanda what I found myself feeling for Button as we sat there by the lake. It was a brand new feeling. And it felt good.

Wanda's the only woman I've had sex with, and to tell the truth, I can't remember much about that. It's been ten years since we've made love. Even when we were doing it, it was a perfunctory sort of thing, never any fireworks, never any of the electricity that you see in the movies. That's my fault, I guess. I must be a pretty awful lover. I never did know much about what I was doing – never cared much either. Sex was something you were supposed to do when you got married. I doubt if I ever gave Wanda an orgasm. Maybe that's why she got tired of me. Maybe that's why she turned away. Maybe I wasn't good enough in bed to make it worth her while.

But to tell the truth, I haven't missed making love. I guess I'm not highly sexed. That's what's so amazing about what happened by the lake. I was watching Button. She had on that pretty pink dress that I like, the one with the puff sleeves. She was tying bits of grass into knots. Wisps of hair hung down across her eyes. She wasn't paying the least bit of attention to me. All of a sudden – *click* – I was head over heels in love. Silly, really, when you think about it. Here I am, thirty-five years old, losing my hair, a lackadaisical bomb-builder, a solitary ornithologist, no experience of women – or almost none – and I'm head over heels in love with my sister-in-law. And for the first time in my life I felt the urge to take a woman in my arms. Of course, I did no such thing. We sat in silence. Button tied little knots of grass and tossed them into the lake. I said, *A penny for your thoughts*, and she said, "Oh, they're not worth a penny."

And the great thing – about sitting so still – a dozen bluebirds descended upon a patch of pokeweed by the lake. The bushes bent under the weight of the birds as they gobbled up the purple berries. We watched the birds gorge themselves, not fifteen feet away. Button brushed the hair from her eyes. She was leaning with one hand on the grass, her legs curled under her skirt. She had removed her sandals. She whispered, "Why aren't the birds frightened of us?" I asked, *Should they be frightened?* She bit her lip. She shrugged. I thought: *Will I ever be happy again?*

Tometta:

I knew writin' that story be a bad idea. I was right proud of it when Missus Cioffi tol' me how good it be, an' that she read it *five* times an' all, but now that Mista Cioffi gone throw it in the stove, it start a awful fight 'tween him an' Button, an' she move on out of his room, out to the sleepin' porch. Course, I'm stuck right square in the middle of it. Yoah shoulda heard Button railin' on 'bout Mista Cioffi, a *bastard* she call him. I never imagine I'd see the day where she cuss like that – was all I could do not to bust out in a big ole smile. That jest ain't like Missus Cioffi. I reckon she'd do well to try an' be like that more of'en. She a lot like Miss Alma in a way, always wantin' to take all the problems of the world on 'erself. Maybe if she stay strong, Mista Cioffi'll see that he ain't hurtin' no one but hisself. I weren't gonna let 'em see that it bothered me none, but it did bother me. That stuck right in my craw when he burn that story.

Miss Alma's back from the hospital now. She come in an' help me peel vegetables fer a spell this mornin'. I think she talked more this mornin' than all the rest of the times we spoke afore. She tol' me how Father O'Neil come an' speak with her ev'ry day in the hospital. Alma, says, "Tometta, he's not like the other priests, he talks to you just like I'm talking to you right now. He's given me a whole new way of looking at things." *How's that?* I ask. "Well, he says I need to build my relationship with God through an appreciation of his creation, not through moritifications of the flesh – not by hurting myself. He said, 'You honor God by looking at a beautiful sunset, smelling the flowers, or by just enjoying the company of others.' Tometta, he has the most beautiful way of expressing things". Alma be beamin', so I says, *Why Miss Alma, I do believe you's sweet on this Father O'Neil.* Well, she turn red as a beet, an' says, "Good heavens, Tometta, he's a priest, it's nothing like *that!* And please stop with the Miss Alma business." *Aw, I jest teasin' ya, Alma,* I says, an' I give 'er a smile. Always struck me odd though, priests not marryin'. Don't the bible say, *Be fruitful and multiply*? An' sho', I see clear as day she be sweet on the man. "You know," she says, "I asked him about maybe becoming a sister. He said he thought I'd make a fine nun, but that I should take some time to find myself before making such an important decision. He thinks I should get out and socialize more, learn to talk to people." I says, *Well, it sounds to be good advice, I always thought you spend too much time alone. You ought try spendin' more time with your fam'ly an' frien's.* Alma says, "To be honest, Tometta, even sitting at dinner with my family makes me shake like a leaf. They all think I'm crazy, and I'm ashamed to say how I feel about most of them. As far as friends go, I simply don't have any." I says, *Well, you can talk with me anytime ya like.* Alma got a sad look on 'er face an' says, "Tometta, I'm sorry. I shouldn't have said I have no friends, I consider you a great friend. I only hope you feel the same for me." She took my hand and our fingers wove together like a beautiful basket. I smile an' says, *I'd say the good Lawd be smilin' down on our frien'ship right now.*

Iggy:

I knew it would come to this. I never could figure why Button an' Vincent stayed together. She's too damn good fer him. Always was. It's not that he don't have his good qualities. He can make me laugh. He knows the time of day. But I can't see a nice gal like Button bein' married to the likes of him. That boy's got hot peppers in his pants. Uses his dick for brains. Vincent's only got one thing on his mind an' it ain't sunshine.

I could've tol' you back in '39 there'd be trouble. I saw Vincent flirtin' with Becca on the day of his own weddin'. Flirtin' with Wanda, too – an' her married. That boy's too damn handsome fer his own good. All that thick black dago hair. Big wop eyes. He could charm the tomatoes off a vine. Swept Button off her feet, he did. Now look at 'em. Button's moved onto the sleepin' porch an' left Buddy in the lurch. Mind you, that be fine by me. If there's gonna be anyone trampin' back an forth through here, it might as well be Button. I've still got a soft spot in my heart fer that girl. Jus' seein' her walk past the bed makes me smile.

An' now ever'one be tellin' me the news. Billy Joe's in the slammer. He'll get the gas chamber, that's sho'. The gas chamber's too good fer the likes of him. They oughta string him up on Market Street an' use him for bazooka practice. They oughta stick a cake of Roger's TNT up his ass an' set it off.

I should've guessed it was Billy Joe that took Teddy Carr. Him an' his dirty pictures. That man is strange as a three-dollar bill. Hangin' aroun' the playground, he was. That's why the *po*lice got suspicious. Got a search warrant fer his house. Turns out the place was filled with guns an' por-no-graph-ic pictures. Found Teddy Carr buried in the basement, naked as a jaybird, black an' blue. The things Billy Joe done to that boy don't bear thinkin' on. The police are over there now, diggin' up the basement an' the backyard. Lookin' fer others. Some colored boys been missin' fer years, an' the *po*lice think Billy Joe may have took 'em too.

Tootsie's all shook up. She figures she might of ended up in Billy Joe's basement next to Teddy Carr. She hasn't told Roger an' Wanda 'bout me sendin' her over to Billy Joe's to borrow a rifle. *Christamighty*, if they knew what I done, they'd throw a fit. Buddy –

he's gone from railin' against the nigras to railin' against perverts. "I should of shot that son-of-a-bitch dead the minute he stepped foot in this house," says Buddy. Becca says she'd turn the gas on Billy Joe herself. Ever'one aroun' here is pissed at me fer havin' Billy Joe as a friend. Lawd knows, he was a frien'ly old coot. He still come to see me when all my other frien's forgot I existed. Seems to me he weren't no diff'rent than the rest of us, only crazier.

Accordin' to the papers, the colored folk are in a uproar. All the time the *po*lice was tearin' around niggatown searchin' for Teddy Carr an' it was a white man that took him all along. The colored folk say the *po*lice are prejudiced, an' they get nothin' from the *po*lice but hassles. An' that's why they's actin' up. Las' night there was all kinds of disturbances. Windows smashed on Market Street. Shots fired at automobiles. A white-owned liquor store was looted down by Terminal Station. Seems to me the situation is gettin' outta hand. Maybe the *po*lice are prejudiced an' maybe they ain't, but either way there ain't no cause to go tearin' down the town. Becca heard that the coloreds are gonna march out to Billy Joe's house some evenin' soon as a protest. Right up Ninth Street they'll march. A "illegal assembly" the papers call it. Somethin' like that can get outta hand. Somethin' like that could turn into a full-scale riot. I'm glad I've got Billy Joe's rifle here undah my mattress. I'm glad I've got my thirteen little soldiers ready fer action.

Tootsie:

Everybody's worried that I'm upset about what happened to Teddy Carr. They're all trying to distract me from thinking about it. Dad woke me up from a perfectly sound sleep to go birding. Tometta asked me to help with the cooking. Mom let me go to the movies with Becca and Lynette. She thought we were going to see "Lassie Come Home," but we saw "Two Girls and a Sailor" instead. It was sensational.

I feel sorry for Teddy Carr, but I feel sorry for Billy Joe Alaska, too. I know I shouldn't feel sorry for Billy Joe, 'cause he did such terrible things and all. But somehow I do. He was lonely and sick. Being lonely and sick made Billy Joe do bad things. The police found three skeletons buried in his back yard. Little kids. The police think the skeletons might be negro children that Billy Joe kidnapped a long time ago. The colored people are upset. They want to know why the police never arrested Billy Joe until a white boy was missing. They say the police never did hardly anything at all when the colored kids disappeared. Buddy says the police will have to move Billy Joe to the Dayton County jail. Buddy says that Billy Joe isn't safe in Chattanooga, with the negroes so upset. Buddy says that with the weather so hot, there's bound to be trouble.

Poor Horst is burning up in the playhouse, so Bitsy decided he couldn't stay cooped up anymore. She smuggled some of Buddy's old clothes out of the house, things from the attic that he doesn't wear anymore, so that Horst could leave the garage. He shaved off his mustache and made his hair brown with shoe polish, and then he snuck out of the garage, and Bitsy and I met him in the schoolyard. We walked downtown. We saw an army show at the Electric Power Board, sponsored by Coca-Cola. There was a bazooka, a handie-talkie, a mine detector, a blood plasma demonstration, some kind of big gun – a howitzer, I think – and Signal Corps pigeons. If you bought a war bond, you got a free Coca-Cola, but we didn't buy a war bond. I liked the pigeons.

Horst liked the ladies in sundresses, that's what I noticed. He hardly even looked at the bazooka or the other stuff, but he sure looked at the pretty girls who were selling war bonds and passing out Coca-Cola. Bitsy noticed, too, how Horst looked at the ladies. And how the ladies looked at Horst. One girl said to him, "What's buzzin', cousin?" and Horst just grinned.

Bitsy didn't say a word all the way home. Horst asked her to come with him to the playhouse – so they could *do it*, I suppose – but Bitsy wouldn't go. Bitsy told Horst she had to go check up on Alma, but she didn't have to go anywhere at all. She went upstairs to her room and cried.

It seems to me that Bitsy and Horst were happier before Horst escaped. It seems to me they were more in love when Horst was in the guardhouse. I used to think that I loved Horst, too. I told him, *Eek leeba dick*, and he said, "Eek leeba dick, Toot-zee." But now I'm not sure I love him anymore. When he was in the guardhouse, he looked cute, with his blonde hair hanging down over his eyes, and his nice teeth, and the way he paid attention to Bitsy, and the little figures he carved for her, and the love notes. It was romantic. Now he's got brown shoe polish in his hair. He's getting fat eating ice cream. And when he isn't eating ice cream he chews on the wooden spoons until they are shreds of splinters. He doesn't make carvings anymore.

Bitsy didn't come down to dinner, so I took her plate upstairs. Her eyes were all red from crying. She said, "I'm probably preggers, and all Horst did was look at the other girls." Sometimes, it seems like *doing it* makes everyone miserable.

Sugar's gone again. Buddy says he has no idea how Sugar got out of her cage. This time I can't find her anywhere.

Button:

Budddy asked, "When are you coming back to our room?" I said, *When you're gone.* He said, "Don't you think you're making a mountain out of a molehill?" I said, *Face it, Buddy, this is not your house, and you're not wanted here anymore.* He said, "Speak for yourself, Miss Know-It-All. I don't hear anyone else asking me to leave." I said, *We're finished, Buddy. It's over. Dead. The end. Kaput. The marriage is ended. I'm sick to the death of you. I can't stand the sight of you. The sooner you pack up and go the better.* He said, "Oh, you'll get over it."

I'll not get over it. I can be stubborn as all get out. I can be ten times more stubborn than Buddy. In a way, though, he's right. It's not easy to stop loving someone. I've put up with Buddy for so long that it's almost a habit. I mean, his childish behavior is part of our relationship, something I go on accepting because it's there. When I said, *Till death do us part,* I meant it. It never occurred to me that we wouldn't always be married. I guess Catholics don't think about divorce. It's not something that's an option. It's like Roger said, *You make your bed and you lie in it.* Besides, I loved him. I suppose in some masochistic way I still love him. Once you love someone – I mean, once you set your mind on being with someone forever, it's not easy to get him out of your system.

When I pass through Iggy's room on the way to the sleeping porch, he always has something to say. He'll say, "I could've told you that Vincent was no good." Or, "That Vincent's been trouble since day one." And you know, I find myself being very defensive for Buddy. I'll say, *That's not so, Iggy.* Or, *It's not all Buddy's fault.* I can't believe it, really, that I'm sticking up for Buddy. It's an automatic reflex, I suppose. I must still care for him in some way. Or maybe I just hate to admit that I made a mistake. Iggy said, "That man uses his dick for brains," and I couldn't help but laugh, because that's exactly Buddy's problem, and the thing is, Buddy's really quite intelligent, I mean, he's got a good enough brain in his head when he isn't being lead around by that thing in his pants. If Buddy had Roger's sense of responsibility – well, he'd be sensational. He could do anything he wanted. Instead, he sits around reading the comics. I mean, can you imagine a thirty year-old man laying on the couch reading *Smilin' Jack*, and he says, "Wow, this Cindy has some tits." I mean, it's like something a fourteen year-old boy would say. Buddy could be anything he wanted to be, and what he wants to be is a fourteen year-old boy.

Roger may not be as handsome as Buddy, but at least he's got something more on his mind than some comic-strip girl's "tits." Roger is – well, to tell the truth, I think Roger is – well, I think he believes he's in love with me. I know that's a crazy thing to say, I mean, he hasn't done or said a single thing that would suggest such a thing, but ever since the day at Lake Winnepesaukah he's been acting strange – moony-eyed and sad whenever he's around me, but very sweet, like he wants to wait on me hand and foot, I mean, it's almost embarrassing, and I hope I'm the only one who has noticed. It's not like I led him on. I did go to Lula Lake with him, and we did have a good time, and I do like being with Roger, and – well, maybe I am starved for grown-up male companionship, but I never led him on. Even if I was interested in Roger, which I'm not, well, after all, he is married to my sister, and although they don't get along any better than me and Buddy, she is my sister, and I would never do anything to come between her and Roger. Besides, if Buddy ever gets out of my life, I don't see myself getting tied down again to another man. I'd love to have an apartment of my own, maybe on the beach in California – San Diego, maybe – a little one-room apartment where I could go walking on the beach in the evenings and watch the sunsets, and a job that would pay the rent. The job doesn't have to be anything important. Working at the candy counter in a theater would be OK. I just can't see myself with another man, I mean, I'm worn out worrying about whether Buddy's ego has been stroked enough, and how many times we have done it this month, and – Buddy said to me, "I read somewhere that the average American couple has sex two-point-three times a week," and, I mean how was I supposed to respond to that? He said, "I'm lucky to get point-three."

I just wish to God this war was over. I can't see Buddy getting out of the house until the war is over. MacArthur is in New Guinea, and Roger says the Japs can't last long now, but it seems to me that the war has been going on forever and always will. I'm sick of hardly ever going anywhere in a car, and of rationing, and of not having butter, and most of all I'm sick of Buddy. I said to him, *The newspaper says they need workers in Hawaii – electricians, carpenters, and steamfitters. You could go to Hawaii and learn how to do something useful.* He said, "When the war's over I'll go to Hawaii, all right but I won't be any goddamn steamfitter. I'll get me a hula girl and raise pineapples." *Pineapples!* Buddy couldn't grow beans on a pile of manure. To tell the truth, I don't care if he gets himself two-point-three hula girls and has sex with each of them two-point-three times a week in a pineapple patch – or ten times a week, for all I care. Just as long as he goes away.

Meanwhile, not only do I have to deal with Buddy, I have Roger to contend with. I was doing the dishes tonight and he came in and said, "Can I dry!' I said, *Suit yourself.* Then I thought that perhaps I sounded a bit standoffish, so I said, *Thanks.* We stood there in silence doing the dishes, me washing and him drying, and I could feel this incredible tension, like his eyes were burning holes in the back of my head, and – well, I know what it is, he thinks he's in love with me, and, like that's all I need, Roger thinking he's in love with me – and he was making me so nervous that I dropped one of Mother's best plates onto the sink and it shattered. He said, "A penny for your thoughts," and I said, *Oh, for God's sake, Roger. Go build a bomb.*

Roger:

There's all kind of rumors about what's going on at Oak Ridge. The guys who've been there say the secrecy is incredible. Nobody knows anything about anything except their own little piece of the job. One thing's sure – they've built a plant that's the size of all the buildings at the Volunteer Ordnance Works *put together*, and nobody knows what it's for. The equipment is like nothing anyone has seen or heard of – miles and miles of pipe and hundreds of steel cylinders. Apparently, huge amounts of TVA power go into the place, and lots of unspecified raw materials, but nothing comes out the other end. One rumor has it that the plant has something to do with uranium, which is radioactive, so I figure maybe it's some kind of poison gas they are producing, or maybe canisters of pellets that will make water supplies radioactive.

I've got my own little secret weapon in the basement, made all by myself. "Roger Goody's Special Mix," I call it. My private recipe for TNT with a built-in catalyst. I've mixed enough of the stuff to make a good-sized test bomb. It's safe and easy to handle. The consistency of bread dough. I've tested milligram quantities in my tank, but to do a final evaluation I'll need a real test range and appropriate instrumentation. That means taking my little loaf of "bread dough" to the plant and letting Mel Kelsen in on the secret. It's hard to know what his reaction will be. Of course, he'll be pleased with my invention, and take credit for it in his reports. He'll be pissed that I lied to him about my private experiments. I'll get the usual lecture on "regulations," and the usual malarkey about "insubordination."

I guess my real problem is, I no longer believe in the war. I know we didn't start the war, and that aggression must be resisted. But I can't read a newspaper anymore without feeling sick. The scale of killing is staggering. Indiscriminate. On those islands out in the Pacific they are using flame-throwers to root Japs out of their entrenchments. Can you imagine what it's like to be toasted in a hole by napalm? And robot bombs are falling on London out of nowhere, with no warning, completely untargeted – they might fall on a hospital or a school as easily as a factory. Newspapers have a way of tidying up the mess of war, of presenting the war news like it was a sports event, disguising the terrible suffering. Whenever the radio announces some Allied victory, Buddy shouts his stupid Jap war cry – *Iki, waki, konki, shookekki*, or whatever it is – like he was in a football stadium and the Tennessee Vols had just made a touchdown and everybody laughs. Propaganda. It's all propaganda. Of course, it has to be propaganda. If people knew what was really going on, they wouldn't have the stomach for it.

Button's the only one around here who doesn't have war fever. She sat by the radio tonight and listened to "Date With Judy," "Fibber McGee and Molly," and "Burns and Allen" for an hour-and-a-half without budging, and when the news came on she scooted to the kitchen. As usual, the supper dishes were sitting there in a heap, so she took it upon herself to do them. I helped. I don't know which is worse – being with Button, or being away from her. She's on my mind all the time. I know she's moved out of Buddy's bed, but I don't know for how long. In any case, she hasn't shown any particular interest in me – except for the time she gave my hand a squeeze at the Miss Chattanooga pageant. I think she enjoys my company, but when I asked her what she was thinking, she gave me the brush-off. "For God's sake, Roger, go build a bomb," she said, but she didn't say it angrily. I think she just wanted to be left alone.

I wanted to tell her about the P.O.W., ask her advice, see what she would do, but I didn't dare do it. There's no point involving her. It's something I will have to work out on my own. But I would like to know what she thinks. Button's a sensible person. If anyone knows what I should do about the German P.O.W., it would be Button.

I can't say exactly what it was that made me look into the playhouse. I heard a noise as I was getting out of the car. I guess I assumed it was Tootsie, and I thought I'd give her a surprise. I climbed the ladder, and – boy, did I get a shock. There was this young man, without a stitch of clothes except for his underpants, and Bitsy is sitting next to him in the uniform she wears at the dry cleaners, and Tootsie is there too. Of course, I didn't know what to think. It never occurred to me that the boy might be the escaped P.O.W. For one thing, he didn't have blond hair or a mustache. I figured he was a boyfriend of Bitsy's, but I couldn't figure out what Tootsie was doing there. I mumbled, *Tootsie, maybe you'd better come with me*, because it didn't seem to be the sort of situation that was appropriate for someone Tootsie's age.

It was Tootsie who told me what's going on. The problem is, what should I do about it? I went again to the playhouse and told Bitsy that I hadn't decided what to do, that I would think about it overnight and tell her in the morning. I promised I would tell her – and her friend too – before I went to the police. Of course, the best thing would be for the boy to leave, either turn himself in or take his chances. That way, no one else would get in trouble. But Tootsie says Bitsy and the German boy are in love, and they want to be together, and the war will be over soon and then everything will be OK. I'd say, she's probably right about the war with Germany being over soon. Paris will fall any day. The Germans can't last long after that. The Allied bombing of the Reich is relentless. I can't imagine that a civilian population can endure that kind of pummeling for long. The attempt on Hitler's life a few weeks ago means the generals are fed up too. I wouldn't be surprised if when Paris falls, the whole Nazi house of cards collapses with it.

But the problem is not just the P.O.W. Nor is Tootsie the problem – she's too young to be considered culpable. The problem is Bitsy. She's going to be in a heap of trouble no matter what happens. The fact that she's only nineteen, and presumably acted under the boy's influence, will go in her favor, but with all the hysteria this town has been experiencing lately, there's no telling what might happen. There's the Billy Joe Alaska thing, which has everyone upset – both the negroes and the whites. The police are still digging in Billy Joe's backyard, and God knows what else they'll find. There's rumors of a negro riot and talk of a march by the negroes to Billy Joe's house, something organized by the negro pastors, which the police have forbidden. There's been crosses burned. And well, there's this business of a supposedly dangerous P.O.W. on the loose. My God, you'd think it was Hitler himself who was running around, or a battalion of trained saboteurs. Every day there's a different story in the newspapers. Somebody saw him in Brainerd. Somebody saw him in the woods near Chickamauga Dam with sticks of dynamite stol'n from a construction site in North Chattanooga. This rumor and that rumor – no end to the rumors. And all the while, he's not five minutes away from where he escaped.

The German boy seems nice enough. A little bewildered, perhaps, but he seems to have made himself at home in Chattanooga. Tootsie says that she and Bitsy have taken the boy – Horst, his name is – downtown a couple of times, and no one is the least suspicious. Believe it or not, they took him to see "The White Cliffs of Dover" at the Tivoli. It's funny when you think about it – everybody running around like chickens with their heads cut off looking for the German, and he's sitting in the Tivoli theater watching Irene Dunne. I can't believe the boy is a threat to anyone. Maybe Tootsie is right. Maybe I ought to just leave them be. God knows the war has caused enough misery – for Americans and Germans. I've spent two years contributing my own fat share to the misery. If Bitsy and her boyfriend can find a modest amount of happiness in a world gone nuts, then maybe I should let them take it.

Buddy:

Women are cold fish. They spend every minute of their lives dolling themselves up, making themselves attractive to men, but when it comes right down to it, they aren't all that interested in sex. Just look at all the stuff in the bathroom of this house. Stockings. Hairnets. Mum deodorant. ODO-RO-NO. Leg make-up. Curlers. Tweezers. Toenail polish. Twenty kinds of soap. Fifty kinds of shampoo. Jeez Louise, a guy can hardly get to the can to take a crap. Cockteasers, that's what they are. Paper dolls. All smoke and no fire.

Of course, it's white women I'm talking about. I wouldn't include Tometta. That girl doesn't give a hoot what she looks like. She only owns two dresses, as far as I can tell. Doesn't wear cosmetics. No Permalift brassiers, no "lastex" girdles – none of that stuff. Just plain old Tometta in a sweat-soaked flour-sack dress, and let me tell you, you've never seen anything prettier in your life. Naturally pretty. That girl's comfortable just being a woman. I could watch her working in the kitchen till the cows come home. I'll tell you this – she's something to behold.

And that William fellow – he's gone now, back to active duty. Good riddance, I'd say. That man is old enough to be her father.

Sometimes I think about what it must of been like back in the old days, before the Civil War, when the master of the house could have his way with a girl like Tometta. Don't get me wrong, I'm not saying that slavery is right, or that we should go back to the old days, or anything like that. But some things were better then. For one thing, a colored girl like Tometta wouldn't be so uppity.

I tried to make it up to her. I didn't know that story of hers was so all-fired important. I said, *Tometta, I'm sorry about that story of yours. Button left it laying around like it was some old notebook waiting to be thrown out.* She said, "It weren't nothin' impo'tant." I said, *Now that William's gone, maybe you and I can be a little friendlier. Get off to a new start, so to speak.* She said, "Mister Cioffi, I'd say we'd get on best if you jest stayed outta the kitchen." That seemed a bit uppity to me, so I said, *You know, Tometta, Mamie says that maybe it's time to ask Eva to move out of the shack, get someone younger and in better health in there to do our cooking and ironing.* It was a lie, of course, Mamie had said no such thing. I just thought I would tease her a bit. Her jaw dropped a mile. She said, "Nana done live in that house all her life. She got nowheres else to go." I said, *Maybe I could talk to Mamie. Maybe if you and I were friendlier, then I'd have a little chat with Mamie. Mamie listens to me, you know.* She said, "Missus Buffon would nevah throw Nana out." I said, *Well, I don't know. Maybe if you'd just open the top of that dress and let me have a peek at your titties, I'd see what I can do.* Well, let me tell you, that girl's got a feisty spirit. Cool as tapwater, she walked over to the stove and picked up a hot flatiron and held it right up to my nose. She said, "Buddy Cioffi, I'd say unless you want your face ironed flatter'n a pancake, you'd best get on outta this kitchen."

I was just teasing. It was a joke. I wasn't actually serious. If I'd said something like that to Becca, or even Lynette, they'd of laughed. They'd of known I was only kidding. That's what I mean by uppity. And imagine Tometta calling me me my first name. That's what I mean when I say the niggers are getting too high and mighty.

Now they're planning a "protest assembly" at Billy Joe's house. I figure they'll come marching up Ninth Street past our house, then turn up Central Avenue to Billy Joe's. It's the "Reverends" and the so-called negro "community leaders" that are planning the assembly. They say it's going to be "peaceful." I'd as soon expect snowflakes in July as expect a colored "protest assembly" to be peaceful. Just ask the folks up in Boston or Detroit how peaceful things have been. The Chattanooga police have obtained a court order banning the assembly, but the negroes say they'll go to Billy Joes's anyway. They say the police paid no attention to reports of missing black kids, and it wasn't until Teddy Carr was kidnapped that the police investigated anything. They say that when Teddy Carr went missing, the police automatically assumed a colored person did it. Well, Jeez Louise, whatdaya expect? The laws of probability say that if you're going to investigate a murder, the place to start is in the negro district. I'm not saying that white people don't commit murders – it's hard to imagine a more horrible crime than what Billy Joe did to Teddy Carr – but it's not worth putting the whole city at risk by staging some "protest assembly" that can lead to nothing but trouble. I'll tell you this, I'm keeping my thirty-eight clean as a whistle.

When those so-called "peaceful protesters" come up Ninth Street I'll be sitting on the front porch as friendly as can be – but I'll have the thirty-eight in my pocket. If one of those niggers so much as sets foot on the sidewalk, I'll take a pot-shot over his head. Anybody that tries to come up the front steps is a dead duck.

Meanwhile, I've got Alma to worry about. The hospital said there's nothing physically or psychiatrically wrong with her, she's just "overwought." She's overwrought, all right – always was. Alma's a classic case of how women and religion don't mix. It's something hormonal. What I'm worried about is that Alma might tell Mamie or Button about me and Wanda. Mamie would have my ass. She'd blame me for Alma going nuts, instead of those priests and nuns who filled her head with nonsense. Button would say, I told you so. Either way, I'd be out on the street. Oh, I'm gonna leave, all right – I've got places to go and things to do – but in my own sweet time. There's no point in giving Button the satisfaction of catching me in the wrong. She's too damn self-righteous, anyways. Always on her high horse, looking down her nose at everyone else.

Not that I admit I was in the wrong. It wasn't me that initiated that little fiasco in Alma's bed. If Wanda had the hots for me, it's not my fault. And, to tell the truth, Button hasn't got cause to complain if I fool around with another woman. It wasn't me, after all, who moved out onto the sleeping porch. Button is determined to humiliate me, to make it look like I'm the one who's been dumped. Wanda says to me today, "Well, Buddy, I see you have the bed all to yourself." I said, *If it wasn't for the cast on my leg, I'd of been out of here a long time ago.* She said, "The only thing you need a cast for is your dick."

Well, let me tell you, that's something for Wanda to worry about, not me. Instead of reminding me that I didn't get it up, she should ask herself why she didn't turn me on. I don't seem to have that problem with anyone else. Just watching Tometta shuck peas gives me a boner. Dancing with Becca last night I had a stiffy to beat the band – this big embarrassing bulge in my slacks. Becca says, "Buddy, if you can't keep that thing of yours under control, we'll just have to stop dancing." That's what I mean about Tometta. With Becca, you can joke about sex, have a little fun, not take everything so seriously. I tease Tometta a little bit and she's ready to flatten my face with an iron. She'd do it, too. You've got to admire her for that, you've got to admire Tometta for being so feisty. Just like you've got to admire Becca for being able to take a joke.

Becca says the girls at Peerless Woolen Mills have heard rumors about the escaped P.O.W. – that he's raping women. She says – according to the rumors – that at least a dozen women in East Chattanooga, East Lake and Rossville have been raped, and all the women report the same blond assailant, with a blond mustache and gray trousers. Becca says the police are keeping it out of the papers because they are afraid of panicking the population. Well, that sounds like crap to me. The population of this city is panicked enough, already. If that Nazi son-of-a-bitch is raping women, then women should be told about it so they can take proper precautions. It's unbelievable that a guy like that can be on the loose for so long, and no one's laid a hand on him. He must surely stand out like a sore thumb. The police are a bunch of nincompoops, pure and simple, that's what I say. Becca wants to carry my revolver in her purse, but there's no way I'm going to let that gun out of my sight. I told her I'd be glad to accompany her anywhere she wants to go. Her friends too, for that matter. The girls have a softball game in Rossville this evening, and I told her I'd come along. No heinie sex-maniac is going to mess with Becca and her friends while I'm around.

Button:

Tometta is sad now that William's gone away. I said, *I know you miss William, Tometta, but he'll be back soon. This war can't last forever.* She said, "William won't be comin' back." I said, *What do you mean, he won't be comin' back?* She said, "Eva had a dream that William was killed when his boat was torpedoed in the Alantic Ocean." I said, *That doesn't mean it will happen, Tometta. It was just a dream.* She said, "Missus Cioffi, Nana ain't nevah knew that William was goin' to Europe in a boat, exceptin' in her dream. But I know that William is goin' 'cross the Atlantic Ocean, cause that's what he tol' me." I said, *That's just plain superstitious. Eva must have heard William mention shipping out to Europe, or maybe you just forgot that you mentioned it. There's certainly a rational explanation. Don't you worry your self for a minute. William's going to be OK.*

It didn't matter what I said to Tometta, because she is convinced that William is not coming back. And, you know, the funny thing is – I have a feeling that she's probably right. I mean, I'm not superstitious, but I have this funny feeling that Tometta knows what she's talking about. So many soldiers are being killed that William will be lucky to come home alive. A negro soldier probably has less chance than most. What surprises me is – Tometta is resigned to it happening, almost like it's fated and there's no sense being upset about it. She loves William – you can see it in their faces when they are swinging in the glider, with Eva between them, each of them holding one of Eva's hands, just swinging and holding Eva's hands – you can see the love light burning in their eyes. I know they were planning on getting married when William gets out of the service. He's is a lot older than Tometta – he must be thirty-five, twice as old as Tometta – but he's as nice as can be – and he always has a happy smile.

Tometta asked me if Mother wanted Eva to move out of the shack. I said, *Where'd such a silly idea ever come into your head?* She said, "I jest thunk, with Nana bein' so sick an' all." I said, *Eva can live there as long as she wants. Why, my lands, Tometta, Eva's been living there as long as I can remember. Why would you even think such a thing.* She said, "It jest come into my head."

I have an idea how it came into her head. It was probably something Buddy said. Buddy is always hanging around Tometta, causing trouble. You'd think with all his prejudice against colored people, he'd have more pride.

I asked Tometta if she had written any more stories. She said, "No, ma'am." I begged her to try again. I suggested that she write about William, and about the war – and Eva's dream. I could tell she was thinking about it, but she didn't say she would do it. I think it's important that Tometta finish high school, and if at all possible go to college. I found the names of all the places where a colored girl could go to college – in the South, I mean, because Tometta would never go to school up North. I told her about Tuskegee, and Macon, and Tugaloo. I told her she'd be sure and get a scholarship, her being so smart and all. I can tell she's thinking about it, but she doesn't say a word, except things like, "Oh, I could never do that." But she *can* do it.

Sometimes I wonder if I'm giving Tometta the attention that would have gone to the child I didn't have – or can't have. Buddy and I tried real hard to have a baby – before he went into the Navy – with no luck, I mean. Every month we made love at the most fertile time, but nothing happened, and since he came back from the Navy we've certainly had sex often enough. I suppose, that one or the other of us isn't able to conceive. I always wanted a child, and I suppose I still want a child, and maybe that's why I've taken such an interest in what happens to Tometta. Heavens knows she's hardly a child, and sometimes I feel like she's older than I am – and certainly the man she wants to marry is older than me – but still, in other ways, she's so innocent, so uncertain, so unaware of the possibilities that are open to her, that I somehow feel responsible for her. She's terribly clever, and she reads all the time – I mean, really serious books – and the story she wrote about going to school was wonderful, and it would be a terrible shame if she ended up doing the cooking and ironing in some white person's house for a dollar a day. That's why I try so hard to encourage her to write stories and go to school.

I suppose there's no point in raising her hopes if she is doomed to disappointment. Maybe I just don't want Tometta to get trapped like I did. I really don't know what I could have done with my life, I mean, I never had any particular dreams or ambitions – serious ambitions, I mean, as opposed to silly daydreams, the kinds of daydreams that little girls have about knights on horseback and romance and all that – and when Buddy came along I guess I was ready to fall in love and get married, but it was a dead end, for Buddy and for me, and here I am thirty years old and I'm still living in the house I was born in, and sometimes it seems like I'll die here too, doing the same old things day after day. In the last couple of years, Buddy has never taken me out *even once*, I mean, just the two of us, like to a movie or out to dinner, or even for a walk to the drug store for a cherry coke or a soda. To tell the truth, that's probably why I enjoyed so much the trip with Roger to Lula Lake, I mean, if just once or twice Buddy had asked me to do something like that, then maybe things wouldn't have come to such an awful pass.

Now that I've left Buddy, I suppose I could go with Roger again, you know, to Lula Lake or wherever – if he asked. Of course, there's still Wanda, but sooner or later I've got to stop thinking of Wanda, I mean, when did she ever think of me? And – to tell the truth – there's *Roger*. Do I really want Roger following after me like a lovesick pup? I know it sounds like maybe I'm imagining it – I mean, about Roger being in love with me – but I'm sure I'm not, and in a way I suppose I'm pleased to have a man paying attention to me in some way other than badgering me about sex, but still – really, I don't know what men want. Maybe it's because I grew up with nothing but sisters, and I hardly even knew my father – I mean, I was only eleven when he died – but sometimes I feel like men belong to another species altogether, or like they are creatures from another planet – I don't have the foggiest idea what makes them tick. I swear to God, if I thought Buddy was a typical man, I would go off and become a nun. And Roger – in some ways he's the opposite of Buddy, I mean, he's almost invisible, he tinkers in the basement or he looks for birds. He was telling me the other day about watching – what was it? – a loghead shrike or something like that – he called it a butcher bird – impaling a frog on a barbed-wire fence, like – you know, like it was the most exciting thing he had ever seen, and I pretended to be interested, but – well, I guess if you didn't see it it just wasn't all that interesting, but, my God, you'd think he'd seen the Beatific Vision, and all the time he's got that soppy "I'm in love" look on his face. I just don't know what men want.

I know what I want. I want peace. I'd like twenty-four hours when I didn't have to worry about anyone but myself. Not about Tometta. Not about Alma. Not about Mother or Iggy or Eva. Especially not about Buddy. And – not about Roger, either.

Just twenty-four hours of peace. Peace and quiet.

Tometta:

There he stood on the porch, jest as I pictured in my mind a thousand times since Nana tol' me of her dream 'bout William, a soldier with his cap in one han' and a big envelope in the other, askin' "Missus Jackson?" Dread done swept ovah me soon as Tootsie come in the kitchen sayin', "Tometta, there's a soldier at the door asking for a Mrs. Jackson. I told him there was no Mrs. Jackson here, but then he said 'a Mrs. Tometta Jackson', so I figure he must mean you." Well, lucky Alma gone with me to the door, 'cause soon as I lay eyes on that poor soldier, my legs give way, an' Alma had to put 'er arm round me to keep me up. He says, "Missus Jackson?" an' he musta seen in my face what I was expectin', cause he quickly says, "Ohh, oh, no, no, no, it ain't that, no, Willie be fine! He jus' ask me to bring you this here package." Well, I burst into tears an' throw my arms around Alma, an' then I cried *Thank ya*, an' threw my arms round the soldier. Poor Tootsie be peerin' outta da house, prob'ly thinkin' she never saw no one so happy to get a package before.

Turns out the soldier knowed William from his ole job, an' jest happen to cross paths with him in England as he was headin' home on special leave. William ask him if he'd bring the package by on account it was *too special* fer the army mail. He tol' me William be doin' jest fine an' is prob'ly in France by now. I tried to get him to come round back fer a lemonade, but he say he gots to be runnin' along, which be jest as well, cause that package be burnin' in my hands to be opened.

I run on back to the kitchen, an' sit down at the table. Alma says, "Open it. Go on, open it." Well, I tear it on open, an' there's a letter an' somethin' wrapped in a white hanky. Inside the hanky is a fancy li'l box, an' I open it on up to find a gold weddin' band inside. By this time, Tootsie is back in the kitchen with Button in tow, an' Alma is sayin', "You've a lot of explaining to do *Mrs. Jackson*."

Settin' in church the next mornin', I's jest starin' at that ring on my finger an' feelin' like the whole world been took off my shoulders. Fer the first time I feel like William be comin' home safe an' sound, an' we gonna have a great life togetha. An' I feel much better havin' tol' Button, Alma an' Tootsie 'bout my weddin'. Button look a bit hurt, but she seem to be real happy fer me.

Well, I got brought back to earth right quick, on account of the church bein' up in arms ovah the murders of them boys. All the negro preachers in town be organizin' a prayer march up to the murderer's house to pray for the boys that got killed. Reveren' Washington be tellin' ever'one when and where to meet, when that hothead Clement Wilson stands up an' shouts out about us havin' to start protectin' our own. Reveren' Washington roared, "Hate begets hate, we must fight hate with kindness, ignorance with truth, and fear with strength. We will be heard. We will be heard as the strong peaceful people we are, as a people who deserve respect, and as a people who demand respect. Anyone who feels any different, best stay home."

You hear about all them riots goin' on in other parts of the country, an' it makes me a might nervous about this march. You ought hear Mr. Cioffi an' them girls go on 'bout the march. They think we's gonna burn the city of Chattanooga to the ground. Mista Cioffi says to Miss Becca, "A single nigger come within an inch of this house, I'll blow his fool head off." An' Miss Becca jest laugh an' says, "Oooh Buddy, we sure are lucky to have you to protect us." I dunno if'n she be makin' fun, or she be as daft as him. An' you think they care that I be in the kitchen, next room away? I made my mind right then I'd be joinin' that march. I ask Nana what she thought of me marchin'. She says, "Honey, the good Lawd will deliver us when he see fit, but I don't s'pose it hurt to remind him we's waitin' now an' ag'in."

Iggy:

Christ a' mighty, when the *po*lice came crashin' inta my room, I knew all hell had broke loose. I'll be damned if there wasn't half-a-dozen officers in my room with pistols pointin' right between my eyes. I was so scared I shit my pants. Poor Button, she got the worst of it – she'd been on the sleepin' porch watchin' the march, so she knew well the shots had come from my room, and she was in there quicker'n a flash – I was tryin' to stuff the rifle under the mattress an' she says, "What in God's name are you doing Iggy, give me that." No sooner did she yank it from my hands, the *po*lice come chargin' in, Button holdin' the gun like Ma Barker, they threw her up 'gainst the wall, an' frisked her up and down, an' made 'er lie on the floor. Hell's bells, all I could think of was Button cryin' on the floor an' me messin' my bed.

The way they stormed in there, you'd a thought she *was* Ma Barker.

Mind you, I wasn't denyin' I shot that rifle. The whole room smelled of powder, an' I sho' wasn't gonna let Button take the blame. They bundled me up an' took me downtown in the paddy wagon. Took Button, too, with Vincent on his crutches, shoutin', "Wait, she's my wife, take me too." They didn't take him. When we got downtown, it was Roger an' Mamie that was there. Roger'd brought Mamie to the station-house in his car. It was Roger that convinced the *po*lice to let Button go.

I can't exactly say as to why I fired off those shots. I reckon the excitement got the best of me. It was hard to tell what was goin' on up there on the hill with the nigras and the cops, an' I guess I figured the best way to keep the coloreds from causin' trouble was to scare 'em off. From my window, you could see the *po*lice lined up across the street, Lawdy, there musta been fifty of 'em, with shotguns an' billy clubs. There musta been twenty times as many nigras that came marchin' up to face 'em. The colored folks was singing some kind of church music, an' they was marchin' arm-in-arm, an' they come right up to where the cops was standin' three deep like a brick wall, they came right up nose-to-nose to the line of *po*licemen an' stood there singin'.

Well, it seem to me the situation was gettin' dangerous, so I figure a warnin' shot or two would scare 'em off an' give the *po*lice a helpin' han', so to speak. I took aim ovah their heads – figured a bullet whizzin' through the air would put the fear of God into 'em – an' mind you, I allowed for the fall of the bullet, cause a twenty-two don't have all that much power, jus' like I did with that goddamn red-headed woodpecker, an' I hit that woodpecker square between the eyes, that's sho, but this time somethin' went wrong, cause the bullet fell too soon an' – as now they tell me – hit a *po*liceman in the butt.

That's whan all hell broke loose. Next thing ya know, the *po*lice are lookin' in this direction, an' there's me settin' in the window gettin' off a second shot, an' this time they could see clear as day where the shot is comin' from, 'cause there must of been a dozen *po*licemen swarmin' toward the house already. Up there on the hill there was pushin' an' shovin' an' all manner of confusion, an' the *po*lice was so distracted that they started to fall back, an' they were carryin' the fellow that I'd shot in the ass, an' the next thing you know, the nigras was movin' ag'in, on down Ninth Street toward Central Avenue an' Billy Joe's house, an' the cops are strung out all ovah the place, an' nobody knows what to do, 'cause suddenly all the attention's on me.

Mind you, it was never my intention to hurt no one, jus' to scare 'em off. Got carried away with the excitement. Anyways, when I saw all the *po*licemen swarmin' toward the house, I jumped into bed an' was stuffin' the rifle under the mattress. That's when Button comes bustin' into the room, an' the next thing I know, the door slams open an' I crap in my pants.

There's Button with the rifle, an' there's my little brass soldiers lined up on the bedside table – eleven of 'em now – two expended shells on the floor, an' it's obvious as hell that I's in big trouble. Button's lyin' on the floor with her hands behind her head, an' some fat, red-faced cop has a shotgun pointed smack at her neck, an' she's sayin', "For God's sake, don't hurt him, he's just a crazy old man," an' one of the cops says, "Christ, it smells like shit in here."

Meanwhile, accordin' to what I hear, poor Vincent had to wobble outta the way when the *po*lice came streamin' up onto the porch, an' he was shoutin', "It wasn't me, it wasn't me," an' him bein' on crutches they don't pay him any attention at all, they just storm into the house, an' head upstairs. By the time they bundle me an' Button downstairs – handcuffed, an' all – the nigras was steamin' past the house singin' away to beat the band, an' the cops done decide it was better to let 'em go than to try an' stop 'em, an' Vincent's shoutin', "My wife had nothing to do with it," an' you can see he's confused, cause he thought he was the only one with a gun, an' I can see as clear as day that he has his thirty-eight in the pocket of his slacks, but the cops don't take any notice at all, 'cause they're too busy eyeballin' Becca an' Lynette who're standin' there next to Buddy in their purdy sunsuits.

Anyways, I don't see what the big fuss is all about. I figure as a lot less people got hurt 'cause of me shootin' than would've got hurt if the cops an' the nigras had squared off there at the top of the hill. That fellow what got shot in the ass is OK, jus' a flesh wound. Button's OK. Vincent's feelin's were hurt that he wasn't the center of attention, but he's OK too. The only one who didn't come outta all this OK is me, cause they done put me inta the psychiatric hospital fer "observation." Button says to 'em, "He's absolutely harmless, if he hadn't have gotten a hold of that rifle he'd be as harmless as a fly." The rifle's the problem. Seems as how they traced it to Billy Joe, an' ever'body knows that Billy Joe is crazy as a loon an' dangerous to boot, so they figure I'm the same. But I'm no Billy Joe, that's fer sho'. I'm no monster. Button's right – I'd never hurt a fly. Jus' got excited is all. Sometimes it seems I've been cooped up in a room all my life, a ole bachelor cooped up in a room, an' when all that excitement start out there on the hill – well, I got carried away. Didn't mean to hurt nobody, I jus' got carried away by the excitement.

Jus' waitin' now. Jus' waitin' to die. It seems as how I've always been waitin' to die, least ways ever since I went to Cuba. That's no way to live a life, but I can't exactly say as where I went wrong. All by myself now. Locked up in this here hospital with a bunch of nut cases. The doctors say I'm not sane nuff to be let go – that I'm likely "to do harm to myself or others." What do they know? What do they know about livin' alone? What do they know about livin' a life all by oneself? I never asked fer much. Never asked fer much at all. Jus' a little bit of love. Jus' a little bit of a feelin' that someone cares.

I miss 'em. I miss that house full of crazy women. Never realized how much I'd miss 'em till they was gone.

Roger:

This family has become notorious. First, Buddy had his picture in the paper when he almost drowned at Warner Park. Now, we've hit the front page. A big photograph of Iggy and Button being led down the front steps by the police, with the rest of us standing in the background looking totally bewildered. *LOCAL MAN FIRES ON NEGRO RIOTERS, POLICEMAN WOUNDED.* If it weren't for the liberation of Paris, Iggy's private war on the Chattanooga police department would have been the top story of the day.

I have to admit, the Times was generous with Iggy. They noted his age. They called him "distraught" and "confused." They didn't suggest malice of intent. He is an old man, they implied, who is losing his marbles. Rather, they blamed the incident on the negroes, for stirring up emotions, and on the police for allowing the crowd to proceed so close to a white neighborhood. "An incident like this was bound to happen," said the editorial. The News-Free Press took a somewhat different tack. Their story made much of the Billy Joe connection, suggesting a rat's nest of intrigue and conspiracy. They blamed the shooting on lax police work. According to them, the police should have somehow traced Billy Joe's rifle to Iggy before the incident was allowed to happen.

Everyone, it seems, is assigning blame. Button blames herself, for not knowing that Iggy had a gun. Buddy blames Button, for not being in her own room "where she belonged," although what that has to do with the shooting is beyond me. Wanda blames the entire family. She calls us a "pack of lunatics." She said, "If it hadn't been Iggy, it would have been Buddy, with his pathetic little pop-gun." She swears the episode is humiliating, and that she'll never go out in public again, although come to think of it, she hardly ever goes out now. Alma thinks what happened is divine retribution for transgressions which she refuses to specify, although she glowers menacingly at Wanda and Buddy. Only Emily Sue blames no one – she seems to have enjoyed the excitement. Mamie refuses to admit that the incident happened at all.

I don't think the police quite know what to do with poor Iggy. Clearly, they can't put him into jail, he's much too frail for that. Apparently, they have decided he's too much of a menace to simply let go. They have charged him with "incitement to riot," "public disorder," "mayhem" – whatever that is – and "assault with a deadly weapon." If he were convicted of all these crimes he would probably qualify for a hundred years in the Tennessee State Penitentiary. As it is, they have dumped him into the county hospital for observation – the nut house, really. Button is infuriated. She knows that Iggy is not crazy – not *really* crazy – and can't imagine why they put him in the county hospital with all those basket cases. Myself, I'm not so sure. I'm inclined to believe that Iggy might feel right at home.

Mostly what I think about now is that German kid out in the garage with the shoe polish in his hair. If this family has become notorious for shooting a policeman in the tail, and for the bizarre connection between Iggy and Billy Joe Alaska, can you imagine the furor if the newspapers discover we have been sheltering the escaped P.O.W., and worse, that the baby of the family is sharing a love nest with Chattanooga's most-wanted villain? This morning, I told Bitsy in no uncertain terms that she must insist that Horst leave the premises. She whined, "Where can he go?" I said, *It doesn't matter, as long as he's out of here.* She said, "They'll shoot him." I said, *No one is going to shoot Horst. They'll stick him in the P.O.W. stockade at Fort Oglethorpe, that's what they'll do. At the very most, they'll take him off that cushy maintenance detail at the cemetery.* I told her I would check the garage this evening, and if Horst was still there, I would throw him out myself.

I've never seen anyone so pitifully confused as Bitsy. She seems desperately to want Horst to stay, and equally desperately she wants him to go. For the life of me, I don't understand what's going on. Does she love him, or what? Tootsie says Bitsy is "madly in love" with the German boy, but when I said I would throw him out I'm sure I detected a glimmer of assent in her eyes. I'm convinced that deep in her heart she wants me to do it. Bitsy doesn't look well. She is thinner than ever, she has black circles under her eyes, and – well, she acts even more scatterbrained than usual. I had thought that Bitsy and Horst contributed a bit of badly needed romance to this unhinged house, but their goofy relationship seems as much off the track as everyone else's. Maybe there's a Buffon gene that keeps the women in this family from finding happiness in love. I suppose it is still too soon to say what will happen to Becca and Lynette, but if their older and younger sisters are any guide, they will fall in love with totally unsuitable men and be miserable forever after.

When I got to work this morning, my colleagues were waiting to rag me – because of the story on the front page of the paper – and to make matters worse, I was half-an-hour late because of my talk with Bitsy. Mel Kelsen started in with his usual lecture, *blah-blah-blah*, an interminable litany of my presumed faults, but this time with an extra air of superciliousness, as if to say, "Well, Roger, you certainly do manage to find yourself in bizarre situations." I simply tuned him out, and went to the lab and started messing around with some new hexamine compounds. At ten-fifteen we were ordered to a screening of new low-level reconnaissance footage from the Pacific showing up-to-date results of our Super-Fort raids on Saipan. A young Air Force reconnaissance expert was at the screen with a pointer, drawing our attention to appalling examples of destruction, with a smug air of satisfaction. I raised my hand and asked, *What would you say were the casualty figures for that last sequence?* He said, matter-of-factly, "Oh, I'd say in that particular residential neighborhood the casualties must have been close to one-hundred percent." I said, *That's astonishingly successful.* He said, "Well, you guys can take a lot of the credit."

I got up and walked out. Just got up and left the room, and they all watched me go. I went to my car, picked up my binoculars, and walked off through the meadows towards the testing range. I saw a timber redbird, and a towhee, and the usual mess of warblers, sparrows, and thrushes. But the most pleasant surprise was to find a catbird nest, fallen onto the ground from a tree – an old, disused nest, almost certainly dating from the time when the government took over that land for the TNT plant. Catbirds are resourceful scavengers, and clues to the nest's age were there in the materials of the nest's construction: a bit of twine, chicken quills, goose down, a scrap of newspaper, a paper doll's dress, a length of partly crocheted wool – the sort of things that would be found on a farm, or a place that was recently a farm, but also stitching thread from nitrate bags, brightly-colored rubber insulation stripped from electrical wires, matted asbestos – the detritus of bombmaking. At one time, the nest undoubtedly contained three or four blue-green catbird eggs, sat upon by a contented catbird momma. It would be no small thing, I thought, to have a place in the country with catbirds nesting by the door, and to hear their crazy catbird music day in and day out. A catbird sings the way it builds its nest – some notes of its own, some notes borrowed from whippoorwills, tanagers, cardinals, or jays – a crazy, inexhaustible repertoire of original and imitative song. It would be no small thing, I thought, to have catbirds nesting near the door, to listen all day long to their borrowed music, and be the willing victim of catbird thievery.

When I returned to the plant, Kelsen was livid. "You're courting dismissal," he fumed. *No need*, I said. *I only returned to clean out my desk.* Well, you should have seen his jaw drop. "You're draft bait, Goody," he said. His nostrils flared and his cheeks flushed. I said, *I'll take my chances.* He followed me right out to the car, railing all the while. As I was backing the car out of my parking spot, he was still shouting, "No more C sticker for your car, Goody. No more C sticker for your car."

And no more bombs. I'll not build another bomb. The war's near enough to over anyway. Let someone else finish the killing. I'll not tell Kelsen about "Roger Goody's Special Mix," and I won't test the stuff I have. I'll figure out some way to render it non-explosive. Let someone else finish the killing. I've had my fill of trinitrotoluene – TNT – in all of its forms and disguises.

Buddy:

I'll tell you this, I had a better chance against Jap bombs at Pearl Harbor than in the Buffon's house. Or in the Buffon's *ex*-house, I should say. No one's going to live in that burned-out shell any time soon.

It wasn't my fault.

I wasn't the one who brought a Nazi onto our property, and I wasn't the one who left the goddamn explosives laying around. Whatever I did, I was only trying to bring a little respect to the family, to counteract the ridicule that Iggy heaped upon us. That crazy old man made this family the laughingstock of Chattanooga. Imagine – shooting a policeman in the ass with a twenty-two! What could Iggy have been thinking? A twenty-two is a kid's gun. A twenty-two is for shooting squirrels. That crazy old coot sits up in his window with a twenty-two and thinks he's Sergeant York – thinks he's going to take on the entire negro population of Chattanooga – and all he manages to do is shoot a policeman in the ass. It's no wonder the family is a laughingstock. That's why I was trying to restore a little respect by catching the escaped P.O.W. Was it my fault Roger had turned the basement into a goddamn minefield?

OK, I feel kind of badly about the German, now that I know he was Bitsy's friend. But it wasn't my fault. Not everybody would have gone after that guy singlehandedly, not knowing if he was armed or not – and me on crutches. You'd think I'd at *least* be given credit for that. I was only doing what the Chattanooga Police Department and the M.P.s hadn't been able to do in weeks of trying.

The police had been searching the entire county, from Rossville to Dayton, and the German was here all along, not a quarter-mile from where he escaped, under our very noses. Bitsy and Roger knew he was here. Bitsy – for crying out loud, *Bitsy!* – was fucking him. Can you imagine that? Nineteen-year-old Bitsy! That dopey little kid has been sleeping with an escaped P.O.W. in *our garage*. It never occurred to me that Bitsy had the foggiest interest in sex, and it turns out she's the hottest little number in the house – fucking a Nazi in the playhouse. Jeez Louise, how do you figure it? Tometta, who looks easy, won't give me the time of day, and Bitsy, who you'd think didn't know her twat from her ear, is Little Miss Come-And-Get-It. I swear to God, I'll never figure it out if I live to be a hundred. Whoever it was who said women are creatures of their hormones got it right as rain. My *baby sister-in-law* – sleeping with an escaped German prisoner! I'd of been less surprised to find out that Eleanor Roosevelt was shacked up with Tojo. You'd think Bitsy would *at least* be patriotic enough to do it with an American.

I only found out what was going on when Bitsy went bonkers at the dinner table. Apparently, Roger had given her an ultimatum to get the German out of the garage, and when he came home from work he checked to see if the playhouse was empty. It was. At dinner, Roger says to Bitsy, "Well, I see our friend is gone," all cryptic like – *wink-wink*, it's our little secret. And – holey-moley, Bitsy just goes nuts. Out of nowhere, she starts weeping like a wrung rag. "He's in the basement," she wails. Roger says, "Shusssh." Everyone's eyes light up, like *What the hell's going on?* I asked, *Who's in the basement?* Roger says, "For God's sake, Bitsy, get control of yourself." I say, *Who's in the basement?* "Horst," wails Bitsy, "Horst is in the basement." *Who in the hell is Horst?* I ask. Roger jumps up from his seat and tries to calm Bitsy down. She blubbers, "He made my ba-ba-baby." Mamie is sitting there shaking her head, like none of this is happening. *Who the hell is Horst?* I ask again. Now Tootsie pipes up. "Horst is the German prisoner," she says, "that escaped." Bitsy stammers, "I didn't mean to d-d-do it, I didn't mean to d-d-do it." Well, I never saw such a scene. Becca and Lynette are looking from one to the other trying to figure out what's going on. Bitsy is blubbering like a goony, "Ba-ba-ba-ba." Roger says, "Everybody stay calm. I'm going to call the police," and he dashes out of the room.

Well, that's all we needed – more policemen in the house. Christ, this time they would probably send the National Guard. So I figured I'd take care of the situation myself. I said to Becca, *Get the you-know-what*. I'll give this to Becca, she didn't waste any time. She was upstairs and down lickety-split with my sweet little baby wrapped up in its clean white cloth. I was waiting at the backdoor. Button's saying, "Don't be a fool, Buddy. Let Roger handle it." *Let Roger handle it!* That chicken-shit's been in on this all along. The thing is, Button can't bear to admit that I can do anything right.

Maybe Becca should tell her what I can do. Maybe Becca should tell her how I handled those smart-assed niggers on the railroad tracks.

I stuck the thirty-eight into my belt and swung down the outside basement steps on my crutch. Becca and Lynette were leaning over the railing, saying, "Be careful, Buddy." Button was yelling, "Buddy, wait for Roger, wait for Roger," like he was the goddamn Messiah. I don't know where Bitsy was – still at the dinner table bawling her eyes out, for all I know. I opened the basement door and slipped into the furnace room. There wasn't a soul to be seen. I shouted, *Come out with your hands up!* and I could hear Becca and Lynette laughing their heads off. *Achtung!* I shouted, mainly because it was the only German I know.

I squeaked open the door to Roger's workshop. It was pitch black in there, and the light switch was on the other side of the room, at the bottom of the stairs coming down from the kitchen. I'll admit my legs were shaking like plucked tines, even the one in the cast. I could barely balance on my crutch. For all I knew, the German was armed and dangerous. The thirty-eight was cocked and ready in my hand. *Come out with your hands up*, I shouted again. Becca yelled down the outside stairs, "Gangbusters!" Lynette shouts, "Come out with your hands up! It's J. Edgar Hoover." OK, so they're making fun, but it's me who's facing the P.O.W. singlehanded, and, let me tell you, I was scared shitless. I moved into the workshop, letting my eyes adjust to the darkness. *Achtung!* I shouted. *Make a move and I'll shoot.*

That's when Tootsie's canary lands on my head.

I was so goddamn startled by the bird that the gun went off in my hand. As luck would have it, the bullet hit a canister containing a patty-cake of Roger's TNT. *Kablooie!* The explosion was unbelievable. I was blown right out the workshop door into the furnace room, with both my legs shattered at the knees. No crutch, can't move, smoke and flame pouring out of the workshop. Everyone outside is screaming. I swear to God I thought I would die. The German comes stumbling out of the workshop looking like death warmed over, his left arm hanging by a thread, and blood all-the-hell over everything. With his good arm he grabs me by the collar and drags me up the outside stairs, drops me snack in the middle of the badminton court, and keels over on top of me. Bitsy's there, yelling, "Horst! Horst!" Button's yelling, "Buddy! Buddy!" My legs are in excruciating pain. The basement is a ball of flame.

I didn't mean to pull the trigger. When that goddamn Sugar landed in my hair, the gun just went off in my hand. I always said that canary was no good. All it ever did was squeak and shit, and now it's burnt the house down. Well, I should say, it was *the canary and Roger* that burned the house down. If it hadn't been for Roger's crazy experiments nothing would have happened. Irresponsible, that's what I say – leaving explosives around the house. Totally irresponsible. Roger has a lot to answer for, that's what I say.

I'll give him this, though, he did manage to get everyone out of the house. Even Alma, who finally lost whatever marbles were still rolling around in her head. Hysterical, she was. Roger carried her out the back door and plonked her down in the glider next to Mamie and Emily Sue. Alma has her fingers in her ears, I think she thought it was the rapture. Mamie's got her eyes closed, shaking her head, refusing to admit that the house is going up in smoke. Emily Sue is blubbering. Like three monkeys, they are – hear no evil, see no evil, speak no evil. Sirens everywhere. Fire trucks roaring up Ninth Street and down the alley. Policemen thick as flies. Me and the German bleeding all over the badminton court.

O.K., so the kid lost his arm, but he hasn't got much else to complain about. The newspapers made him into a big hero. Can you believe it – that guy is an enemy soldier, and the newspapers make him out as a hero for saving *my* life? As if I needed saving. I would of got out of the basement somehow, although right now I can't imagine exactly how. *A love story*, that's how the papers are playing it. Star-crossed lovers, Bitsy and Horst, like some goddamn Romeo and Juliette. And not just the Chattanooga papers, but nationally. On the radio, too. H. B. Kountenborn. William R. Morrow. Apparently we're close enough to winning this war that people are ready to start feeling sentimental. **"CUPID'S CASUALTIES OF WAR: BOBBYSOXER FALLS FOR P.O.W." "EILEEN AND HORST: ROMANCE TRANSCENDS WAR."** The German's picture is everywhere, even in Life magazine, grinning like a baboon. His hospital room is stuffed with flowers. Women send him loveletters and proposals of marriage. I heard Becca say to Lynette, "Isn't he just too good-looking for words." "A real killeroo," says Lynette.

Damned if I can figure it out. A few days ago, those girls were prepared to believe the German was a rapist, a saboteur, a Nazi monster. Now he's God's gift to women.

That goddamn Horst came out of this thing smelling like a rose. The only real causalities were me and the canary.

Button:

The spell of hot weather has finally broken, and luckily for Buddy. The entire lower half of his body is in traction, casts up both legs to the hips. If the temperature were still in the nineties, Buddy would be absolutely dying of the heat.

I felt badly about Buddy. I wondered if maybe I had been too harsh with him. I thought maybe this accident is just the thing to bring about a change and help us recapture what we used to have. I was willing to give it another try.

I brought him flowers. I put them in a vase on his bedside table at the hospital. He didn't say anything, but his eyes were so pathetic, so alone, so grateful, that I felt my old love for him coming back. I said, *Buddy, I'm willing to give it another try if you are.* He nodded. I said, *I don't know where we went astray. It was good when we first got married.* He nodded again. I said, *When you get out of the hospital, we can get our own place again, our own little apartment, and start over.* He smiled. I said, *Maybe we could adopt a kid.* Big tears welled up in the corners of his eyes. I leaned over and kissed him on the forehead. I held his water glass so he could sip. I wiped his brow with a wet cloth. I said, *I love you, Buddy.*

I can't imagine what I was thinking, I mean, really, I must have been out of my mind. I even reached under the sheet and gave his thing a squeeze, a little love-squeeze, and I winked, and he grinned, and I thought, *well, I'll try harder too*, I mean, I'll try to be more like he wants me to be, and – when he gets out of the hospital – if he wants to have sex ten times a day standing on our heads, well, then you know, I'd try to go along, because I hated to see our marriage break up, and seeing Buddy laid up there so helpless, unable to move, with his legs all strapped up in those harnesses, and his eyes so sad, I just thought anything would be worth it if we could make it work again.

I can't imagine what I was thinking.

I was sitting there thinking these things when in walks the nurse to take Buddy's temperature, and it's Sandra, Becca's friend from North Chattanooga, and she's holding Buddy's wrist, taking his pulse, and he has the thermometer in his mouth, and I'm looking at him, and he's looking at her, and his eyes are lit up like hundred-watt bulbs, and the sweet sadness is gone, and she takes the thermometer out of his mouth and reads it and sticks it in her pocket, and writes down his temperature and his pulse, and tidies up the sheets, and says, "Buddy, you be good now, you hear," and to me she says, "Make sure he stays still," and she leaves the room.

And Buddy says, "Have you ever seen such fantastic knockers?"

I couldn't believe it.

I mean, I just stood there shaking my head in disbelief. Buddy says, "Oh, come on, it's just an observation." I said, *Buddy, I'm leaving now, and I never want to see your face again. When you're discharged from the hospital, you can go to your father's. I'll go by and see your father now, and tell him you will be coming to live with him.* And I left.

In the lobby, I met Becca and Lynette on the way up to see Buddy. I said, *He's all yours.*

I suppose it's just as well that it's over with Buddy. It would have been impossible for Mother if Buddy and I got our own apartment. I mean, if it weren't for me I don't know how the family would ever get settled again. Roger is a rock, of course. Roger is helpful, especially with his car. But I'm the only one who can sort things out for Mother. I'm the only one who can get her to face the reality of what she has to do.

We found a rental house in Brainerd, with an option to buy when the insurance money comes through on the old house – *if it comes through*, I mean, there's some question about the business of the TNT in the basement. I don't like the new house. It's a boring old suburban house, with no character at all, on one floor, with not nearly as much room as we had on Ninth Street, and no neighborhood at all, I mean, nothing interesting is going on, just other boring old houses, and there are no stores where you can walk to, and if you want to go downtown it's a forty-minute bus ride, but Becca and Lynette like it because "it's away from the coloreds," and it's a good place for Alma because it's a clean break from the past and already she is brighter and happier, and Bitsy likes it because it's a "more stylish address," and Mother acts as if she has lived there all her life – like the house on Ninth Street never existed at all. Iggy is still at the psychiatric hospital. Wanda insisted that she and Roger and Tootsie have a place of their own, so they are renting a house in

East Lake while Roger looks for a new job. He is waiting for the Draft Board to sort out his change in status.

Wanda is furious because I insisted that we give the shack to Eva, I mean, that we separate off that little piece of land with the shack and give it to Eva when we sell the burned-out house on Ninth Street. Becca and Lynette agree with Wanda. They say it will be much harder to sell the property with Eva living in the shack. They say we won't get nearly as much money for the property. They say we'll never be able to sell the property to white people. But Mother and Roger agree with me. There's no way I'll let Eva be thrown out of the house she has lived in all her life.

I had a note from Tometta thanking me for giving the shack to Eva. She said that William is in Europe, fighting on the front lines, and now she's confident he'll come home. God love her, how awful it must have been for her in that house that she didn't even want to tell us she got married. She has written a new story, called "Eva's Dream," about her and William. And asked if she can send it to me to read. She says that when William gets home, they will move up North, and she wants to keep writing stories, and William wants her to keep writing stories too.

I hate the new house, but everyone else seems happy enough. Heaven knows, I don't miss Buddy. I share a room with Emily Sue, but I seem to have more privacy than when I lived with Buddy. I have my salt-and-pepper shakers on display – all three-hundred-and-twenty-six sets – on the windowsill and on the dresser and bureau, and Roger put up some special shelves just for my shakers, and it's wonderful to see them all, and Emily Sue likes them too, and she pats them and doesn't pick them up, and I don't have to worry about anyone breaking them for spite.

I do miss Roger. I didn't realize how much I liked having him around until he wasn't here anymore. And I miss Tootsie, too. I hope that Roger and Wanda have better luck than me and Buddy. I really don't think it's Roger's fault that things have been going so badly for them. I don't know what Wanda's problem is. Whatever it is she wants, it clearly isn't Roger, and that's no fault of his. He shows up here in Brainerd every chance he gets. He says, "I was just in the neighborhood," or "I thought I'd stop by and see if anything needed to be done" – but I know he really comes to see me. I don't know what to do about Roger. I don't want to be a problem in his marriage, and, really, you know, right now I have enough to worry about without having to deal with another man. I just love being alone for a change, and having a roommate who never talks, and not having to worry about making a man happy. Roger has asked me to go birding with him on Saturday, down to Chattanooga Valley, and I said I would go. I know it is probably a mistake, and if Wanda finds out, my name will be mud, and there's no sense in making Roger more lovesick than he already is – but to tell the truth, I want to go. I had such a good time when we went to Lula Lake. It's the only really pleasant outing I've had in as long as I can remember. I mean, it's not like we're running away to California, or anything like that. I mean, why shouldn't I go? Why do I have to think about others all the time.

Just for once, I'd like to do something for myself.

Roger:

Its Latin name is *Mimus polyglottos*, which means "many tongued mimic." Of course, I'm talking about the mockingbird we have in residence on the gable of our house in East Lake. I've never heard a louder, more incessant singer. All day long, starting at sunrise, he warbles, trills, whistles, coos – imperiously drowning out any other bird in the neighborhood that dares to open its beak. Tanagers and catbirds are soon put to quiet by our noisy mimic. Come to think of it, sometimes that mockingbird wakes in the middle of the night and begins singing, as if even sleep is not enough to contain his excitement.

The mockingbird is driving Wanda crazy, or so she says. She asked me to drive it away, but of course there is no way to do it, and I wouldn't do it if I could. She throws stones at it, but there is small chance she'll hit it. She said, "Where is Iggy with his rifle now that we need him?" She blames me for the bird. Because I'm an amateur ornithologist, she blames me for the mockingbird and the noise it makes. She says, "It's me or the bird, Roger. Take your pick."

I wish I *could* take my pick – there's no doubt which I prefer. If Wanda would walk away I'd be happy. I'd ask Button to move in here with me and Tootsie. Button wouldn't mind the mockingbird. Or if she did, she wouldn't make such a fuss about it.

But I don't imagine that Wanda will leave. Where would she go? And it's not fair to Tootsie for me to wish away her mother, although it is difficult to see that Wanda is much of a mother. Tootsie seems to bother Wanda almost as much as the mockingbird. For the life of me, I don't know why Wanda stays with us.

But stay she does. She sits around the house each morning in her breakfast coat listening to Don McNeill on the radio and reading movie magazines – although she never goes to the movies, not even to "Going My Way" – and drinking endless cups of coffee. In the afternoon, she goes into the backyard to take the sun, in the skimpiest outfits she can find, and lays herself out in the one place where she can be seen from every one of the neighbors' houses. Of course, there are no young or middle-aged men to see her – they are either at work or in the service – but when Wanda is out there sunning herself, teenage boys suddenly find reason to play in neighboring backyards, and old men leave their rocking chairs to trim the hedges or mow the grass.

You've got to wonder what she's up to – pure exhibitionism, as far as I can see. She lies there on display for all the world, fuming at the mockingbird, getting browner and browner and crankier and crankier. She is irritated by the bird, she is irritated by her husband, she is irritated by her child. I can only hope that the war ends soon. If I'm drafted and killed on some godforsaken Pacific island, I can't imagine what will happen to Tootsie.

Of course, Tootsie is bored out of her mind now that she doesn't have Becca and Lynette and Bitsy and all the rest. I think she has forgotten how to play with children of her own age – if she ever knew. I told her she could invite friends over for her birthday celebration on September sixth, but she said no, so we went to Brainerd for the party. School has begun, and I'm hoping she will make new chums at school. I would have liked for Tootsie to go to the public elementary school right here in East Lake, but of course Wanda insisted that she travel all the way downtown to Notre Dame. The long journey back and forth each day will only make it harder for Tootsie to find playmates. This is a crucial time of life for Tootsie. She's had her first period. I was astonished when she told me – as casually as if she were announcing a toothache or a trip to the playground. I suppose I shouldn't have been surprised, after all the things she has been through with her aunts. She certainly knows more about sex than I did at her age. She asked me if Wanda and I "do it," and I answered, *Not anymore*. It was a strange and melancholy conversation – almost impossible to imagine that a twelve-year-old girl would ask such a question, or that I should be required to provide such an equally poignant answer. She shrugged her shoulders as if to say, "Don't worry, Dad, things will work out." I take Tootsie to the Brainerd house every Sunday, and she likes that. Now that the Buffons live so far out of town the soldiers from the USO don't come for Sunday dinner anymore, so it's just Tootsie and me. Of course, I'm glad to be there, as it gives me a chance to see Button.

Button came with me to Chattanooga Valley on Saturday. I picked her up at sunrise – a spectacular morning, full of mist and color, the North Georgia sky tinted an extraordinary yellow. It was threatening rain for the first time in six weeks, but ultimately the day turned out bright and brisk. We parked the car near Flintstone and walked through farmland up along Rock Creek to where the woods start up the mountain. We were below the place on the mountain where we walked on our morning at Lula Lake. In fact, Rock Creek is the same branch that flows through the lake.

We didn't say much – Button was quiet, introspective. She walked with her hands thrust deep into the pockets of her slacks. Her cardigan was tossed about her shoulders and buttoned at the neck. Until the sun burned off the mist I could see gooseflesh on her bare arms, but she seemed not to mind the chill. I had brought an extra pair of binoculars for Button to use, though I'm convinced she only put them to her eyes to please me. I explained how the mountains made this place perfect for migrants, like a funnel that gathers up the birds going north and south, and concentrates them into a few square miles of fields and forest. The day was perfect for birding. Within minutes we had seen half-a-dozen warblers – Nashville, hooded, blackburnian, blue-winged, myrtle, and palm. Near an old barn we saw a ruby-throated hummingbird feeding on honeysuckle. Button was keenly interested in the hummingbird – she wondered that the bird could move its wings so fast, all the while staying in the same place – but our other sightings elicited only minor interest.

Nevertheless, she seemed happy, taking in *absolutely everything* in a vague, dreamy sort of way. Again, there was something about her that reminded me of Floweree, my sister; perhaps it was her ability to feed upon life without actually seeming to touch it, as the hummingbird fed upon the trumpets of honeysuckle. We reached the woods where the land starts rising, and followed the creek upstream. As we climbed, the stream leapt from ledge to ledge on its downward journey, and although birds became less numerous than in the open lowlands, Button seemed happier. At one point, where the path climbed steeply over rocks, I gave her my hand – and she took it. When the path leveled out again I was reluctant to let her hand go, but she took that decision for me, retrieving it with the pretense of brushing back her hair.

There was much I wanted to say, things I wanted to ask, and declarations of affection I was inclined to make, but her self-contained manner did not invite them, so we walked mostly in silence. When we came to a broad flat rock at the side of a pool she asked to rest. We sat. She took off her shoes and dangled her feet into the water. I said, *Button, I wish it was you I married.*

She did not respond for a long time, then she said, "We make our beds." At first I didn't understand, then I remembered what I had said to her when we were coming home from taking Alma to the hospital, my grandmother's expression. I said, *Surely it must be possible to have a second chance at happiness. You and I could be happy.* She said nothing. I said, *You know that I love you.* She said, a bit wearily, "I know."

She said, "You're sweet, Roger. And I care for you too, perhaps not in the same way you care for me, but – I enjoy your company." She shrugged. Then she said, "Perhaps we could be happy. But – it's not possible. You have Wanda, and Wanda is my sister. Aside from that there is no way I could come away with you, even if I wanted to. Mother needs me. She is too old to run things on her own. She will need me all the more as she becomes infirm. God knows what will become of Iggy; certainly they won't keep him in that hospital forever. I'm the only one who visits him, and he's terribly alone. There is no one else to care for Emily Sue. Alma's better, thank God, but she still needs help. Bitsy is still certain she is pregnant. Since Horst was moved to the P.O.W. hospital at Fort Olgethorpe, he has made no attempt to get in touch with her and ignores her letters. God forbid if Bitsy's pregnant, she hasn't the temperament to take care of a baby. Who is going care for all these people, if not me?"

I had no answer.

I said, *I could help you. I could live with you. We could do the job together.* She shook her head, resignedly. I said, *At least we would have each other.*

She allowed an eddy of the stream to stir her fingers. There was not much to be said. We both knew that until the war was over there was nothing to be done. Nor was there much to be done even then, unless Wanda could be reconciled to a new arrangement. Button looked into my eyes – a long, searching gaze. I could see that she was measuring, adding up the debits and credits of love, trying to decide if throwing in her lot with me would add to the sum of her happiness or merely compound her troubles. Either way, the difference was likely to be marginal – or so it seemed in the bottom line I read in her eyes. Somewhere nearby we heard a vireo – *Are you weary? Why is it? We can cheer you.* She recognized the song and remembered the words with which I had rendered it. She touched my hand. Her fingers were cool from the stream. We smiled.

www.ingramcontent.com/pod-product-compliance
Lightning Source LLC
Chambersburg PA
CBHW031405250626
47155CB00004B/1418